MY   515098
                    18.95
McConnell   Oct90
The frog king

DATE DUE			

THE FROG KING

THE FROG KING

FRANK McCONNELL

Walker and Company
New York

First published in the United States of America in 1990
by Walker Publishing Company, Inc.

Published simultaneously in Canada by Thomas Allen & Son
Canada, Limited, Markham, Ontario

Library of Congress Cataloging-in-Publication Data
McConnell, Frank D., 1942–
The Frog King / Frank McConnell
ISBN 0-8027-5748-0
I. Title.
PS3563.C3437F7   1990
813'.54—dc20   89-70761
CIP

Printed in the United States of America
2 4 6 8 10 9 7 5 3 1

For Celeste, with my love,
and, with ours,
in memory of our friend John.

California
Tumbles into the sea.
That'll be the day
I move back to Annandale.

—Steely Dan

$\bigtriangledown$

CHAPTER ONE

Тнеу were trying to kill me, and I had to pee.

Southern California, to a Chicago boy, isn't so much scary as it's—what?—hallucinatory, dreamlike, wiggy, *not there*, you know? I mean, you're not supposed to be able to smell magnolias or jasmine and such when you wake up on a February morning; that only happens to the characters you see in movies and TV shows set in southern California. And the guy in the liquor store who sells you your six of Coors shouldn't be wearing a flowered purple shirt open to the navel and shorts, like a kinky boy's camp counsellor: that's strictly "Magnum P.I." (yeah, I know, I know: but from the center of the world—Chicago—California and Hawaii might as well be the same place). And nobody—*nobody*—really hopes the Lakers, for Chrissake, will do better in the playoffs than the Bulls or the Celtics. Nobody in the real world, that is: only people like Johnny Carson and Jack Nicholson and Meryl Streep, and they don't really exist, now do they?

That's what I mean. The place isn't there, because you've been there so often in the movies when you knew it was snowing like three sonsofbitches outside, that once you get there you don't *feel* there. Forget all the sociological bull you've heard on "Sixty Minutes" or whatever about the

1

apocalyptic city or the new interpersonalism or whatever, and new urban and home definitions of space. California's weird and wiggy, folks, just because it's so familiar. The average American—hell, the average Berliner—has probably gone there more in the movies than he's gone to the grocery crosstown in what we jokingly call "real life." It's *not* new: like your grammar school revisited twenty years later or your wife's body on your twenty-fifth anniversary, it's so well known as to be a new kind of strange.

At least that, or something like that, was what was going through my mind when, not too long ago, I found myself crouching among the garbage cans out behind Golden State Liquors Number Six—just off scenic Lake Cachuma Pass— in Santa Barbara. I was being shot at—Jesus, shot at like your basic Jim Rockford, and I've been a detective for years and I almost never get shot at. I was smelling magnolias or whatever the hell they were in February, and the Lakers had just destroyed the Celtics, and I was being shot at just like in a goddamn movie and I was scared out of my ass. In Chicago, when they shoot at you, they have to be very good because about all they can get off is one shot before the cops get interested. It's why cities and streets and high- density populations are so nice. But here, in a stinking- rich suburb of L.A. trying to make believe it was a sleepy small town, I could be in for a replay of the gunfight at the OK Corral, for all I knew. And I didn't even know who was shooting at me, though I thought I knew why.

I did what I always do in situations of extreme danger. I gagged and then I yelled.

"Hey, goddammit," I yelled. "You really want me to tag a murder charge on all the other shit you're facing? Come on, you can talk or walk away or whatever. Just stop shooting, okay? I don't even know who the fuck you are! Come on, okay?"

Another shot—the third—gonged into a garbage can maybe five feet from where I was crouching. Oh, yeah; it was eleven-thirty at night, the liquor store had closed (another California weirdness—can you believe it?), and there was only one, maybe fifty-watt bulb out back. So my attempt to reason with my assassin had, mainly, given him or her a better sense of where to aim. With enough guys like me, we could have lost in Vietnam in half the time.

I spidered around the corner of the big blue dumpster bin that stood behind the garbage cans, hyperventilating all the way. The bastard—or bastardette—shooting at me hadn't said anything, I thought. Maybe this wasn't connected with the case I was working on. Maybe it was just your random, mindless West Coast violence that we all read about in the *National Enquirer* in line at the supermarket: another cute surfer kid on speed out to win his Charlie Manson merit badge. God, I thought, don't let me end up another California story in the *Enquirer*. If that happens to you, instead of going to heaven, you end up a movie of the week.

And why wasn't he/she/it closing in for the kill? If this was to do with my case, then it knew I was a detective and probably figured I had a gun, which I did, back in Skokie, Illinois, in my bottom desk drawer, unloaded and uncleaned since, I guess, the last Apollo mission. If it was just a Manson scout, then it had no reason to think I was carrying, and maybe just wanted to scare the hell out of me.

If so, the merit badge was a lead-pipe cinch.

Five minutes or so passed. No, they didn't seem like hours, they seemed like *minutes*, which when you're waiting to part company with your ass is entirely long enough, thank you. Golden State Liquors was part of one of those little, scraggly-butt "shopping centers" that line California highways, a Seven-Eleven, barber shop, bait store, liquor store and maybe Japanese restaurant in an acre or two of scrubland that the cops, dammit, don't patrol after closing time. It crossed my mind that if Chicago had had more little islands like this, I'd have gotten laid a lot earlier and a lot more often when I was in high school. This while I was still hyperventilating and sweating: maybe that's what they mean by your life flashing before your eyes.

So if I could break the back window of the store I could set off a burglar alarm. But the window was five feet off the ground and I didn't have a stick or a stone. I had come there to meet somebody about something pretty serious, but either he or she was already there, trying to kill me, or had been scared off by whoever *was* trying to kill me, or was late, or—what the hell did I know?—had dropped dead or decided to take in *The Rocky Horror Picture Show*, it being a Friday night and all. Anyhow, the total message was that help was not about to be on the way. And I didn't even know if my assailant (I love that word, it sounds so damned *nice*— like "safe sex," you know?) was even still out there. I was sweating enough that by now I could feel the moisture talking back to me through the tweed jacket I was wearing. And I discovered something else, something that they also don't tell you about in those pull-the-grenade-pin-with-your-teeth-and-fire-the-Uzi-with-your-left-hand-while-yo u-brandish-the-cutlass-with-your-right happy horseshit hero films.

I had to pee. Bad.

So, faced with one of the worse dilemmas any man can face—a maybe crazy killer out there in the dark and a full bladder, and unarmed, yet—I fell back again on the technique that saved my bacon in all those schoolyard fights all those years ago and that hasn't let me down since. I yelled once more and this time I lied, too.

That's how long five minutes can be, by the way.

"Awright, you sonofabitch," I hollered into the night. "You wanna fuck with me? I tell you what, you asshole. Your ass is *grass*! You wanna fuck with me? I fuck with *you*, is what I do. You come here, you pansy-ass. You shoot at me again, I blow your head off. I shoot till I blow your fuckin' head off, you goddam shitface asshole. Come on! Come on! You fuckin' pansy asshole"—I was screaming by now, by the way, and I even think I was standing up. What's that dumb song from the show, *The King and I*? Oh, yeah, "Whistle a Happy Tune." "And no one will suspect you're afraid," I think it goes.

"You fuckin' pansy asshole," I repeated myself for effect. "I'll take your goddam head off, and then I'll break your ankles. Just come on, you . . ."

There was a light in my face. I stopped trying to impress anybody. "Are you all right, sir?" said the voice behind the light shining in my face, and I didn't have to try to look behind the light to see that it was a cop. After all these years, even given the difference between Chicago and California, that voice of all voices you can tell.

"Yeah. Yeah," I said, as I heard a car start not too far away and roll off. "Look, some bastard was shooting at me here, and I was hollering because I didn't know what else to do, you know? and . . ."

"Yes, sir," the cop said, with all that lizardlike politeness they use when they know they're going to get at least a book and a print out of this one. "Yes, sir. We had a report of gunfire from this area, so we came to investigate. And we find you, shouting obscenities at no one we can find and looking"—okay, okay, I'd had a few— "looking intoxicated. Are you sure that you don't have a gun yourself, sir?"

What are you going to do? Pull off a smartass Bogey-style

wisecrack at the expense of an officer of the law of a state you don't even live in? Or be submissive?

Go ahead. Guess.

"No gun," I said, trying to keep my arms as far away from my body as possible. "Just a big scare. Some bastard was shooting at me, you know? Now I'm from Chicago, man, and in Chicago if some sonofabitch shoots at you, you're the one gets to register the complaint. You're the one . . ."

"Yes, sir," he said. I might as well have been talking to a test pattern—if you're old enough or lonely enough to know what a test pattern is. "Do you have any ID? Driver's license, credit cards, like that?" As I reached into my left pants pocket, I could see him tense and glance over his shoulder at his partner, whom I couldn't see but who I knew was somewhere back in the night.

"It's okay," I said quickly. "Just my wallet. Here, I'll get it with my right hand." And I did. I couldn't have been more respectful or cooperative if I had been a damn hostess in Disneyland, with a Mickey Mouse head on my head and a map to the Haunted Castle crammed in my fist. I was polite, I was downright respectful. I was almost slavish.

Naturally, I got busted, Double-D, drunk and disorderly in most parts of the world, although in the land that give us Jerry Brown and Tommy LaSorda, of course it would have a number and a sillier name meaning the same thing.

But, like my dad and any number of my classmates always told me, a bust is a bust, right?

$\triangledown$

CHAPTER TWO

Now WHAT DO I want to tell you about first: what happened after my Double-D bust or how I got there in the first place?

Okay. After. But just a little bit after, say up to when I found out that the Brother of Satan wasn't going to carve me into sushi.

Friday night in Santa Barbara—Friday night *anywhere*— the fuzz is out in force for drunk drivers. They wait outside restaurants, they lurk outside bars, they cruise suburban streets where snockered ol' daddy may be cruising home to li'l wifey and the kids, and they make out like bandits. They screw up a surprising number of lives, and they get to feel pious as all hell because, as we all know, driving drunk is next to child molesting on the scale of things Americans just won't stand. Never mind that "drunk" is a word with about as clear a definition as "nice," and that most of the folks busted are at least as competent to drive as many of the folks who aren't. Never mind that the DUI (driving under the influence) collar is mainly a sophisticated form of urban tax collecting, and never mind that Ron and Nancy and their heir like the issue because it's so much easier to piss and moan about than the ozone layer, or world hunger, or

apartheid, or any of those nasty old issues that make you
scared. I mean, shucks: get them drunk drivers off the road
and stop our kids from smoking pot, and we'll be right back
in the fifties, dig?

Sorry: I sound like I'm giving a sermon. Maybe I am, and
the moral is be careful, but don't be silly.

I'll tell you what I mean by "silly." The cops asked me if
I had a car, which of course I did, parked out in front of
Golden State, and confiscated my keys (it was a rented
Datsun and I didn't like it anyway), and drove me, hand-
cuffed behind my back, two miles to a station for a breath-
alyzer test. I still hadn't had a chance to pee, so I figured my
chances would be better with giving head than with a golden
shower. All the way, by the way, I was trying to tell the two
failed quarterbacks driving the car (one was a failed lady
quarterback) that somebody had been trying to, like, blow
my *head* clean off. But no dice or, as they say in the Mexican
Marines, *el tougho shito*.

El tougho shito, too, with the breath test. I checked out
at point one-oh which is four beers and almost okay for
driving, but which is also enough for a Double-D in the state
that gave us the avocado and the med-fly. So I was printed
and photoed—Garnish, Harold, 750-B Avers, Skokie, Illinois—and put in the tank for the required four hours.

Now that is silly. Sorry, Ron and Nancy, if you're reading
this. I always thought you took a cute picture.

Into the tank. By now it's maybe twelve-thirty, one—
when you're doing the Man's time it's all his time, anyhow—
and I'm printed and photoed, as I said. There are mug shots
of me in three states, and in only one of those states did I
really deserve a mug shot—never mind which one.

The tank is a special place. I wouldn't recommend it for
a first date or a wedding reception, but it's one of the really

secure places in the world, by which I mean one of the places where you can actually trust people. Because if you're there—on the inside, I mean—you're there because you're a loser, at least for today. You screwed the pooch, and everybody else there knows you screwed the pooch, and you know that they all did, too. It makes for an amazingly low-bullshit level of conversation. I mean, forget your hundred shares of Amalgamated Wombat or your picture in *People* or that fantastic Eurasian seventeen-year-old who swears you're hotter than Attila the Hun on a skateboard. You're inside and you. can't. get. out. until. they. let. you. Anyone admitted, a quarter for a phone call optional, cigarettes—if you've got the good sense to share them—better than gold.

I made sure I had a cigarette, unlit, in my mouth when the cop ushered me into the cell, and I lit it as the door slid shut behind me. (By the way, you know all that romantic, melodramatic stuff you've read or seen about "the cell door clanged shut behind him," all that corny shit? It's all true—and I was looking at four *hours*, dig.) The ten or twelve other guys in the tank stared at me with the polite disinterest of shared humiliation. But they knew I was a smoker, and also that I was not a hoarder. In fact, I had two full packs in my jacket. Christ, I'd probably never been more of a capitalist in my whole life.

First thing I did, I finally got to take my pee. The open urinal was, naturally, clogged with milk cartons and paper and such, but it still improved my attitude toward the world considerably. Then I was ready to make my phone call.

Forget the "one phone call" business from all the television shows. If you're a misdemeanor and not a felony, there's a pay phone in your cell and you can talk to your heart's content as long as the change holds out. The funny thing is how few guys do make more than one call. Bikers, executive types, little old men, makes no difference: they make their one phone call to get picked up at kickout time, and then settle around the wall to wait. As I said, when you're in, you're in.

I had only one call to make, anyhow, to my boss—well, my employer, Bridget O'Toole who I knew would be fretting about me like a hen trying to hatch a roc's egg. And I hate it when she frets—she is to fretting what Wayne Gretzky is to the slap shot. If I don't reassure her we shift into what any kid from St. Eulogius Elementary School will recognize as guilt-feedback meltdown.

How many ex-nuns does it take to change a lightbulb? Why, Harry Garnish, (sniffle) how could you ask such a hurtful question?

"Harry, is that you?" she gasped before I could say anything. "I've been going crazy with worry."

"It's me, Bridget, and you can stop going crazy. The meeting didn't take place, but I wound up getting shot at— I'm perfectly okay," I added hastily, hearing the beginning of a four-liter intake of breath on the other end of the line. "I'm perfectly okay, but the cops seem to think I imagined getting shot at, so I'm in the drunk tank at the Santa Barbara County Jail, and I'll be out in four hours and call a cab back home, so just go to sleep, okay?"

"I will *not*," she huffed indignantly. Come on, fess up: how many people do you know who can really *huff*? "I'll get dressed and I'll be right down there. Did you tell them about your blood pressure? Did you take your pill today? How are they treating you? You know . . ."

"Bridget," I edgewised. "Listen. Four hours. That's how long I'm going to be here. You can't do anything except warm a chair down here for all that time. All I'm going to do is just sit on my butt and wait for the lady in leather to call my name and open the door. And you can't drive, anyway."

I didn't bother to add that, given Bridget's bulk and her normal speed, by the time she finished getting dressed I'd probably be half-way to kickout anyhow.

But she was adamant—if you can say "adamant" about somebody whose presence gives you the impression you're talking to the world's largest gefilte fish.

"I'll be there," she said in her firmest tone—and after all her years of teaching seventh graders or whatever, that can be pretty damned firm. "Don't worry about a ride. I'm sure Kim or David can get me there, and they'll be glad to wait with me. Now you just relax, Harry—and don't worry about anything." And she hung up before I could remark that, since Kim and David were the cute about-to-be-married kids who were our clients and the reason we were in California in the first place, they might not be too choked up about having to bail out one of their detectives at three in the morning from the drunk tank. Now I did have something to worry about. It's the nun in Bridget. They get so used to being driven everywhere by other people that eventually they look on the world not just as the people of God but as one big free public transport system.

The hell with calling back, I thought. I picked out a place to sit along the wall that promised me the least hassle for the next three and a half hours of waiting (that's right— you're always counting): between a bald oldtimer on the nod who might have weighed a hundred pounds and smelled almost as ripe as the tank itself, and a nervous keen teen with sculpted modified punk blonde hair and a paisley short-sleeve shirt who had probably just had to call daddy to explain why he wouldn't be home tonight with the BMW. Between the zonked-out homeless and the screwed-up spoiled; from what I'd seen of Santa Barbara it wasn't only nice quiet drunk tank company, it was goddam allegorical.

I settled down, nodded at my neighbors, and fished out a pack of Marlboro Lights—since I was in California I figured I'd go on a health kick—and silently waved them around to the rest of the gang. No takers.

Well, almost no takers. "Yeah. I'll have one," said a voice from across the cell. And there, stumping toward me, was the Brother of Satan. And oh, shit, I thought to myself, poor ol' Harry's a goner.

I knew he was the Brother of Satan because it said so on his chest, in a big purple tattoo that could take up the top half of the front page of the *Chicago Tribune*, if the *Tribune's* front page also had a lot of thick black hair.

He wasn't wearing a shirt, just one of those leather vests that say, all by themselves, you better get on the other side of the street. Plus assorted snakes and skeletons tattooed up and down his arms, plus a gold earring in his left ear and jet-black moustache that would have made any mama walrus proud. He stood over me and silently extended his hand for the cigarette.

To repeat myself: oh, shit, I thought.

He lit the cigarette with a WW-II vintage Zippo he fished out of his vest pocket, took a long, loving drag and settled down on his haunches right in front of me. Old homeless on my left just kept on staring straight ahead and young spoiled on my right suddenly discovered something fascinating as hell about his fingernails: this was one of the boys he'd been told definitely *not* to play with.

"Aah," said the Brother, exhaling. "Nothing like it when you want it."

"Here," I said, holding out the pack. "Take a couple more." Maybe he would go away.

He looked at me for a minute with eyes that I swear to

God twinkled, except I don't think black that deep can twinkle.

"No, thanks, man," he smiled. One of his front teeth was missing. "You know what Oscar Wilde said about a cigarette."

Huh?

"Yeah, ol' Osacar said that the real pleasure of a cigarette is that it always leaves you perfectly unsatisfied." He guffawed. "Goddam, ain't that a kick?"

Now, wait just a minute, I thought. I was ready for your average helping of West Coast strange—and from Chicago that's a pretty big helping—but a biker with death engravings all over his body quoting Oscar Wilde was a bit much even for me, and I've seen a *lot* of television.

"Hey, man," he said, filling up my silence, dragging away at his cigarette. He was one of those guys who can talk and smoke at the same time—it's sort of like chewing with your mouth open. "I hope you don't mind or take offense or anything, but you know this is kind of a small tank, and I like heard you talking on the phone to your old lady—that was your old lady, Bridget, right?—and your tale really caught me—like the ancient fuckin' mariner, you know? So you were shot at, huh? And the pigs wouldn't buy it, so here you are doing supershort time, which is, I mean, the worst kind of time you can do, for *nada*. Fascinating," he said with the faraway stare of a chessplayer in endgame. "Yeah, I guess I will have another," reaching out for a cigarette. "I'm Arcadio. And you?" His hands changed from the grab-a-cig to the handshake position.

"Uh, Harry," I said, as homeless and pampered edged away from us. "Harry Garnish." Then, on impulse as I shook his hand, I said, "Are those tattoos for serious, or are you just trying to get a date for the prom?"

I won't say his laugh was "cosmic" (a word I later learned

from him in any number of roadside bars to apply to anything from ideas of God to the ass of the latest probably seventeen, pretending to be twenty-one, stone cutie to walk in). No, it wasn't "cosmic," but it was generous and loud enough to wake up the dozen dozing drunks in the tank, who looked in the direction of the whoop from hell, checked out the snakes and daggers on his arms, and went discreetly back on the nod.

"BULLfuck, man," he strangled out at the end of his laugh. Bullfuck? I thought. Maybe they even spoke a different language out here. "You really don't give much of a shit about anything, do you? Good. I like a guy who doesn't scare."

Now where the hell did he get that idea? I wondered as my lower intestine said to my higher, "Man, this is bad—we gotta split."

"Brothers of Satan?" he went on. "Well, hell, it's a gang, you know? You never heard of us? Naah, you wouldn't of, unless you were from around here. And you ain't, are you," looking me over again with that chessplayer stare, making a comment, not asking a question.

"Chicago," I said, because if you say "Skokie" they always say "Oh, yeah, where's that—near Chicago?" and then you wind up explaining that, well, it is Chicago, actually . . . and like that.

"Ah, yeah. I got family in Skokie: you know Skokie? Anyhow, I figured you weren't Californian. Those tweeds and that tie, you know. And you gave your last name, too; that's real back East." "Back East," I had already learned, to a Californian meant any part of the planet on the sunrise side of the painted desert or the sunset side of Catalina. "Well, mine's Molina. Arcadio Molina. Back off, dude, you wanna keep your teeth and make it through the night."

That last was growled, almost over his shoulder, at a beet-colored hulk in a cowboy hat with a jockey-short bulge hanging out of his open fly who had just been let into the cell and stumble-stumped over to us, drawn probably by the smell of tobacco. The dude took one look at my new pal Arcadio's tattoos and then, as he had suggested, backed off.

"At your service," grinned Arcadio, turning back to me. "So look, man, I'm interested. How come you get your sweet Chicago ass shot at all the way out here, and how come the pigs don't dig your tale. Come on, man—I like stories. Hey, you got another cigarette?"

Now go ahead and tell me that a private investigator working on a case has a moral and ethical, not to mention legal obligation to keep details of the case confidential. That's how Bridget O'Toole would put it and, if you pushed her, she'd even tell you the difference between "moral," "ethical" and "legal"—three different ways of saying "you *got* to," as far as I'm concerned.

Go ahead and tell me that if I was going to spill to anybody, it should have been to the cops when they booked me for being disorderly which I wasn't and drunk which I wasn't hardly, so I wouldn't wind up in the tank. Right: *you* get busted by the Man sometime and then you tell *me* how many inches you're going to give him so he can make you feel even shittier than he's already made you feel.

And tell me, for crying out loud, that a grungy refugee from the fifth remake of *The Texas Chainsaw Massacre* was the last, the very last person in the world to tell the tale to.

So fine. So you're feeling the cold stone floor chill your ass and you're looking at three hours of waiting with nothing but talk and cigarettes to fill the blank till they let you out and you feel stupid and pissed off for getting yourself in this situation in the first place. What would *you* do?

What I did, anyhow, was tell ol' Arcadio what I'm about to tell you—changing the names, of course, because you only trust your cellmates *while* they're your cellmates—and feeding him almost as many Marlboro Lights as I smoked myself.

The ancient fuckin' mariner, I thought: with palm trees and tacos, yet.

$\bigtriangledown$

CHAPTER THREE

SPEAKING OF ANCIENT MARINERS: O'Toole Investigations, Inc. is a sinking ship. We're housed in one of those concrete-slab buildings that are almost as much a part of the mid-western landscape as Gulf signs and dead skunks in the road: just above Ben Gross Dry Cleaners and an ex-dancing academy that's now, I'm sorry to be the one to bring the bad news, a Theosophy Reading Room. A whole suite of rooms, right? Three offices the size of Greyhound terminal johns and a reception room with all the class of a Motel 6 Lobby (which is where most of our business comes from, anyway). Just off McCormick on Church Street, which is a hell of a good location if you're into Jack in the Box fast food or Happy Foods grocery shopping or the Mister Wheels bicycle store, but not if you want to find a reputable private detective to track down your erring wife or your lost investment in Arizona beachfront property. And Ben Gross may be the world's worst dry cleaner, and I don't even know what Theosophy *is*.

Like I said, a sinking ship.

We don't make money. We have what Steve Yussman, our accountant, calls a "negative cash flow." That means we don't make money. Steve just puts it that way because he's pathologically *nice*—an orthodox Jew from Louisville, he signs his notes "Shalom, y'all." Nevertheless, we don't make money.

Mind you, we used to make money. That was when Martin O'Toole ran the O'Toole Agency. Martin was born in Londonderry, Ireland (as opposed to what—Londonderry, Cleveland?), lost a few toes, so he said, fighting for home rule, and finally wound up being a Chicago cop—not an easy thing to do because you had to be fat *and* Catholic *and* tough in those days—about the time that Anton Cermak, then mayor of the City of the Big Shoulders, took a slug intended for Franklin D. Roosevelt, then president of the Guardian of World Democracy, and in his death leapt from mediocrity to legend: there's a street named after him.

A few days before he took the slug, Cermak signed, along with a lot of other papers he probably didn't read, a proclamation that Officer Martin Coolan O'Toole had been promoted to the rank of sergeant. Thinking back, that may have been the beginning of my bad luck. Because a few years after Cermak signed the promotion, Martin decided he had enough money to start a nice little detective agency of his own on the North Shore and still take care of his sickly wife and his chubby little girl who, even then I figure, was probably showing symptoms of piety. So the agency was formed, and the chubby little girl went into a convent, and the sickly wife died, and Martin hired me, and I was sure I'd take over the agency when he decided to step down because, what the hell, I did my job well, and it was easier than what my own old man wanted me to be, which was a pipefitter.

And then Martin had a stroke, and his chubby daughter—now Sister Juanita, a.k.a. Bridget O'Toole—came out of the nunnery to oversee the business until it could be put in order. Suddenly I was as they say in a feculent estuary deprived of means of locomotion, wondering when my life would get back on the, not too goddamned ambitious course I'd plotted for it.

So that was the situation—as I explained to my good friend Arcadio—the morning I walked into O'Toole Investigations to find myself—temporarily, of course—in command of the American Dream.

There was a message for me from Brenda, our eighty-six proof receptionist, to see Bridget. So, after dropping off my lunch on my desk—a Big Herm's hot dog with tomatoes, sauerkraut and peppers and two cans of Rolling Rock—I saw Bridget. Bridget's office isn't as big as the Garfield Arboretum, but it looks like it has about as many plants per square inch and after a few minutes there you begin to worry about a chlorophyll overdose.

As usual, I settled in the chair across from her desk, lit a cigarette—I think I'm the only person who uses the little ashtray she keeps on her desk—and checked out Phil, the moribund philodendron in the corner who is the only plant old Martin had, the feeble patriarch of Bridget's other salad. He didn't look much worse than usual.

"You rang?" I said to Bridget. It was one of my wittier days.

"Harry . . ." She beamed at me from the folds and rumples of a banana-popsicle-colored muumuu, if that's the word for a big dress that looks like it's been dropped over the body by the same winch-and-pulley gizmo you use to hoist a Chevrolet transmission.

"Harry, do you think you could run the agency on your own for a while?" she asked.

My first thought—honest to Pete—was that I should have bought three cans of Rolling Rock for lunch.

"Uh, yeah, I guess I could manage, Bridget," I said, staring at the burning end of my cigarette. "What's the story?"

"Well," she said. "I know this is rather sudden, and I'm afraid it may be an imposition on you, but, you know, I have been doing this job for some time now—"

"Hey, Bridget, hey," I smiled in my best weasel-like imitation-of-friendliness. ("Some time now" was, by me, too long by half, thanks and write when you get work.) "Hey, Bridget, I understand. You want to go back to the— what— nunnery and such, and I can sympathize with that, and believe me, everything will be handled here just like you would—"

"Oh, *no*, Harry," she said, eighty-sixing, by the way, my short romance with the American Dream. "I don't mean to leave the agency completely! My goodness, why else would I have applied for, and been examined for, that private investigator's license? No. Until—until Father comes back, you can be sure there'll be an O'Toole at O'Toole Agency. I was only speaking of leaving for a few weeks, you know."

I hadn't known. And once she said "Father" in that especially mournful tone of voice, and once I saw her fat face fall as she pronounced the word, I knew I didn't have a chance. Hell, I wasn't even playing the same game. All I wanted was to run a private detective agency. I wanted to run it because it's an easy way to make money. *You* know— people are always screwing people they're not supposed to be screwing, and people are always running away from debts— else why the hell call them debts? And other people are always ready to pay other people to find out what the first set of people have been doing behind the other set of peoples' backs. Didn't Barbra Streisand have a song about that? Anyway, it's not a bad living if you don't mind staying up late and if you don't mind trading in sleaze, innuendo, and ruined reputations. And do you? Remember what I said about reading the *Enquirer* in the supermarket line?

But then Bridget said "Father," and it came back to me that for her, this was "Father's" business, and father had taken such loving care of mother and had been so proud of her on her First Communion and when she took her final vows, and therefore it was a noble calling, maybe even an extension of her vocation (yeah, she actually thinks and talks about "vocations" instead of "lifestyles," which is what the Rolex and blow-dry priests who have written books talk about to Bryant or Oprah or Phil on TV).

Never mind that the Martin O'Toole I knew and worked with was a cynical, funny old bastard who used to mumble, between puffs of his pipe and sips of his Jameson's, things like, "Harry, dear boy, did it never strike you that the phrase, 'human nature' is one of the great self-contradictions?"

No: the Martin she knew was the real Martin, as far as she was concerned: straight out of Spencer Tracy with a dash of Pat O'Brien and a Cagney/Crosby salad on the side. It wasn't even worth the trouble to argue with her. When the Irish decide to be self-deluded, they don't do it by halves (me, I'm Czech).

So, to my mad boss, while exchanging another of many exasperated stares with Phil the bitter, I said, "Oh. Oh. Just a couple of weeks. Where are you going, Bridget?"

"California!" she exclaimed, the way I guess my turnip-farming ancestors said they were going to "America!"

"Santa Barbara!" she reexclaimed. "I'm so excited! Harry, I'm going to be a mother!"

Phil, I suppose, fainted, but Phil couldn't see, as I could, the sly squint and lopsided smile as she said it—reminding me, and not for the first time, of old Martin's way with a joke. So I just did what I used to do when the mood was upon Martin. I said nothing.

"Yes, a mother," she went on after it was obvious I was
going to outwait her. "Kimberly Molloy was a lovely young
novice when I was a counsellor at our Rockford convent.
Bright, serious, completely without any of those corny clichés
about being a sister."

"Huh?" I inquired.

"Oh, *you* know," she smiled. "All that silly stuff about us
being either so spiritual we can't change a distributor cap or
so cute we induce tachycardia, like—what are those little
dolls?—oh, yes. Like smurfs in wimples."

I laughed knowingly along with her. *I* sure wasn't taken
in by such bullshit. And besides, I can't change a distributor
cap and I don't know what tachycardia is.

"I'll tell you, Harry," she said, still laughing, "when I first
saw *The Sound of Music* it made me so angry, and at the
same time was so ridiculous, that I started laughing too loud
and was asked by the usher to leave the theater. The other
sisters were mortified."

We laughed again, she reminiscent, I bemused. At least
it gave me a minute to adjust to the image of Bridget in full
uniform getting rousted for guffawing at, of all things, St.
Julie Andrews. A rerun of "The Flying Nun," I figured, would
probably have induced tachycardia.

"Anyway," she went on. "Kimberly Molloy was just a
dream of a novice, except for one thing. No vocation."

"Uh, excuse me, Bridget," I said. "This is all real fascinating, and you're the professional, nunwise. But what do
you mean, 'no vocation?' Like, she didn't emit some kind of
light or something?"

"Harry, don't be obtuse," she scowled (I think the "nunwise" got her). "*You* know what a vocation is."

I did? I thought.

"Oh, call it 'calling' if you want," she went on. "It's only the road you're clearly on, like walking along the easiest path through the sand to Lake Michigan. The only hard part is not fooling yourself about where the path lies. And Kim and I went through—oh, dear, I don't know how many—sessions before she agreed that the sisterhood wasn't really her way."

"Yeah," I half-yawned. "Too worldly, right?"

Bridget's face can go through some pretty amazing changes, sort of like those stop-action films you see on public television; tulips opening, caterpillars turning into butterflies, all that. This time she went into a phase I'd call surprised-at-stupidity.

"Not worldly enough," she said. "I said she was an ideal novice. But there was something—well, I suppose—something too conventional about her expectations for happiness to be satisfied by the kind of life we lead. She was idealistic enough for what *people* call 'the real world'—just not tough enough for any other."

When she starts to talk like that, I start to wonder if the Rolling Rock in my office is getting warm. "Okay, Bridget," I said. "I take it you kicked her out of the convent. I've got some phone calls to make, and I'd also like to finish up on my case files for the month. Does all this have something to do with Santa Barbara, and with your becoming a mother?"

So it was mean. She likes to talk, and I usually can listen to anything, it's part of my job, dig, but with her sometimes I get the feeling I'm playing poker and I've forgotten what's wild this hand.

"Oh," she said, face fallen and making me of course feel like a hairball. "I'm sorry, Harry, I know I run on. It's just that Kim, after she left the convent, went to California. She got a few jobs in Los Angeles—I think she even did some modelling—and then she went to work for a real estate agent in Santa Barbara. Very well-off, I understand. David

Pescatore. And, well"—that Martin O'Toole smile again—
"in Kim's *worldly* fashion, they fell in love, and they're to be
married in three weeks, and Kim—did I tell you she's an
orphan?—Kim has asked me to stand in for her mother at
the ceremony. It's really rather wonderful, don't you think?"

Peachy, I thought, and said so. You know the way you
say, "Hey, that's *great!*" when your friend tells you he's just
come across a mint condition 1952 Mickey Mantle, and you
don't even *like* baseball cards?

Anyway, I sounded sincere enough to Bridget. I usually do
to most people, maybe because they've never seen me when
I really was. "Yes," she beamed. "It really is one of those
happy ending beginnings. And after the wedding, I'm going
to stay out in California—for just a little while—to help Kim
settle in. You see, David has a daughter by a—previous
marriage, and she thinks she might need some, well, some
moral support for the first few days."

I winked at Phil. I don't care how hip you are or how many
times you've been around how many tracks: if you're a
Catholic from Bridget's generation, or from mine, you can
not say the words, "previous marriage," without that little
intake of breath before you bring them out together.

"So," she went on, "I may be away for a month or more.
I'm sure you and Knobby can handle things wonderfully, but
I did want to make sure it would be all right with you."

Now I know damned few bosses who ask permission from
their employees to take time off. But how many bosses have
nun training? It's not a business, see, it's really more like a
family where we're all very considerate of one another and if
one of us needs a favor, why then it would be almost
unthinkable to say "no," right? Take it from me: if Lee
Iacocca had done some time in a convent, he could have
made Chrysler run like "The Waltons."

One throw or bugger all, I was what you might call taken—taken, don't you know—by the prospect of Bridget moving in for just a little while to help somebody else. Because I knew what Bridget's idea of a "little while" was, and because the idea of "handling things wonderfully" with Knobby while she was gone made me just all atwitter with anticipation, like when you finally corner the raccoon between the garbage cans in the back yard.

I'll tell you about Knobby when the time comes.

So I told her that everything would be cool, and made a few of the dumb little jokes you always make in Chicago or, I guess, in New York or Philadelphia or St. Louis when somebody tells you they're going out to California. Nobody ever goes *to* California, you know? You go *out* to California. Check it out; it's because we think of it as a different planet. As I was to find out, in its way, it is.

With a nod to Phil, I shambled back to my office and my by now too-cool Big Herm's and too-warm Rolling Rock, musing (I like that word) on fate. Here I was, for a while at least, about to get to run the detective agency I had always wanted to run, and all because a pretty young novice had fallen in love with a previously married, rich guy who had a kid and was about to enter bliss in la-la-land with him.

Why, I thought, fliptopping my first Rolling Rock, did it all sound so familiar?

The hills were alive. I just wasn't listening.

▽

CHAPTER FOUR

A COUPLE OF WEEKS later it was the end of January and Bridget was gone.

Now when I talk about Chicago I make it sound like it's always winter there (this I told my pal Arcadio who, I figured, probably knew that snow came in crystals but probably wasn't too sure if they were water or alkaloid); but that's an exaggeration. Sort of.

We have seasons. I mean, you can tell what time of year it is by looking out your window. In L.A. I gather, you have to check *TV Guide* to see if they're rerunning *Picnic* or *Miracle on 34th Street* that week.

We have spring, though you've got to stay alert to catch it: a few silly weeks like prepubescent cheerleaders between April's last snowfall and June's first thunderstorm. And summer: the streets buckle from last winter's deposited moisture, the tornado watches get hurrieder, you start to worry if the air conditioner can make it all the way through (when *was* the last time you cleaned the fucking filter?), and the White Sox lose. The Cubs, forget it. And fall: forget all about burning orange leaves and pumpkins, we get a fall where the air is fresh like you never remembered it could be, where the cold kisses you on the cheek as you leave your door, and where you could jump up and shout thank you, *jeezus* if you didn't know Chicago, and if you didn't know what's next.

Because what we've mainly got, is we've got winter.

The city is built for winter, and winter isn't a season, winter is a state of expectation. It's watching the late-night weather report to see if you'll be able to drive to work the next morning; it's making sure there's Hormel Chili in the larder and enough beer in case a blizzard hits. Winter is just knowing that old mother Nature, whatever the hell *you* want, is sooner or later going to *mess* with you.

Keeps you alert, does winter. At least, Chicago winter.

Now they built New York (this is the Garnish history of American cities—at no extra charge, no one will visit your home, etc.)—they built New York so that it could make believe it was European with a few minor differences— *new* York, you dig? And they built Los Angeles, about which I was going to find out a lot in a little while, so that it could make believe it was a paradise on earth, the city of the goddam angels. Okay on both counts. Everybody gets to make believe because, basically, nobody gets to do anything else. But the new Europe couldn't quite cut the climate and the complexity and the size, and the city of the angels couldn't quite cut *being* paradise. And in the middle of the continent and in the middle of history they built Chicago, where I've lived all my life and I still don't know what it's named for, but which was built and rebuilt with a mind for winter, expecting anything because it already knows the worst.

Right. That's what Brother Declan called "nature imagery" when he made us read *Wuthering Heights* in sophomore English, and I don't like it any more than you do. It's just that you've got to know how the city feels, because no other city feels that way. I mean, if you do know it, and you've been away for a while, you can come back, step on to Michigan Avenue at the top, by Watertower Place, and I swear to God you can feel the city's balls humming: and they're resonating with *yours*.

Anyway, it was dead winter and Bridget was gone and I was, as we say hoping nobody in the room pisses their pants laughing, in charge of things. I know I make it sound like we get almost no business at all at the agency. But that's only because it's the truth.

What I love about detective movies and TV shows is how the detective always explains to his client, who usually looks like Suzanne Pleshette, that it's a dirty, boring business, and then ten minutes later he's firing a .357 or a Baretta at a black Maserati laying rubber into the night. And then by the end the guy is either in Suzanne's pants or by her graveside, looking noble. This is, already, boring?

No. My job is boring. One of my really big concerns is shoes that will last long and not hurt when I'm following a guy and his other-than wife from lunch at the Blackhawk to a single room at the Drake. They usually stop to look in all the shop windows, it's usually too cold or too hot, and they're, of course, walking on air but I am walking on pavement, K-Mart leather, and if I remembered that morning, Doctor Scholl's. Or drinks: that's a big one. You've got to know just how many drinks to stand a guy at a bar so he'll start telling you these really *outrageous* stories about his best friend, and just how many to let yourself have so you'll remember the stories. Or keeping reliable batteries in a reliable instamatic: the divorce lawyers I know never criticize your shot-composition or ask about the film speed.

See what I mean? So maybe I react to the detective movies the way Bridget does to *The Sound of Music*. But no, that's not quite true. I react the way everybody else does who thinks their job sort of sucks. I love them, because I like to make believe that no job really *is* boring. I want to believe that someday, somewhere, a garage door will open or I'll turn a corner and there they'll all be, Suzanne and the goddamn Maserati and the really *fun* bad guys, waiting for me to come out and play.

"Who cleans a privy in God's name," said a monk, one of my teachers told me, "dignifies himself and the action thereby." Okay—but wouldn't, don't *you* want a tip?

So. Let me tell you about my month.

Divorce cases: four, three male and one female instance of infidelity, which brought in good bread and which didn't take up a hell of a lot of time, since nobody is dumber than when they think they're being clever cheating on a spouse. And you'd be surprised at how often the cheaters are almost glad to be caught. Maybe it's easier than walking into the family room and saying, "Dear, this marriage is killing me and I want out." In which case Motel 6 should apply for matching federal funds as a family therapy service.

Pet cases: two. People, especially older people who live alone, are always worried about that mean little kid down the block or the weird dude in apartment 5B who has it in for their Siamese Siegfried or their Doberman Muffin. You tell them to go to the cops, of course: but if the cops don't give them relief—and when do they?—what you do is you sigh, say okay, let me talk to 5B and you explain to him that this little old lady is scared for her friend. He usually grunts and says yeah, I got you and you reassure her and she feels better and you get twenty bucks or a loaf of home-baked bread or, on one memorable occasion, a fifth of Dewar's.

Hey—I said I wasn't "Miami Vice."

And speaking of "Miami Vice." Cocaine is the glamorous,

dangerous, sexy and expensive drug of the day, right? Tina
Turner in a vial. Everything you always wanted to do to your
head but were always afraid to try. Well, maybe. Besides pets
and adulteries we get the occasional industrial case, the
embezzler or the guy who may be selling business secrets
and such, a hangover, I guess, from the Martin O'Toole days
when the agency actually looked like it could turn a profit
some day. Anyhow, over the last few years more and more
of these guys turn out to be screwing the boss because they're
feeding their noses, and guess what: funky and glamorous
is just what they're not. They're little guys, assistant grocery
managers and brewery shipping clerks whose kids have bed-
wetting problems and who you *know* get meatloaf and
nagged twice a week, wanting to feel like a Gold Card for
fifteen minutes at—what? I never keep up with the market
rates—a hundred bucks a snort, say. I tracked down one
turkey doing a line off a toilet seat in a MacDonald's john
in Logansport, Indiana. (He'd stolen a few grand from Her-
nadi Industrial Felt, an old associate of Martin's.) He tried
to break *my* nose when I found him, and it was sort of fun,
because after he's been doing coke long enough, a guy is
usually weak or fucked-up enough that even I can beat the
shit out of him. I did.

A dealer friend of mine says, "Nobody does nothing, man,
but they don't know what they're doing." And, hell, I've got
no moral objections to the shit. I just can't even afford
Glenlivet. And I do, I guess, object to a drug that draws
wimps, keeps them wimpy, and also makes their noses run.

And that was my month running the circus. Oh, there
were good parts: like, I got to give Knobby all the really
sleazebag jobs (I'll tell you about Knobby when the time
comes). And, of course, on February 2 Ben Gross and I had
our annual Once and Future Party.

Ben, the world's worst dry cleaner, was born and raised in Berlin—"very near what is now—*ptah!*—Marx-Engels Platz," he likes to say. He came to Chicago in 1949 after spending some time as a guest of the National Socialist Party because he'd had the bad luck to be circumcised. And he joined America, but he married baseball.

So, every February 2, he comes over to my apartment and drinks tea while I drink Scotch—he brings his own tea in a thermos, he doesn't trust me—and we toast the hundredth-and-whatever anniversary of the founding of the National Baseball League. Because that first year, Chicago won the pennant.

["Yeah," said my pal Arcadio in the tank, taking my pack without asking. "I dig the aura, man—but how'd you get *out* here? And who's this fuckin' Knobby?"

I took the cigarette—*my* cigarette—he offered me. "You got someplace else to go?" I asked. "I'll get to it. I'll get to it."

The surfer boy had found himself a lone spot on the other side of the cell. The derelict who smelled like Gary in July was awake, staring straight ahead, either seeing God or pretending not to be listening to me.]

Naturally, Ben always outlasts me on our Once and Future celebrations. I fall asleep, he tucks me in on the couch with my rat's-ass afghan, whispers (I'm never really *that* asleep) "*Sei gesund*, Harry," and lets himself out.

That, by the way, also pretty much covers my sex life for the period under discussion.

So the next day, Feb 3, I woke up—or, at least, I got up—with a Muhammad Ali-class hangover. Feb 3 was also—you think about things like this when you're really, righteously hung—*The Day the Music Died*, when in 1959 Buddy Holly went to glory on a plane and, if you ask me, took half the fun of rock and roll with him. A tapioca day, we call it in Chicago—as in "tapped out." In California they call it "bad vibes," which makes, of course, no sense at all.

But sick or sane, screwed-up or plugged-in, I'm one consistent bastard. I thumbed a cassette into my player, switched on—what else?—"Peggy Sue"—and checked the refrigerator. My Guardian Angel—I like to think of him as a grifter in a brown suit named Murray, and I think he smokes Roi-Tan cigarillos—old Murray had left two eggs in the fridge, which went, raw, into a schooner of V-8 with Worcestershire sauce and Tabasco, which went, with four aspirin, down my throat in a single gulp. The Willie Nelson Breakfast Special.

After a while, hearing "Rave On" on the tape, I felt heroic enough to call the office and tell them I'd be late. Since it was already 9:15 a.m., this was not exactly classified information. But a manager, after all, has responsibilities.

Brenda was overjoyed to hear from me. "Overjoyed" is Brenda's more or less permanent state, and part of her problem, but today she had something like a reason.

"Harry!" she exploded and, I swear to God, in my hypersensitive hungover state I almost caught a whiff of Jim Beam out of the mouthpiece. "Bridget's been trying to call you all day. From *California*! Whatchathink*a*that?"

What*I*thought*a*that, for the hundredth time, was that Brenda ought to be working for the federal government, with job habits like hers. And my head still hurt, and now it was making a whining noise.

"Brenda," I said through the hurt. "Bridget's got my home number. Why couldn't she call *that* all the fuckin' way from California?"

Silence at the other end. Oh no, I thought. I forgot that Brenda, no matter how ripped she might be, hated what she called "no words." She was even worse about it than Bridget. And the whining in my head, I realized, wasn't in my head. It was a scratching, like fingernails on a blackboard, on my door. It was the Bandit, here for his morning collection. Cradling the phone in the crook of my neck, I let him in.

"Harry," said Brenda, punishment time over, "you know Bridget hates to disturb people at home. But she did leave a number where she can be reached. She said you could call collect."

"Okay, kiddo," I said. "I'll be in when I can."

"That's fine," she said stiffly—no, the *other* kind of stiff. "Peter can handle things." And hung up.

"Peter" is "Peter Conn," the name his parents gave Knobby in their understandable delusion that they had produced a person. So Knobby could run the business without me, I had to call Bridget, the Bandit was staring at me accusingly, and my head felt like it was fixing to hurt more. Buddy was singing about how easy it is to fall in love (so doggone easy). I turned him off and put in another cassette. Thelonious Monk, also dead, was playing "Well, You Needn't."

Right. Better for a tapioca morning.

CHAPTER FIVE

Bandit, OF COURSE, IS a cat; or at least he's trying real hard to be a cat. I started feeding him a few years ago because he kept coming around and he looked and acted like a used bunch of HandiWipes. I mean you could have used him to clean your dipstick and he wouldn't have complained.

He's still like that, except now he knows there's one place he can come and not be used for a dipstick rag. Cats are a pain in the ass, but everybody deserves at least that much, am I right?

So he stared at me. I found some sliced salami, grated it (he's got bad teeth), put it in a bowl with some olive oil (it helps what's left of his coat), and turned on MTV (he enjoys videos).

"Have a ball, fuckface," I said as he settled on my afghan, licking oil off his paws and digging Twisted Sister.

There was a little Scotch left and, for once, I decided it ought to stay left, lit a cigarette, and reached for the phone. As I touched the receiver, it rang. Just like you do when that happens, I jumped a mile—or enough to turn Bandit's head.

"Hello," I barked. "Harry Garnish."

I could hear the carrier wave, that background shush, that seems to bear the weight of continental distances and stick them right in your ear.

"Harry?" said a reasonable imitation of Bridget's voice. They always do that. You say "Harry" and they say "Harry?" I think it means that, after all these years, we still don't trust the damned thing.

"Harry, Bridget," I said. "I was just going to call you."

"I'm so glad I reached you. I'm awfully sorry for calling you at home, but—oh, I'm not disturbing anything, am I?"

"Bridget, you couldn't be disturbing less of anything if you tried. What's up?"

MTV had switched to Whitney Houston being gifted and facile. Bandit had turned his back to the set and buried his nose in his paws. Smart cat. *Good* cat.

There was a sharp intake of breath on the other end of the line. I know that sounds corny, but Bridget has so much breath to take *in*.

"Harry," she said again. "Something has happened."

No shit, I thought.

"Something has happened," I said.

"Yes. I don't think we should talk about particulars on the phone, but it's quite serious, and quite alarming. And I really believe we need you out here. Harry, can you possibly fly to Los Angeles today. There's a flight out of O'Hare at four- thirty, and you'd be picked up at the airport here . . ."

"Bridget, hold it!" I said decisively enough to make Bandit raise his head a second time. "*Today*, for Ch-for crying out loud? What about the agency? What about—what about—"

"Oh," she cut in, "Knobby can run things for a while, I'm sure. And, Harry, it's Kim and David. They need us. We need you. Now your ticket is already paid for, and you can pick it up at O'Hare. The United desk. Will you come?"

Now, a couple of things were going through what I like to call my mind, and the first was, that if Bridget hadn't interrupted me with her heartfelt "Will you come?" I wouldn't have known what to say anyway. Besides the agency, what *was* keeping me in Chicago today or any other day? I had that complicated a personal life, already? I *had* a personal life, already? One of my closer friends was staring at me at the moment, and he thought of me as a food source. A vending machine with body odor.

The second thing was a little more professional. "My ticket is prepaid?" I said. "Look, is this business—I mean, you know, is this an agency job, or are we talking about performing one of the corporal works of mercy? This is important, Bridge."

She hates it when I call her "Bridge."

Her voice, even over the transcontinental electrosurf, got harder. "If you need to hear it, yes, it's agency business, although you should know, Harold, that I would not have called you at home if it weren't also a matter of personal concern."

I hate it when she calls me "Harold." And uses subjunctives.

"David's child has disappeared," she went on. "There has been no ransom note, no information at all. The police have been called, of course, but Kim and David are *very* distraught. Kim naturally turned to me, and I suggested that you could be a great help—a great solace—to them. I—"

"*Meshuggeneh,*" I said.

"I beg your pardon?"

"It means crazy. Look, I know you care about this kid, Kim. But kidnappings and disappearances and all that shit are stuff for the cops, Bridget. And, hell, there must be a thousand P.I.'s out there who know the territory, which you and I don't, so what does anybody expect us to do? Unh-unh; we'd be wasting their time and not earning our money."

"And easing their minds and letting them feel that at least

somebody—however new to 'the territory'—cared about their problem and that their sorrow was in—well, in a *family*. Harry, you'll help just by being here. You'll help *me*."

Glorious. I was being coaxed and seduced into a job I didn't want by my own sixtyish and elephantine boss. Bogart had Mary Astor, though, didn't he now? I tried to look dramatically at the February Chicago sky outside my window. But the ice crystals formed on the inside were too thick.

"Four-thirty, United terminal?" I said. "Okay, I've got some things to take care of, but—"

"Oh, thank you, Harry," she said, "we'll be at your gate in L.A." Over and out.

Christ. Bandit. There he was, sleeping through Eric Clapton not knowing that his food source was going to disappear for a while. I found my next-door neighbor, the retired butcher Mr. Thompson—he was watching MTV, too—and asked him to look out for the cat for a few days. When I offered him ten bucks for Bandit fodder, he grunted. "Hey," he said. "You pay somebody for a favor, then it ain't a fuckin favor. Cat'll be jake. Take care."

I threw some pants and socks and such into my one suitcase—not forgetting the four fingers of J&B left in the bottle— and scribbled the following note:

"Dear Knobby: I'm going to be gone for a few days, so that leaves you in charge of the agency. You've got the case files, you know the routine, and you know our prices. I'll be back soon, and I'll check you out on everything. Everything. So be careful, even though I hope you won't. Between firing your ass and making some money, I'd rather make money. I think. So, Knobby: don't fuck up. Love, Harry."

Tell me I'm not executive material.

As I'd hoped, Knobby wasn't at the agency, so I left my note for him with Brenda, juggled my appointment schedule, and kissed her on the forehead (it hadn't been Jim Beam over the phone: Tanqueray, or I'm a low dying dog). I still had a few hours left before I had to be at O'Hare, so I went in search of Ben Gross. But the door of his shop had a sign saying he was closed because of illness; I guessed he must have caught one of his eternal colds coming home from our party. Ben's the *Weltmeister*, as he likes to say, of the hacking cough. So I walked to my bank—it was starting to sleet—and took $300 out of the automatic teller. I didn't think I had that much in my account, but who wants to piss into the wind—or the computer?

The shuttle bus to O'Hare leaves from in front of the Orrington Hotel, among other places, every hour. The Orrington is walking distance from my bank, and is one of the great, dilapidated but still elegant and courteous hotels on the North Shore—sort of like a dotty and beautiful old Evanston matron who still insists on sherry at five and believes in Nelson Rockefeller. It also has a nice warm bar on the second floor.

When I walked in, the only people there were the bartender, a bullet-headed dude with boxer's shoulders who's always been known as "Torch," Janie, one of the nicer and funnier hookers in the neighborhood, and a visibly nervous pinstripe suit sitting at the table with Janie. The day the Orrington bar is overcrowded, you'll know the Republicans are having their convention in Evanston.

"Piña Colada, Torch," I said, sitting at the bar. "Hi, Janie."

"*Piña* fucking *Colada*?" squealed Janie in her seduce-me-I'm-the-babysitter voice. "You gotta be kidding, Harry. Jesus, Torch, don't serve this man. He's got shit on the brain, or something."

Pinstripe, who'd been buying Janie Wild Turkey straight

with no ice (Janie's a pal), looked edgy and tapped a filter cigarette on the wrong end. Janie's a *nice* hooker—not necessarily the most *successful* hooker.

"Training, sugar," I smiled at her as Torch, a block of disapproval, put my glass in front of me. "I'm going to California." I took a sip, shuddered, and put it back down.

"On the house, man," grinned Torch as he took the glop away. "You want a Heineken's?"

"California? Glorioski," chirped Janie as I nodded gratefully at Torch. Really—she says "glorioski." "You gonna see Beverly Hills and Malibu and all that stuff? Wow, I'd like to be going there. Whatcha going there for? Oh, yeah. Harry, this is Mr.—Mr. Crews, from Louisville. Clyde, this is my friend Mr. Garnish. Clyde?"

But Mr. Crews from Louisville was already on his feet, mumbling something about being late for something, and flapping enough bills to cover the tip onto the table.

"Janie, Janie," said Torch as pinstripe left the bar. "You gotta learn to distinguish business from social events."

"Yeah," she sighed, finishing her Wild Turkey. "Harry, you shouldn't of come in just then."

"Sorry, kid," I said. "Buy you one?"

"Nah," she smiled. "I gotta go back trolling. There's some computer salesmen or something in town this week. You now what a—a microship is, Harry? Anyway, sweetie, have a nice time in California."

"It's microchip," said Torch to her retreating, very cute butt. "The essential element in computer technology."

"Thanks, Janie," said I at the same time. "I'll see you when I get back, okay?"

And that was my going-away party, that and one more Heineken and no conversation from the Torch. I caught the shuttle, found my gate in the new, weird Disneyland and

disco terminal they put up to deface O'Hara, and five hours
and a couple of Bloody Marys later walked down the ramp
into the City of Angels.

I was also walking into something else. But what it was,
I didn't really know when I was telling all this to Arcadio in
the tank, so I won't tell you now. No, that had to wait until
after we both got sprung.

$\triangledown$

CHAPTER SIX

EVER TRY TO LOCATE the exact moment when *The Wizard of Oz* switches from black and white to color? I don't mean the time in the story, I mean the time when you're watching it, the exact damn *frame* where Dorothy starts seeing things in color. Try it sometime: it's when she goes to the door of the house after the tornado, but they cheat you with a reverse-angle shot and you're never sure where the color *starts*. In fact, maybe you start seeing Dorothy in color before she starts seeing other things in color. A pisser.

And that's what it's like flying into L.A. The Chicago sky looks like the washwater in an honest bar, you take off, have a little vodka and imitation tomato juice, and you wake up coasting down into an overcast Garden of Eden. On the approach, for crying out loud, while you wait for your ears to stop hurting, you can see the palm trees. And you remember that *they're* aliens here, too; or, as a bumper sticker I later saw put it, "Welcome to California. Now go home."

And I would have, too. I was tired, logy from the Bloody Marys, and anxious for nothing so much as a soft bed and four more Excedrins. The stewardess who smiled me off the plane told me to have a nice day, which struck me as odd to

41

say at seven p.m. until I realized it was only five in L.A. Bandit, I thought, I don't think we're in Illinois anymore.

And there was the good witch of the Midwest, Bridget, waiting to welcome me at the ramp in what looked like a paisley horse-blanket. "Harry," she said, giving me an ample hug, the double of the one she had given me when I saw her off at O'Hare. "Thank you for coming. Did you have a good flight?" And, before I could answer, "Harry, this is Kim and David. Dears, this is Harry that I've told you so much about."

Kim looked like a Kim. I mean, she could have understudied for Tinkerbell, small-boned and five-two on a good day, brown hair in a pageboy and brown eyes that should have made her top-heavy. Her hand, when I took it, acted like it wanted to get away as quickly as possible. I wasn't so tired that I didn't remember the immortal words of Roy Orbison: rrowwworrr.

David was another story: actually, damn near another story tall. Lanky and quick in his movements, sort of like Jimmy Stewart on speed. Pinstripe suit, too—remembering the Orrington, I loved it—with an open-neck, floppy collar I- hope-you-think-I'm-silk shirt. I didn't like him.

"Harry," he said as he shook my hand firmly—I remembered that he sold real estate for a living. "We're so glad you could make time for our—uh, problem. Do you have any luggage to claim, or should we just get going to Santa Barbara? It's a good two-hour drive, this time of day."

I was thinking what an asshole he was: his daughter disappears, he calls in a nobody from three thousand miles away for help on the advice of a bulbous refugee from—well, from *The Sound of Music*—and he calls it a "problem"? And then I thought that I was the nobody, and that I was as goddamn silly being there as he was for asking me, and maybe more so, because I *knew* it was silly. Remember those nightmares where it's opening night, you're the lead in the school play, and you haven't even read the script?

"Thanks, David," I said. "No luggage but this. But look, before we drive to Santa Barbara, is there anything like a bar in this place? I'd like to get my land legs back and talk to you folks a little. And that's hard in a car, no?"

His face fell a little when I said "bar," and I could see Bridget in the background raise her eyebrows and deliver a micro-no and a macro-sigh (believe me, I've calibrated them). Anyhow, we found ourselves soon seated around a well- hidden and dark-as-the-movies L.A.X. bar—pictures of, guess what, film stars all around the walls—with our drinks: Perrier for David, reluctant (I hoped) Perrier for Kim, a Manhattan for Bridget, and another Bloody for the ol' toastmaster.

By the way, before I go on with the story . . .

["What story?" said Arcadio. "Man, I want to hear how you got in the fuckin *tank!*"

"Shut up and smoke," I told him. We were old pals by now. "I'm telling the tale, and anyhow they're my cigarettes."

"They ain't nobody's fuckin cigarettes, doofus," he said. "They're all gone."

"Oh," I said. "Okay, I'll hurry up."]

By the way, before I go on with the story: always order Bloody Marys in airports. They're better in airports than anywhere else. Why? Simple. Real bartenders always like to make drinks "their own," like to add that extra something that makes it distinctive—which can mean unfamiliar, which can mean bad. And an airport bar is, for a bartender, like an advance post on a battlefield: no chance to send around the corner for something you don't have. So for Bloodys, you've got pre-made mix, loaded with Tabasco and pepper, and no chance to personalize it. And you can also always toss in that extra half-shot of vodka, because the boss in an airport bar doesn't usually check the day's receipts against the bottle levels. Like Chrysler and the Big Mac, the airport Bloody is a triumph of mass-production, the LeBaron of booze.

I sucked mine up through a little plastic straw, signalled the waitress for another, popped the lime wedge in my mouth, and looked at David, who hadn't touched his Perrier. Maybe he was wondering if it was low-cal.

"Right," I said, looking at Kim, who was looking at the remains of my Bloody. "Now, about what David here calls your problem. You called the cops, I hear. No help, I hear. So one question, which I asked Bridget here but I want *your* answer. Why did you call *me*? I mean, folks, this is a hell of a time to bring it up, but you don't know me and I don't know you and I sure don't know California. Are you sure— sorry, Bridget—are you sure you're going about this the right way?"

"Oh!" "Oh!" they both began, David a beat later than Kim. But it was David who went on.

"We called the police," he said. "Last night—no, the night before last. Jennifer didn't come home, and we called the police and gave them a full description—when did the officer's come, honey, around eight? Yes. And they were nice, and concerned, and all, but they said all they could do was post a lookout, send out bulletins, things like that. They even suggested Jen might be a runaway. She's fourteen, you know, and one of the officers told us how a lot of girls around that age, well—"

"David!" Kim finally spoke, flushing. "You know it couldn't be that. We've talked about that."

"Okay, honey," he said, and I swear to God he patted her hand, just like Robert Young or Bill Cosby. "So you see,

Harry, we had nowhere to turn, until Bridget suggested that she and you might—"

"Yeah," I grunted, sucking up the last of Bloody two (okay, four, counting the plane. Sue me.) "Sorry, David, but I don't see a damned thing. I mean, I know this is rotten for you all, and people in rotten situations sometimes do things that aren't all that smart. Okay: I flew out here on your dime, man, and I'm not real sure why I did. But I have to tell you—now *listen*—I'm not sure I can be any help to you at all, and maybe I should just catch the return flight to Chicago. I don't know, Bridget," I said to what was becoming a great and not very friendly stone face. "This all just feels wrong, you know?"

"But you *can't* go back," said Kim, her eyes getting, impossibly, even larger. "Juanita—I mean, Bridget—told us we could trust you to keep things, to keep things—"

"To keep things in the family," said Bridget, with that tone of finality in her voice it must have taken years in the classroom to perfect. "Be still, Kim. Harry is only making sure you understand the—the parameters of our venture. And he realizes"—shifting, no aiming her glance at me—"that now that he's here he has, in effect, accepted a retainer for his—our—services, and is therefore at least honor- bound to deliver some kind of satisfaction for them."

Goddamn. I wished the parameters of *my* venture were still feeding my cat and watching MTV while the ice made patterns on the window.

"And there are some considerations," she went on, "that Harry doesn't know yet, and that I didn't want to tell him on the phone. David?" she said in that "Have you done your homework?" tone from her Sister Juanita days. It still works.

"Well," began David, glancing around nervously at the other tables. "I'd wanted to tell you this in a more private place, but—"

I didn't bother to tell him that an airport bar is one of the most private places this side—or maybe the other side—of the CIA, and a damn sight more private than your home with its eight or ten easily tapped appliances. Hell, I knew a guy who used to make regular drops for the Organization in the Tartan Bar at O'Hare. Never a hitch. Of course, he finally got jugged by the fed, but that was only because on his way to one nighttime drop he was stopped for having a burned-out headlight. Nothing *really* works, right?

"Anyway," nervous David went on. "The thing is, Harry—and we don't want the police to know this—I'm pretty sure I know where Jen is. Who's got her." Meaningful stare.

Seriously, now: sometimes I think there are no people, only statistics. You hang around divorce cases, missing kids, all that stuff long enough, you can almost write the script.

I stared back. "Jennifer's mother?" I said.

Only Bridget wasn't surprised at my stunning intuition. "How—how did you—" David began.

"Stunning intuition," I said. "Never mind. Have you got any proof? And where is the mother and what does she do?"

Lucky for me the guy was only drinking cave water. He went all purple, and actually slammed the table—like he had to before he could spit out what he then shouted.

"She's a whore," he shouted, while I tried again to wish myself somewhere else, "She's a dirty, filthy whore, and her name is Carla. Carla Bolero. Carla the cunt. You've heard of her?"

Well, somebody in the bar had, or at least had heard David's poetic description of her. Remember what I said about airport bars being private? With old David, forget it. While Kim and Bridget tried to make soothing, now-don't-make-a-fuss noises at him, and the waitress stared apprehensively at our table, a guy from two tables away came over to us. He was short, fat, and he had a face like the inside of a good London Broil. He had a Marguerita in his right hand and he was wearing a cowboy hat and boots with his gray suit.

"Hey, Mister," he said, looking down at David. "I don't mean to break up your little party, but you oughta know, this here's a public place, and there's ladies here, and they don't appreciate that kind of language."

Tex Ritter, I thought. From back when they used to show old Westerns on TV in the afternoon. And he was right. "You're right, sir," I began. "We're sorry, and—"

"Shut up, Harry!" shouted David. "You want me to keep my voice down, you cracker? You never heard the word cunt before? Well, maybe you should learn it—maybe everybody here should—"

The brave little fat man was carefully putting down his drink and his mouth was getting tight. He *was* a brave little fat man. And I was seated just right at the table to come between them. "Now, now, David," I said, rising, leaning over him, and smiling at Tex. "Let's just—"

And I drove the middle three fingers of my left hand straight up under where I figured David's rib cage would be. He went purpler—is that a word?—and sat real still, staring straight ahead trying not to barf up his Perrier. That's a strong impulse.

"Let's just pay up and go on our way. Can I buy you a drink, sir?" to Tex.

Tex's smile was almost as much fun to get as Bridget's solemn nod. Everybody in the bar, assured that it had just been a minor misunderstanding—I fight dirty and I fight quiet—was going back to their ordinary chatter. The waitress was back on her inscrutable orbit.

"No, thank you, son," he said, "Thank you." and went back to his table.

"Well," I said brightly, sitting back down. "Shall we go?"

Kim was stroking David's hair and staring from me to Bridget and back like she'd just been magically transported into Mutual of Omaha's "Wild Kingdom." David seemed to be remembering how to breathe.

"Right," I said. "Well, let's go. David, you drive: you haven't been drinking." And I helped him to his feet and supported him out of the bar—which, I noticed on the way out, was called "The John Wayne." As we passed the automatic doors into the California sunshine of the parking lot, I stage-whispered in his ear, "Okay, you neurotic sonofabitch, if you still want it, consider me hired." He still couldn't talk, but he gulped and nodded.

Sentimental old me.

$\triangledown$

CHAPTER SEVEN

As it turned out, Kim drove, with David slumped on the back seat beside me staring out the window. Nobody spoke until we got out of the L.A.X. parking lot, and the L.A.X. parking lot is the size of some of the more opulent North Chicago suburbs. Hell, a drive-in Taco Bell could probably do pretty well for itself there.

"Mind if I smoke?" I asked as we pulled onto the Santa Anonyma Freeway (they all look alike and they all go in great big semicircles, as near as I ever got to figuring it). Nobody spoke.

"Okay," I said. "I was wrong. I'm sorry. David, you want to take a free shot at me, you're entitled. Look, folks, really—I almost never assault clients on the first date. But that little guy back there was fixing for trouble and, David, you *were* just a tad unhinged. So—"

"It's all right Mr. Garnish," said Kim, eyes on the road. "You probably saved us some trouble. But you'll excuse me if I don't say thank you." The iciest. But she was for Chrissake *engaged*: so why did I feel snorkeled?

"No, honey," said David, and massaged her neck. She arched her back the way kittens do when they're stroked. (Lesson one: always let the woman drive, they're so damn *cute* when they do that.) "Thank you, Harry. You did the

49

right thing." And he held out his hand, the manly, noble-enough-to-admit-a-mistake wuss. I shook it.

"Well done," said Bridget (in a pig's wazoo, thought Harry). "And now, children, perhaps we can fill Harry in on the details of this—misfortune."

And so they did, all the way north to Santa Barbara. Driving seemed to calm the happy couple down a few degrees. I later found out that most Californians regard highway driving as a relaxing activity: further proof that there's something they don't want you to know about in the water supply. Anyhow, I got the story.

The story was that David hadn't always been in the real estate business. Some years earlier, he'd been hotshot talent agent, producer, film broker or something in L.A. I couldn't follow what he said about how he made a living, except it sounded even less like real work than what I do to make a living: one of those guys who, if they ever get an Academy Award for something grin their asses off in designer tuxedos and thank everybody from their orthodontist to their guru and make sure you either run out of beer or fall asleep before they get to Best Picture.

So. Old David, to hear him tell it, was pretty good at his job and he had contacts at Orion, MCA, Paramount, and a bunch of other important places I didn't know about, and he also had a wife and, in the course of things, a kid. The wife was an actress from, so help me, Little Rock, Arkansas: Karin Bryant, whose name David changed to Cora Bolivar because he thought that name suited her dark, Spanish looks better than her Irish name, even though she *was* Irish, and because he really thought she could score with it. Go figure. The kid they named Jennifer, because, I guess, in those years everybody was naming their kid Jennifer, and she was now fourteen years old.

Yeah. That was the second time I'd heard it, too, and it just then sunk in. Old David *was* old David, or at least my age, and I feel old. But he didn't look it. No beer gut, a spring in his walk (when he hadn't been just hit in the gut), no pouches under the eyes. Just—tan. Real tan.

And while David was staying young, Cora Bolivar was getting experience. Not a lot of work, but experience, and not the kind of experience David was too thrilled about. I guess she did look Spanish, and I guess the new name made her look more so, but the problem was, the parts she got were, well, *Spanish* parts. You know: a few lines as a big-city whore on a "Kojak," a few lines as a spitfire Mexican peasant on "The Big Valley," like that. (I wondered about David's judgment, even if he was in the business: hell, even I knew what a "Spanish type" meant on TV.)

So much for the jobs. The experience part was sadder or funnier. It seems the folks who make the movies believe the clichés they make almost as much as the folks they make them for. Weird: like finding out the president of American Tobacco smokes four packs a day, or that a TV preacher *doesn't* finesse the Sixth Commandment. Cora got herself come on to by a lot of what David called the "sleaze element" in town. There were a lot of parties, a lot of business propositions, a lot of quarrels after the parties and the propositions, and finally a lot of that special bitterness— bullshit, that special hate—you only get between two married people. So Cora, maybe for spite, took some of the propositions seriously and they led to some real, starring film roles—in the kind of films where the Vaseline budget is higher than the wardrobe budget. That's when Cora Bolivar became Carla Bolero. David mentioned one of the movies, *The Sweeter Elixir* with special disgust. Before long, she—

["Jeezus, *The Sweeter Elixir!*" exploded Arcadio—who by now had told me to call him by his "brother name," Cado. "Jeezus," said Cado. "You're talking about Carla fuckin' *Bolero!*"

Remember, till now I'd been changing the names in my little drunk tank show and tell. Who knew I was talking to a film historian?

"She's bitchin', man. I mean, Jeezus, she's bitchin'. You ever *see The Sweeter Elixir*? She gets down with these two dudes and—dig this—the other bitch, I mean at the *same time*, baby. You know *her*? Bitchin'. Hey— you want a smoke, Harry?" And he fished a fresh pack of Camels out of somewhere in his leather vest.

I just stared. Then I took a Camel, and went on.]

Before long, she had got herself a pretty long list of credits, and was even getting interviews in fan magazines. Yeah, they have fan magazines for fuck films, though you won't see them at your local drugstore, unless of course you live in a neighborhood of very special people.

When David called them "fuck films" as we drove along the Pacific at sunset, I saw Kim wince in the rear-view mirror. Bridget just watched the big water roll on by. The landscape, nearing Santa Barbara, was getting to be something not even the Disney people at their best could catch: a sky of, I swear to God, apricot, reflecting back off the mountains to the right and making the ocean to the left look thick enough to walk on. The world was ice cream and maple syrup. Bitchin'.

The rest of the story was as full of surprises as a TV dinner. David found out—if he hadn't suspected all along—one soap-opera afternoon (opened the mail, recognized the company name on a check for Karin/Cora/Carla, and blah, blah, blah). So he wound up with a divorce and custody of the kid. Physical *and* legal custody, which is important, and unusual, and about as close as you can come to telling the mommy or the daddy on the short end that they have ceased to exist. I must have raised my eyebrows or something because David smiled to himself at the memory.

"That's right, *complete* custody," he said to the back of Kim's neck. "She didn't want a court fight, not with clips from her so-called 'performances' and selections from her so-called 'interviews,' I can tell you that."

Schmuck, I couldn't block the thought: Kim must have been one hell of a too-long time in that convent.

So. Divorce, Carla disappearing into the X-rated sunset, David and little Jennifer moving to Santa Barbara to lick their (mainly his—the kid was only six) wounds, and get into the real estate business on the side; Kim coming on the scene, getting to be fast friends with little Jennifer who was by now, like, fourteen, and Kim and David finding out that they both loved not only Jen, but Lionel Ritchie, Stephen King, white Zinfandel, Waterford crystal, and Menudo (what the hell was *that*? I wondered. A singer, a town, or a recipe?). Anyway you get the picture and can write the rest of the scene yourself.

By this time we were parked in front of David's house. It was up in those apricot ice cream hills around Santa Barbara, it was surrounded by palm trees that all looked like they had some disease—is there tree dandruff?—and you had to walk up twenty yards of twisting, eight-degree grade to get to the front door. I figured it must be prime property. David offered to take my bag, and I accepted.

The kitchen, where we wound up sitting, was not as big as my favorite Mexican restaurant back in Chicago—okay, Skokie— but it was almost, and it looked the same. You know: what looked like children's drawings, but framed, of orange chickens on the walls, along with pots and pans and wicker baskets that had obviously never been used. And a couple of clay figures with big bellies and too many teeth: K-Mart Aztec.

"Uh—another Bloody Mary, Harry?" asked David, standing by a refrigerator as large as the national debt. I told him I'd settle for a beer, and he looked relieved.

"And a question," I said. "Have you called your wife—"

"*Ex*-wife," he said, handing me a Corona and a glass. A glass, yet. In the kitchen.

"Right. *Ex*-wife. Well, have you? And if not, why not?"

"No," he said. "I only communicate with her—which is not often—through her 'talent' agency." You could hear the quotation marks. "And we—I—thought that you might be the best person—you know, a professional—to contact her. I— we—told the police that we didn't know her whereabouts, so naturally I didn't want to compromise that by talking to her, you see."

I've always wanted to do a really good Danny Thomas coffee-spit—remember "Make Room for Daddy"?—and I managed a fair one with my beer at that line. What you do is, you try to laugh and swallow at the same time.

"You're kidding, right?" I said, wiping Corona off my jaw. "Okay—people under pressure don't always act sensibly, but come on, campers. You gave false information to the cops, the kid's mother might not even know that the kid is missing, so you buy me—*me*, for Chrissake—a ticket to fly out here and make it all right. David—this is not what I call being on top of things. And Bridget "—by God, I thought, *I* finally get a chance to scold *her*— "you're what David here calls a "professional"; it says so on your private eye secret decoder ring. *You* go along with this waltz? We could be talking lose your license, here."

Everybody started to talk at once, but Kim wound up playing lead. Bitterness will do that for you.

"Your *license!*" she said. "Your *license!* Mr. Garnish, a little girl is missing, and she may be frightened or—or— Mr. Garnish, you keep telling us we shouldn't have brought you here, and maybe you're right. All you've done since you got off the plane is drink and treat us like we're fools. We're *not* fools."

"Hey," I began—

"*No!*" she explained. "Sis—Bridget has gone along with this *waltz* because she cares about us and because she knows we're in pain and she wants to help us. David *knows* his—wife, he *knows* this is the kind of thing she would do to stop our marriage. You think Jen's picture won't be in the *News-Press* tomorrow as missing? You think we haven't done everything to get her found? But she *is* an awful woman. The mother. And I'm very sorry, Mr. Garnish, but we don't know what else to do. Oh—have it your way. We're all so stupid. Go home. You obviously don't give a—a *turd* about any of this."

"Harry—" began Bridget.

"Fuck it," I interrupted.

"Turd" was the word. That did it, I mean. She could have said I didn't give a good goddamn or a shit or a rat's ass or a flying fuck about any of this, and I probably *would* have taken the next flight back to Chicago, delightedly damning Bridget all the way. But "turd"? Jesus, the kid didn't even know how to swear. It was so damned innocent, so vulnerable. "You're be-*yoo*tiful when you're mad," John Wayne or whoever always said to Maureen O'Hara or whoever in all those Westerns.

You need me to spell it out? I'd told David he was my client after I'd invaded his solar plexis. But now I decided I would really try to find Jennifer. For Kim.

"Fuck it," I repeated. "Sorry, Bridget. Sorry, gang. Okay, that was my last escape attempt. You're in deep yogurt, and I'll float with you, if you want me to stay."

Kim nodded. David nodded. Bridget stared.

"Right. Deal," I said. Now, what do you want me to do?"

"Well," said David. "Could you, do you think, get in touch with *her* tomorrow? Through her agency, I mean?"

I knew he was going to say that. I just wanted to hear it. I also insist on playing out the last tricks even when I know I'm going down four spades doubled and redoubled. We Czechs have been conquered so many times, we've sort of gotten to be connoisseurs of the experience.

"Sure thing, Sparky," I said. "Is there another Corona? And who sleeps where? It's about four a.m. in Chicago."

∇

CHAPTER EIGHT

Where we slept was Kim and David in the master bedroom (nice going, Second Vatican Council), Bridget in Jennifer's room, and me on the couch in the den. Why do they call it a den, by the way? It must be a class thing: by me, a room with a couch and a TV and easy access to the fridge is, already, a living room. Oh, well, I'll probably never be able to afford a den of my own.

Now you should know by now that morning is not my really really favorite time of day. And in California, let me tell you, in February, it's even more of a swift pain. It's *warm* and it's *sunny* and it's *cheerful* and while the rest of the continent is freezing its ass off it's *temperate*. It's like watching Mister Rodgers after you've just got a phone call that your grandmother died.

That's how I felt when I shambled, in yesterday's clothes, out to coffee and bacon and scrambled eggs, which Bridget of course had fixed. And scrambled eggs as everybody knows are only barely edible with ketchup, and David, naturally, being an upscale kind of dude wouldn't have anything as plebeian as ketchup in his house, so after a hearty helping of scrambled eggs and Doctor John's Louisiana Hot Sauce— that's all there was, folks—with the roof of my mouth trying to secede from the rest of my body, I picked up the kitchen phone and made The Great Phone Call.

The Great Phone Call was to the Sybaris Agency, Inc., in L.A. ("*East* L.A., sniffed David as he handed me the phone number. I didn't, at the time, know why the hell he was sniffing). So I punched it—you don't want to hear this, but the kitchen phone was a Mickey Mouse with the buttons between where his heart and balls should be—and took a deep breath.

No sweat getting Carla's number from the Sybaris receptionist. It's something I learned from Old Martin O'Toole, who knew how to lie like Joe Tex knew how to sing blues. You don't tell how you need to get in touch with the mark because you've got insurance money from their deceased cousin in Fargo, North Dakota or any of that "cinematic foofaraw," as Martin used to call it.

"No, boyo," he would say. "Keep to *sancta simplicitas*, which is Church Latin for the one dependable side of human nature, which is of course the petty side. Now, what's the one thing about your life that you find most embarrassin' but not truly shameful? Why, that your toilet is broken, of course. It's such a lovely, *tacky* problem, and it gives just the right twinge of superiority to all your associates whose toilets aren't, just at the time, broken. So you say you're the plumber, you've lost the marks' home number and you need to discuss the price of some further emergency repairs. Your informant is, on the face o' things, doing the mark a favor— Lord knows we all need plumbin' repairs—and lets the informant bask in causin' a little—just a little—minor inconvenience, for Lord knows nobody *wants* to hear from the plumber. Trust me, Harry. It works like a bloody charm."

And so it did, for the umpteenth time. I always give the plumber's name as Harry Goodman—Benny's brother, of course, who played bass with the band during the classic years.

At Carla Bolero's I got an answering machine and a surprise. "This is Karin Bryant," said a soft voice with just a little lisp—what had I expected, I wondered, Rita Moreno doing "Louie, Louie?" "If you leave your name and business after the beep, I'll call you back." Beep.

"Miz Bryant," I said. "Or Miz Bolero, whatever. My name is Garnish, and I'm representing Mr. Pescatore and Kim Molloy. It's about your daughter, Jennifer. I think you know what I'm talking about. Anyway, I'm at—" I gave the number— "and I or somebody will be here all day."

"Well?" said David and Kim together as I grabbed the milk carton off the table.

"Well, now we wait. That is, if she hasn't flown with Jennifer to Zimbabwe or somewhere. Or we drive to her apartment—I got the address, you know how to find a street called North Normandy in L.A.?—or, back to square one, my man, you call the cops back and let them do what you pay them for. And, get this folks, if that lady *hasn't* got your kid, she's in for a hell of a shock when she gets that message—and you could be in for a hell of a lawsuit for endangering Jennifer. You think of that?"

Moods change. I mean, did you ever wake up next to last night's love goddess and realize she was actually the screw-o-matic from Ronco? That's why I don't like mornings. They nag at you, whispering that last night—hell, all your last nights—you could've, may've, been just *wrong*.

Anyhow, I was changing my mind about getting involved in the whole circus again, and Kim and David and, yes, Bridget, were all beginning to explain to me how for every-body's sake, especially Jennifer's, we *have* to see this thing through. Kim finally got so exasperated that she said she had to lie down for a while, and went to her room.

I sat thinking that the milk wasn't cold enough—you've got to keep it just below freezing for it to be drinkable—when the phone rang. I took it without asking.

"Mr. Garnish?" said the telephone.

"Miz Bolero?" I said. "Or Bryant? Whatever. Thanks for calling back."

"There's a liquor store on—on Calle Real, by Cachuma Pass. Can you be there? Tonight? Around eleven o'clock. Oh—you have to come alone."

There was a funny—what?—shyness, I don't know—about the speech. "Miz Bolero," I said. "I'll be there. Look—this is about Jennifer, am I right?"

"Yes," she said. "Thank you." Click.

[Click went the electric lock on the cell door and "Molina" said the little bald man in blue who poked his head in. "Time, Molina."

"Righteous," said Cado, and grunted to his feet. "Harry," he said down to me, "thanks for passing the time. Sorry you didn't get to finish your story, but it was fun. Good luck, man. You come in like a half hour after me, so relax—you're on the short end."

"Uh—yeah, man," I said. Okay, okay, I *was* a little hurt. The kid and the old derelict had been sprung sometime before, and I hadn't even noticed. "Take care, Cado," I said.

"Dig it. Leave us go, Chauncey," he said to the waiting cop as he strolled to the door. And, as he reached it, not turning around, "Hey, Chicago!" he shouted, tossing the Camel pack over his shoulder. He didn't see me catch it, either, just said, "Good hands—better'n the fuckin' Cubs" as he walked into the other part of the world.]

David thought I should have "backup" for the meeting—I guess he'd been watching "Hill Street Blues"—and when I

and Bridget—acting professional for once—insisted that it
was silly, he insisted on renting me a car for my stay in sunny
Cal, just in case events took me on a joyride. I hate cars
almost as much as I hate cats, and I really hated the idea of
driving in what looked like, to me, a bumper-car course with
palm trees.

But there was nothing to do until the eleven o'clock
meeting, and you always want nervous children to be occu-
pied, so after I washed the breakfast dishes (yeah, I'm a
sweetheart) we all drove down to the nearest place trying
harder to serve us and I got a Datsun to worry about. Then
Kim and David said they had to go in to the office for a while,
and they'd be back for dinner, and I said I'd drive Bridget
around for a while, just getting used to the car.

Now, if the L.A. freeways are designed for missing your
turnoff at impossibly high speeds, the streets of Santa Barbara—where, I understand, L.A. people go to live and make
believe they don't inhabit the King Kong of urban blight
areas—are designed to make you feel you ought to be riding
a donkey. Except you're driving a Datsun. Seriously—in the
high-rent part of town (and that's the whole damn town),
the public buildings look like haciendas from Disneyland,
the Taco Bells look like public buildings, and the streets are
guaranteed, old-Spanish, put down in the late sixties cobblestone. "Conspicuous consumption." Ben Gross explained the idea to me once: you prove to yourself that you're
really rich by affording to live in a town that kills one
complete suspension system a year.

So while Bridget and I bumped and ground our way around
town I tried to get out of her why she was being so silly about
all this. With no luck.

"Harry," was all she basically said, "Kim means a lot to me.
And I want to ensure that she—survives this ordeal with some

of the happiness she deserves. Can't you just accept that?"

Well, yeah. Enough. Back to David's house, where there was Corona in the fridge and Bridget decided to take a nap and I decided to check out "Geraldo." Good deal: today was women who fell in love with convicted serial killers. If old Geraldo won't pass your time, man, you're in serious trouble.

David came back—Kim had to handle a closing in Oxnard, which I gathered was forty minutes south and would keep her away from the pre-homestead till after I'd gone on my little trip, so we went out to a Mexican restaurant. The conversation was *bupkis*—what's there to talk about when you're waiting to find out what to talk about?—and Menudo is a soup made out of cow's guts and barley, which is not half bad if you like Mexican food that tastes bland enough to be Kosher for Passover.

I'd driven by Golden State Liquors to make sure I knew where it was. I'd had three Coronas to make sure I was dumb enough to go through with the meeting but awake enough to save my ass, if the need arose. I said goodbye to Bridget and David at his front door. "Don't wait up," I told them. "I'll ring the bell, two shorts and one long." Nobody laughed.

I got to Golden State right before it closed and figured, what the hell, I could afford an airport miniature of tequila while I waited. They closed up. I sucked tequila and waited outside (okay, so I could afford a couple). At around eleven-ten there was a noise sort of like when you crack your knuckle, except I hadn't cracked my knuckle and at the same time a little bit of concrete six feet away from me went ding. I dropped my teek (abandoning the worm) and dived for the nearest garbage can.

Click. I was lighting my third Camel when baldy stuck his head in the cell and said, "Garnish. Time."

"Thanks," I said, got up, and thought about leaving the

pack of Camels on the floor for the next poor busted bastard. Then I decided, fuck him, put the pack in my pocket, and left the tank.

They're always real careful about returning your stuff to you—you have to check it and sign for it—and in Santa Barbara you don't get to see anybody until you leave the police parking lot, this kind of no-man's land between the tank and planet Earth. And, sure enough, as I walked out of the lot, there was Bridget, and there was David, and there was Kim. And there, doing a little dance with his hands in his pockets—it's cold at night in California, if all you wear is a leather jacket—was Cado.

"Hey, Chicago!" he said. "Your friends here said I could stick around to see you sprung. And I bet you're enough of a sonofabitch you kept them Camels, right? Gimme one, hey."

∇

CHAPTER NINE

Y OU SPEND A LOT of your time thinking that everybody else knows what's going on, and you don't want to let them know *you* don't know? Like, life is a surprise birthday party and you've been invited but you can't remember who the guest of honor is?

Well, anyway, I do that a lot. And that's the way I felt when I saw Cado in the lot, grinning his ass off in the middle of a stern David, an annoyed Kim, and a—what the hell *is* the word?—an enigmatic Bridget O'Toole.

"Hey, Cado," I said, offering him one of his own cigarettes. "Hey, Bridget. David. Kim." They all just looked at me—except Cado, who was lighting his cigarette and smiling and nodding at me like I'd just told the funniest joke since the one about the guy who walks into a bar with an alligator on a leash and a baseball bat.

Well, damned if I was going to be cheated of my moment. I hadn't flown three thousand miles on a whim, screwed up a kidnapping investigation that wasn't my business in the first place, and gotten busted in, for Christ sake, a *new* state, for *nothing*.

"I suppose you're wondering why I asked you all here tonight," I began, beaming at them.

Right on cue, Cado guffawed, Kim—her tiny fists clench-
ed—stared at the sky in exasperation, David just stared, and
Bridget barked.

"Harry," she barked. "It's very early Saturday morning,
and I don't think any of us are in the mood for old-movie
trivia. Mr.—Molina?"—grinning nod from Cado—"yes, Mr.
Molina here has told us that you told him about our—
problem." *That* she said with a cock of the eyebrow that,
even in the bad light of the parking lot, I could read as saying
something like, "How the *hell* could you get drunk or dumb
enough to let this creepozoid and probably psychotic loser
into the game?" But I've been dealing with her for years, now,
and I knew all—okay, most of—the moves. I just looked at
her blandly, your basic cabbage-patch private investigator.

"Yeah, ponch," interrupted Cado, dragging on his Camel
and doing, I swear to God, an elaborate dance without
moving anything but his shoulders. "I dug from your tale
that this"—tagging Bridget absolutely with the slightest
gesture of his cigarette—ever watch Solti conduct the Chicago symphony?—"had to be your boss you was telling me
about, and I figured, what the ff—what the heck, I might as
well hang around and see, maybe I could be some help to
you good folks in your, like, time of need, you dig?"

Like I said before, inside and outside the tank are, or are
supposed to be, different worlds. *Really*: if you've never been
there, I probably can't tell you about it. But you make
friends, and I mean *friends*, behind the door— trust me, the
door is everything when you're behind it— that you just
want to forget on this—your—our—side. Of the door.

So there I stood, breathing fog into the smog of a chilly
southern California a.m., wondering how I'd been stupid
enough to spill my truckload to a dude I wouldn't have given
a match to on Michigan Avenue and knowing that it was

just because we *hadn't* met on Michigan Avenue but in one of the few honest places in the world, in the tank, behind the door, and I made—sonofabitch!—a moral choice.

"Cado's okay," I said to Bridget. "If it's cool with Kim and David, Cado's okay with me."

You get weird looks and then you get *weird* looks, am I right? Cado tried to give me a high five, which I pretended to ignore, Bridget gave me that you-didn't-do-your-geography-home-work-because-you-were-reading-*Hustler* look, and Kim and David looked at one another and then at Bridget and then at Cado and then at me.

"Well," said David. Did you ever know an asshole who didn't begin a concession by saying "well?"

"Well," harumphed David. "Mr. Molina, since Harry here vouches for you, we thank you for your interest. But—"

"Hey, no buts, bro," crowed Cado, and now he was dancing with the whole top half of his body. Not to mention that his accent had gotten stronger. "You know"—it sounded like *dju*naah—"I don't got nothin better to do than help you find your little *chula*. I mean I just be passin' through, dju*naah*? And ol' Harry, here, he's good folks, so why not I help you like, much as I can—hey, like I'll stay out of your way, just be there, you know, if you need me."

Never mind that this did not sound like the same cat who, a few hours earlier, had told me about Oscar Wilde's theory of cigarettes. At the time I was too tired to notice, and later it didn't seem to make a hell of a lot of difference anyway.

"Well," said David again, "the thing is, after this—I mean, a shooting and all—I don't really know if we should, ahh, keep on this way. Maybe the police—"

"Nonsense," said Bridget, as I knew she would, goddammit. "The police should certainly take a stronger interest in this business now, but that doesn't mean Harry and I can't—"

"Dig!" said Cado. "I mean, hey, man—I can call you Dave?—it's your *daughter*, right? I say we oughta—"

"Christ!" I shouted. They stared at me. "Look, campers, this is just one hell of a fascinating discussion, and by the way I vote with David. But it's *real* early in the morning, and I've spent the last four hours smoking two packs of cigarettes in a king-size latrine and my head hurts and this place, don't you know, gives me da *blues*. Can we get the hell away from here?"

Everybody got solicitous, except Cado, who looked sort of disappointed that I'd let a little thing like an all-night bust rattle me. So we began piling into David's car when my new and, apparently he thought, best buddy sang out again.

"Hey, Dave," said Cado. "Look, I can't ride with you guys, I gotta pick up my hog at the impound lot. But I usually sleep down by the fig tree, there. If I'm gonna help you folks, how's about I crash in your backyard tonight? You gotta backyard, right? I got my gear and all on my hog, and I won't bug you guys till you call me. What say?"

David looked like he'd swallowed a fishbone—or an avocado pit. Kim, who hadn't yet said a word, gave David, who wasn't looking at her, one of those looks you see wives—in her case, I guess, wives j.g.—give husbands sometimes. It's the one that says something like, "You're the man in the family, but you foul up on *this* one and you'd best know you're in the seriously deep and I mean *deep* yogurt." Like I say, David wasn't looking at her. But he knew he was getting The Look.

Me, I was wishing for one of the few times in my life that I didn't smoke.

And the Bridget smiled. "Mr. Molina—may I call you Arcadio?—that's, I'm sure you know, a very unusual request. But you are, after all—well, privy to our problem. And I've never had reason to mistrust Harry's judgment of people, and perhaps you *can* help us, if you don't mind abiding by our suggestions about what you should and—well, shouldn't do. If Kim and David don't mind my interfering, I think we should accept your offer."

Now both Kim *and* David looked like those big-eye paintings you see for sale at K-Mart. Probably I did, too: Bridget trusted *my* judgment of people? I was damned if *I* did. Cado once again grinned his ass off. It seemed to be one of his best things.

With all the enthusiasm of a teenager in the confessional, David gave Cado his address and began telling him how to get there.

"Righteous, Dave," interrupted Cado. "No sweat, I *know* this town. Okay, guys," giving us all the clenched-fist salute (damn, I thought, they still did that out here?), "I'll catch y'all up. Hey, Chicago, catch you back at the ranch." And he walked off into the night.

"Bridget," said Kim as we drove out of the lot. "Do you really think—"

"Kim," said Bridget, taking her hand. "Dear Kim. And dear David. Please don't be bothered about Arcadio. Believe me, I'll do everything in my power to help find Jennifer, and nothing that I think could possibly hurt you. The young man *is* a little—daunting, but he seems good-hearted and I really think he may be of some help. I know this sounds empty, but trust me. Trust *us*, right, Harry?"

But dear Harry was pretending to be asleep, not just to stay out of the conversation but because he couldn't remember being this tired, and knew he was too tired to really sleep. So he pretended to sleep and pretended to dream: of featherbeds and mountains of Excedrin, and then of whether Alka-Seltzer was soluble in Dewar's and then—sometimes you get lucky—he *was* asleep.

$\triangledown$

CHAPTER TEN

So I ASSUME, PROFESSIONAL deducer that I am, that on the way back to David's everybody talked about what had happened and what to do next, and that I got into David's house, took a bath, and got into bed. At least, when I woke up next—nope, the same—morning, I was *in* bed, and I didn't smell like the inside of a camel's mouth. I assume all that, but I'm damned if I can remember any of it.

And anyway I woke up too early. There was a knock on my door, I jolted straight up out of what must have been REM sleep, shouted—wouldn't you?—"Fuck it!" and there, through a widening crack into the door, was Bridget's face, a full moon at—what was it?—Jesus, 9:30 a.m.

"Oh, Harry, I'm sorry to wake you, but there are some policemen here, and they'd like to talk with you, dear.'

"*Maah*velous," I moaned. "Tell them I'll be out in a minute, okay, Bridget?" The door closed.

It's a beautiful day in the neighborhood, I thought as I got out of bed and looked for last night's clothes which, I figured, should be somewhere around the floor. Ever have one of those mornings when it's hard to find the floor? But they weren't there. Instead, neatly folded on the top of the TV, were a fresh pair of pants, shirt, underwear, and, perched on top like the cherry on a sundae, socks. And hanging from the doorknob with, I swear to God, a handkerchief in the breast pocket, was my other, fresh jacket.

Nuns, I thought as I got dressed. Ex-nuns. Two of them, now, dammit. Who the *hell* would fold *socks*?

In the living room, seated with coffee cups in their hands, were Bridget and the sort-of happy couple. Standing, cupless, by the fireplace (yeah, really—they build fireplaces in a town where the climate varies about as much as in a Howard Johnson's lobby) were George and Lenny from *Of Mice and Men*: a short, slim, greying elf in a suit and a burgundy polo shirt, and on the other side of the hearth, unbalancing the composition, a grim-faced and I mean *big* mother with a black moustache that would have made Groucho swoon, in a copsuit complete with a holster that looked big enough, if you drove over it, it could wreck your suspension.

"I'm John Carroll. Lieutenant John Carroll, Santa Barbara P.D.," the elf said in a reedy voice, not bothering to flash his tin at me. "You are Harold Garnish?"

"I are," I said. "For a long time now. Excuse me, Lieutenant," yawning, "can I sit down?"

"Oh, sure. Sorry," said John Carroll—and he actually looked like he *was* sorry. "I know you had a—well, let's say a rough night. Like some coffee?" Kim was already on her feet.

"Don't use it, thanks," I said. "Is there maybe a Coke?" Kim bustled off.

"Right," said Carroll. "Mr. Garnish, this"—indicating black moustache—"is Officer Helgerson. Now, I'd like to ask you—ask you *all*, in fact," nodding at the other folks in the room, "a few questions about Mr. Garnish's arrest last night and about, Mr. Pescatore, your daughter's disappearance. I—well, there's no way to say this gracefully," and he smiled at us, the kind of smile where you can almost read the stage direction, *Lieutenant smiles*, "the fact is, we're a little—concerned—at the main office. Mr. Garnish listed this house as his address when he was—detained—last night, and of course his Private Investigator's license from"—leafing through his notebook with a piano player's slender fingers—"yes, from Illinois went into the computer along with his other data. And *then* the computer—it's programmed for this sort of thing—matched the address with Mr. Pescatore's missing person report, and, well"—smiling and spreading his hands like Astaire at the end of a solo—"we're a trifle concerned about the possible connections here."

I was watching Officer Helgerson. He hadn't moved during Carroll's routine. I mean, I could see him breathe, but he hadn't *blinked*. Unless he blinked only when *I* blinked. And he wasn't just big, he was *fit*. No gut. Your Chicago cop always has at least a little bit of gut, and it makes the big town kind of homey, because it says, even if they have to bust you, what the hell, they've got pants that don't fit anymore, too. They, like, get cavities and don't know how to fix the sink, and they have to bust you because they're the Man, wearing the Man's colors, but what the fuck: it's only business.

Nossir. I don't trust cops that don't have a gut. What's the word? Officer Helgerson *intimidated* me. And Lieutenant Carroll was his boss.

"Now," went on Carroll, as Kim handed me a glass of Coke with crushed ice and—of course—a wedge of lemon in it. "Now, you understand that this is an unofficial—well, let's call it informal—business. At this point. But, of course, if anyone would rather have a lawyer present or— well—"and he finished the sentence with that fluttering hand-movement the Brits are so good at, the one that says, hey, there's maybe some nagging little problems with what I'm suggesting that might bug people with tiny minds, but folks like us sail above all that bullshit, don't we? Carroll was very good at it, too.

Good enough, at least, for David, who nodded understandingly and said, "Well, Lieutenant, I don't think that'll be necessary. After all, all we want to do—all of us—is get Jennifer back. I'm glad you're here, in fact."

But not good enough for everybody. "Oh, man, you just gotta be jokin, what?"

You're right: that came from Cado, stomping in from the kitchen looking like an extra from *Easy Rider* and holding a tallboy of Miller Genuine Draft like it was a cross to ward off vampires.

Heads swiveled, David rose to his feet, Officer Helgerson uncrossed his arms and let his right hand hang next to his *big* holster—I saw him blink!—and, maybe most important of all, Carroll kept on smiling. But thinner.

"Excuse me, sir," he said. "I don't know who you are, but this is a police matter, and you're interfering with its progress. Now, if you'd identify yourself—"

"Lieutenant," said Bridget, rising to her feet—well, she doesn't rise, really, she kind of surges—"this is Mr. Molina, an—acquaintance—who's—visiting." It was the feeblest I'd ever heard her sound.

Carroll looked at David in his slacks, real-estate blazer, and turtleneck, Kim in her white blouse and corduroy blue skirt, Bridget in her paisley hot-air balloon with a gold cross at the neck, and then at Cado. Helgerson just looked at me.

"An acquaintance. Visiting" Carroll nodded, still smiling. "And Mr. Molina, just how do you know these good people?" There might have been a little extra emphasis on the word, *good*, or maybe I was being paranoid: I usually am before the Lowenbrau lamp is lit.

"The tank, I bet," came a rumble. "Probably met Garnish in the tank." *Helgerson speaks!* I thought, noticing that he was still looking just at me.

"Hmmm," Carroll nodded again, all—what?— *professorial.* "You know, no offense, Mr. Molina—Mr. Molina *would* look more, well, in place in the tank than, well . . ." looking around at the fireplace, the knicknacks on the end tables, and the prints—you got it, Picasso's *The Lovers* was among them—on the walls. "What about it, Mr. Garnish? Is Mr. Molina here one of your many recent cellmates?"

"Hey, General," said Cado before I could answer. "I'm over here, dig? And I can talk for myself, you know? You said this was informal? So *be* informal, already. I gotta right to worry about the little girl too, don't I?"

I said "Fuck it!"—inwardly—for the second time that morning and Bridget gave a barely audible grunt, which means "Fuck it!" in Bridgetese. Carroll, whose smile was now about as comforting as a paper cut, said, "Right. Richard?" And Helgerson, at the magic word, crossed to Cado. He had a couple of inches on Cado, and took his arm without taking his arm. Cops can do that, you know. "Sir," he said, nodding toward the kitchen, "would you come with me, please?"

"Aww, *shit*, man," said Cado. "Another ff—another bust?"

"No bust, Mr. Molina," said Carroll. "But your presence here is not required. In fact your presence here is a damnable nuisance." Ever notice that? You say *damnable* and it means you've got all the bets covered, you say *damn* or *goddamn* and it means you don't. "And Officer Helgerson needs to get some information from you. Alone."

While he was saying this, Helgerson, silent, gently took the beer can out of Cado's hand, set it on an end table, and shoved him without touching him into the kitchen and out the back door into the yard. It was like a ventriloquist act: the Muppet from Hell.

"And now," said Carroll as we heard the back door close. "Your biker friend, Mr. Garnish, has actually saved us all a lot of time. I'll come to the point." He put his hands in his jacket pockets and sent what was left of his smile back to the props department.

"Mr. Pescatore," he began. "Miss Molloy. Please believe me, we are very, *very* concerned about Jennifer. I know it must seem to you as if we're dragging our feet, and you're just another case in a long line of cases. But we don't work like that. If you haven't heard anything from us, it's because we simply have nothing yet to tell you, and we don't believe"—glance at me, then at Bridget, then back at me—"in raising false hopes. But we *are* part of the most sophisticated police network in the country. S.B.P.D. is in the loop with L.A.P.D. *and* with C.H.P., and, you have to believe this, that loop is working *at this moment* to find your daughter, Mr. Pescatore. May I call you David?"

I liked that alphabet soup and "in the loop." It was so damned reassuring: like, you know, the oil spill is approaching the Florida keys or the reactor is two inches of dirty and leaking water away from a mushroom-shaped "incident," but a hand-picked Presidential fact-finding team is on its way *at this moment* to the site . . . .

"Lieutenant," began David.

"Please," he interrupted. "Let me finish. And I'm *John*, okay?" The smile made a curtain call. "David, it's obvious and it's what worried us that you've retained Miss"—glance at Bridget—"Ms. O'Toole and Mr. Garnish here to try to find your daughter. Now, now"—waving an elegant hand as Kim and David started to murmur—"I know that Ms. O'Toole has been visiting you and is a friend of the family.

But she *does* run a detective agency back East, and Mr. Garnish, who does not *seem* to be a friend of the family, *is* her employee—"

Honey, I thought: clover honey. I'd get a half pint of clover honey and, when he was asleep, I'd siphon it into the tank of the fucking Volvo he probably drove.

"—and," he went on, unaware that his doom was being plotted, "and Mr. Garnish has managed, in a very short time here, to open up your problem to a—well," nodding toward the back yard, "to a character *I* certainly wouldn't trust. Now, I can't tell you what to do, David. But I do urge you, for your own sake, to trust *us*. These private investigations—"

"But, Lieutenant," said David. "Kidnapping is serious, and, well—"

"We don't know that it *is* kidnapping," snapped Carroll. "Unless there's something more you have to tell us?"

"No. No," said Kim, holding up her little palm like a cop stopping traffic. "It's just that—"

"Kim!" snapped Bridget, and she snapped better than Carroll. "Since Lieutenant Carroll doesn't deign to address Harry or me directly, would you please show him the receipt I gave you for your retainer paid to O'Toole Agency?"

Kim looked confused. "But, Bridget," she stammered. "There's no—I don't—"

"Of course you don't," said Bridget. "You don't understand what I'm talking about because there is— *was*—no retainer paid to O'Toole Agency. There is no retainer *to* O'Toole because there is no investigation *by* O'Toole. We are an accredited, professional enterprise, and without an initial, recorded transaction, we do not function—we do not *exist*—as an investigative agency. Now, will you please inform Lieutenant Carroll—you can call him John—that I am a lady in advanced middle age who has not seen California, who likes to consider herself not only a concerned friend of yours but, until proven otherwise, a citizen free not just to appreciate the hospitality of this lovely state, but to share in your anxiety. And Mr. Garnish is *my* longtime friend— not, you may tell John, my "employee"—and is here out of his kind wish to support *me* through this trial. Or—ask Mr. Carroll—is shared grief considered grounds for conspiracy in California?"

Remember how Jack Benny used to put three fingers to his cheek (three fingers is funnier than two, Benny always said), do a slow take, and say, *"Well!"*? Carroll didn't do the three-finger bit, but he got the same effect by staring at the carpet and picking an imaginary piece of lint off his jacket sleeve.

"Of course," he finally said. "Ms. O'Toole, Mr. Garnish. You understand that we're only here because *we're* concerned, too. No one wants to start any sort of harrassment. God, the situation is awful enough for you two, Kim and David. But there *is*"—looking at his fingernails—"there *is* this business of Mr. Garnish's initial report to the arresting officers last night. Mr. Garnish, you *did* say that you had been shot at when you were found behind Golden State Liquors shouting obscenities into the darkness. Now, you see, that *does* make us wonder if there is, say, any connection between your arrest and—well, *you* know—anything to do with—uh— Jennifer's disappearance?"

That was it. That was the hook, that was why they were there, and that was my ticket out of it all and back to Chicago and Bandit and Janie and the Orrington Bar and a little more Janie. That was my chance to get everybody *off* the hook by *taking* the hook and return us all to normal space and time, where disappearances are handled and usually—well, what the hell, sometimes—solved by the people society pays to handle them.

Dig: all I had to say was yes, some bastard *had* been shooting at me, and what happens? My upcoming D&D rap gets shoveled into the circuit court landfill, Carroll has a good reason to tell me and maybe Bridget to get our asses *into* interrogation and then *back* to Lake Michigan, the cops twig to the possible involvement of Carla Bolero, and everything is back to the rule book, as manageable as meatloaf or miniature golf.

And that's what I thought would be best, and everybody was looking at me. I could *do* it, man: one word.

Of course, I screwed up. Maybe because Bridget—who was, for her, lying her ass off, and that's a lot of ass—had called me her "friend," not her "employee." Maybe because I was pissed off at getting shot at and then not being believed by the cops because of a blood count of one-oh. I don't *know* why: you want people who do things for *reasons*, go read novels.

"Yeah. Well," I said, sucking down the last of the Coke. "I guess I was a little looped last night. I do that sometimes"—giving him my best awshit-I'm-sorry-tremulous-drunk-grin, which wasn't all that hard to manage—"and I guess, well, you know, fucked up like that and all, maybe a car backfired, whatever. And Cado—that is, Molina—well, hell, Lieutenant, you know what it's like in the tank, you get talking, a guy's all at once your best friend. Boy," I said, lighting a cigarette and willing my hands to tremble, "I must've been parboiled."

Not that he bought it, but then again he didn't have much choice except to make believe he *did* buy it. He sighed, and so did I before I could stop myself. Goddammit, we were saying to one another: no miniature golf today.

"You tested at point one, Mr. Garnish," he said. "That's not what I would call 'parboiled,' and it's not usually a level that induces paranoid delusions. But then"—cocking an eye not at me but at Bridget—"maybe you have a low tolerance. Richard?"

And there, in the kitchen entry, filling the kitchen entry, right on cue, was Officer Helgerson. Do cops have little transistorized telepathy chips in their skulls, or what?

"Squared away, Lieutenant," said Helgerson.

"Then, we won't be bothering you folks anymore," said Carroll. It's got to be: the telepathy chips, I mean. "Mr. Pescatore? Believe me, we'll let you know as soon as we can anything at all we find out. And—try not to give up hope, can you do that? A lot of people are on your side here."

Kim and David made suitably submissive and grateful noises—the kind you and I make when the operator says, yes, she will connect us to the district supervisor about last month's phone bill.

Me he advised to take care of my bust as soon as possible, since I was going to be in California such a short time. That basically means, in coptalk, don't sweat, get out of town, and if you skip before trial we'll extradite the very first thing after we pardon Sirhan Sirhan. Bridget he looked at for a minute, and said, "Well, I probably will see you again, Ms. O'Toole: enjoy your visit here." And then he glided out of the house, with Helgerson in his wake. Such a small man for such a large wake.

We all stared at one another and I, noticing that it was now 11:00 a.m. was wondering if Cado had left any beer in the fridge, when in walked the Calfskin Kid himself, with two beers, one of which he handed to me.

"Hey," said Cado to everybody and nobody, "was that some bogus takedown, or what? Anyhoo, campers, they got dog *heuvos* from us and we're still a team, ain't it so?"

And then Bridget said something that, even at the time, I thought was funny.

"Hello, Cado," she said. "You had a pleasant talk with the officer? Good. And Yes, I suppose we are a team, now. And no, I think Mr. Carroll and Mr. Helgerson got exactly what they came here for."

"Now. How shall we all spend our Saturday?"

CHAPTER ELEVEN

AND THIS IS HOW we all decided to spend our Saturday, except me. (I didn't *decide* a damn thing).

David and Kim had to put in an appearance at Pescatore Realty. "Weekends are our peak business days," David told me sagely. Right: when else can the poor yobs sweating forty a week find time to spend a day cruising neighborhoods looking for a place that'll make them sweat a little more, because *this* one's got an automatic lawn sprinkler or an electric kitchen or it's close to "good" schools?

Anyhoo, as Cado liked to say. Kim and David were off to sell black holes to people who wanted to be sucked into them, and Bridget said that she was going to go along with them, just to, as she put it, "try to get the feeling of the business, its rhythm, and appreciate the situation." Solid, I thought: I was planning to re-appreciate my bed, just as soon as everybody got the hell out of the house. Cado, for all I cared, could impregnate the family cat—if they had a family cat—as long as he was quiet about it and let me sleep.

But—like all those guys and ladies say to one another all the time on afternoon TV—it just wasn't meant to be. "Harry," Bridget said. "I think you should go to Los Angeles,

and see if you can find out anything from—well, exploring—
Miss Bolero's residence."

You caught it. There was a direct suggestion of breaking
and entering, and if somebody had taped it, we could *just for
talking about it* have done some serious time, just like Nixon
and Halderman . . . .

Okay. Scratch that. We could have done some serious
time.

Not that I brought up anything that complicated as an
objection. "Bridget!" I said. "I'm hardly awake, L.A. is a
hundred miles away, and I don't even know my way *around*
the damn town! And it's already almost noon! And the cops
still have my damn car from last night!"

And that, folks, is why you can *always* have too many
friends. David could pick up my rented Datsun, or arrange
to have my rented Datsun picked up, from the impound lot,
and Kim, shyly, told me that she knew Carla's L.A. address
and David, jumping back in to cover Kim's blush (for that I
liked him) told me he could draw me a map if I needed one,
and then, the olive in the martini and the rim-shot after the
punch-line, Cado said:

"Hey, no worries, I know L.A. like the back of my hand.
Better. I never look at the back of my hand. And we can go
on my bike, dig, leave right now and save time getting your
car back. You ever ride a bike, Chicago?"

"Uh," I said, and I was never more eloquent.

"Walk in the park," he said. "All you gotta do's hang on.
I even got a spare pair of goggles. Let's boogie, hah?"

I hate driving even in the city with the sanest grid pattern
in the world (thanks again, Mrs. O'Leary), so I figured L.A.
would really do it to me, so: what the hell.

"Bitchin'!" said Cado. "We are outta here. Oh, hey, yeah,
Miss Bridget: what happens if the lady's, you know, *there*?"

"That's *right!*" said David, like he'd just discovered the formula for nylon. "What if Carla's there?"

"No problem," I said. "Then Cado and I just come on like a couple—what?—survey takers, Bible students—"

"*Cado?*" Bridget smiled, and I smiled back.

"Hey, Bridge," I said. "Be cool. This be El-*lay*, dig."

"*Bitchin,*" laughed Cado, turning it into a four- syllable word. "C'mon, Chicago—showtime."

Now a few years ago some guy wrote a book—I'm serious— about motorcycles and Zen. Ben Gross loaned it to me, told me I'd enjoy it—Ben can't figure why everybody doesn't enjoy everything anybody writes—and I couldn't figure if it was a novel or a very *long* sermonette. But it gets mystical as hell about how riding a cycle is the communion of nature and technology, and the landscape embraces you, and the wind in your hair and God peeking over the horizon, like that. One line I remember, something like "it's as easy to find the Buddha in a motorcycle engine as in the heart of the lotus."

I say *wrongo*. At least the motorcycle part. I don't know from hearts of lotus.

Cado's bike was, he told me proudly, a 1200 cc. Harley— "customized up the ass, baby!"I assume that 1200 cc. is fairly high up the meanmother scale, bikewise. *Got* to be: the damn thing had bulges and twists of tubing under the seat that looked as powerful and dangerous as a panther's butt right before it springs (so I watch PBS nature specials— sue me). And the front wheel was canted out at, I don't know, a forty-degree angle, so that, even sitting parked in David's back yard, the bastard looked like it was moving, or at least pawing the ground.

And it was painted pink. Pink, with green stripes along

the tubing and around the bulges. A Baskin-Robbins pterodactyl in threat display. That I was going to ride.

"Jesus!" I said as Cado handed me a pair of goggles and
John Wayned onto the seat. "Th' fuck am I supposed to hang
on *to*?"

"*Me*, lover," he grinned. "Just lock your hands around my
sexy little belly and worry not, cause *I* ain't goin' *nowhere*,
bro." Kickstart, three full throttles that I figured could have
saved me the money I paid for my vasectomy, Cado turns
and hollers, "Relax, Chicago, you're ridin' with an urban
fighter pilot!"— goddamn if *that* didn't ease my mind—and
we're off, down the yard, onto the street, onto Highway 101,
and I realize—I've seen motorcycles my whole life, okay, but
now I realize—that we're doing over sixty m.p.h. on the
downslope of a continental shelf, and that we're doing it not
in anything but perched *on* something that only has two,
count them *two wheels*. I mean, it can, like, fall *over*.

I don't know. Maybe the Buddha was somewhere in the
1200 cc's. Tell you the truth, I forgot to look.

Seriously: do you have any idea how *big* a Peterbilt with
a refrigerator hitch on the back looks when you're riding the
white line between it on the left and a Winnebago on the
right?

That was around Ventura, thirty or so miles south of
Santa Barbara, where 101 hugs the side of the mountains
and the Pacific is a sheer drop off on the right. By the time
we got to Camarillo, about halfway there, I was relatively
sure we might not fall over—we hadn't so far—and I even
took the risk of looking at the countryside. Camarillo is a
nice little town—flat, like the Midwest—with long roads
branching off the highway and low buildings and rows of
palm trees that make it look like those romantic Army
barracks from World War II movies. We passed a turnoff

marked CAMARILLO STATE HOSPITAL, and I thought, damn! This is *the* Camarillo: this is where Charlie Parker was locked up for the last six months of his terrible 1947 California tour, strung out and suicidal, and out of that pain and shame brought a masterpiece and the first jazz record I ever heard, 'Relaxin' at Camarillo."

If I'd had a hat, I would have tipped it, for Parker. Funny, that's the first time being in California *meant* a damn thing to me.

Then up the Conejo Grade, which is steep enough it's like slipping into slow-motion, unless you're sitting on a 1200 cc. Harley: fishtailing between the semis and the Volvos, you could almost hear them saying, "I think I can, I think I can." And then down into L.A.

I told you that you always talk about going *out* to California. Well, out there, you always go *down* to L.A. And it really *is* down. Since when God was in kindergarten, these continental plates have been mashing together, and what they've done is make a connected series of shallow soup bowls—or maybe a Salvador Dali muffin pan—and it's in the hollows that people cooked up all the not-quite-the-same muffins that, together, are the City.

Carla Bolero's particular part of the big muffin was a bungalow on a street of bungalows shaded, if that's the word, by mangy palms that made me think, with a twinge, of Phil back home. Cado coasted down the street to check the address, and then parked around the block. When he shut off the engine, the sudden silence felt like having water in your years.

"Yeah," I said, fumbling for a cigarette. "Nice ride. Good time. Now, here's the way we're going to play this thing—"

"Wait, man. Look!" Cado interrupted, grinning and pointing upwards.

Through the anorexic palm trees I saw a green and brown hill topped by a white concrete structure that looked like it was auditioning for the role of Roman fortress in a Biblical movie, and stumbling over its lines.

"Yeah?" I said.

"That's *it*, man," said Cado, staring at it. *"Griffith Park Observatory!* Damn!"

"Yeah?" I said.

He looked at me—for the first time—with disappointment in his eyes.

"Griffith *Park*, man. James *Dean*? *Rebel Without a Cause*? Jesus, Chicago, this is where it all started. Remember Dean and Natalie Wood and Sal Mineo telling all the grownups—who? Jim Backus?—to just fuck off? *Sonofabitch*," and he stared back, reverently, at the building on the hill.

Okay. I had Camarillo, and Cado had Griffith Park, and I couldn't say that my holy place was holier than his. Maybe that was the problem here. California was so full of ghosts that *every*place could be somebody's holy place—and a sad one.

The question of the hour, though, was what ghosts, if any, we could find at Carla Bolero's place.

I told Cado to wait down the block while I rang the bell—I could hear it sound inside the house—five or six times, checked in as many windows as I could, and strolled back to my accomplice.

"Nobody home," I told him. "Look, I'm going to find a basement door, something, around back. Now in about five minutes you come to the front, all natural, and—"

"Aww, *hey*," whined Cado, twisting his torso with his hands in his pockets—I think he was still thinking about James Dean—"California bungalow, there *ain't* a basement door, on account there ain't a *basement*."

"Oh, yeah. Right," I said.

"Course," he went on, "you might find a crawlspace, you like black widows and shit. But you can't get from there into the fuckin' house. Now—"

"All right, Cado," I said. "I'll just find a back door. Now in five, ten minutes you mosey to the front, ring, and I'll let you in, okay?"

No, I don't carry one of those little leather cases full of little scalpels and dental tools you see in the Bond movies, but I've found you can do pretty well with credit cards, big safety pins, and patience. I had the back door just about licked when it swung inward, taking my safety pin in its lock and sending my Adam's apple into my mouth. And there stood Cado, saying, "You rang, sir?"

Never mind what I said then, or what he, laughing, said back.

I'd never been in a porn queen's house before, but this one had as much personality as a Holiday Inn room: same style furniture, as far as I could tell, all greens and blues. A bottle of Chardonnay in the fridge, along with a salami and a loaf of bread. Ten or twelve tapes in a box by the cassette player-radio ("Jesus," sniffed Cado, "she likes Phil fuckin Collins?") Bed unmade ("Wow," breathed Cado, "hey, man, Carla Bolero's *bed*!") Nothing personal: no photos, knick-nacks.

And no clothes in the closet, or in the dresser drawers.

"She skipped!" said Cado. "Hey, Harry, maybe we oughta call Santa Barb, see if maybe Miss Bridget wants to twig the cops on this, somethin."

"Hang on a sec," I said, closing the last dresser drawer. The answer phone was on the bedtable, and I pushed the "playback" button. Nothing. I flipped open the cassette chamber, and it was empty.

"Okay, Cado," I said. "Let's take a short walk, smoke a cigarette, think about this a minute. What's her agency? Sybaris. I wonder if anybody'd be there on a Saturday."

We left through the front door, and there, on the stoop, was a man who looked about as old as E.T. and about the same size, holding an orange and black cat that should have tipped the little guy over. In the crook of his right arm, that is. In his left hand he was holding what couldn't have been less than thirty years old, and couldn't have been more than a .22 caliber, but was very definitely a revolver. And his left hand wasn't trembling.

"Okay, you mugs," he said. *Mugs?* I thought. "I might call the bulls, or I might just take care of you gonniffs myself— and I'd be in my rights, too, no mistake about that. But first I want to know just what right you got messing around Carla's house. Back in the house—and slow, facing me."

My fellow mug at least knew that a tiny gun was still a gun. He backed up right beside me, and, as we recrossed the threshhold, whispered out of the side of his mouth, "Harry— what'd he mean by 'the bulls?'"

"Cado," I whispered out of the side of mine, "Just shut up, okay?"

$\triangledown$

CHAPTER TWELVE

"ALL RIGHT," SAID E.T. "Sit down, and if you want to keep your gazongas, don't make any sudden moves." As he sat, the cat jumped out of his arm and trotted off toward the kitchen. Maybe it could smell the Chardonnay.

"Hey, man," began Cado—

"You just shut up, buster," said our host. "And my name isn't 'man,' it's Bruce Hewitt. To you, *Mister* Hewitt. And I want to know why you're messing around in my neighbor's place. Are you the guys that were making all that damn noise here last night?"

"Mr. Hewitt," I said. "If you want to call the police, go ahead: and they will arrest us, because we were—sorry, sir—breaking and entering. But if Carla Bolero is your neighbor, and if she's your friend, that might end up getting her in worse trouble than it would us."

"Smooth customer, aren't you?" he said, with a little smile. "But now just why should I believe you, sport?" And he hitched his shoulders like early Richard Widmark.

And, by God, that's *it!* I thought: the little guy was talking and acting like a forties film. Not that that made his revolver less real.

I took a chance on getting the dialogue right. "Because,
Mr. Hewitt, that's the only way it plays. I'm a private eye,
see—name's Garnish. I work out of Chicago, mainly—and
I'm on a case. You want to see my papers? No?"

"What kind of case?" Hewitt asked. His eyes had bright-
ened, just a little, and his gun—I hoped—had tilted a little
bit toward the carpet.

"Well, now, Mr. Hewitt, you know I can't tell you that"
I smiled. "Hey—you mind if I smoke? Thanks. The thing
is"— exhaling and talking at the same time like the real cool
cat I was—"the thing is, it's pretty serious business, and one
of the things I'm trying to do is talk to Miss Bolero without
getting her involved with the cops. You just have to trust me
on this," I lied, "but she's in no danger from me. Things are
just a little—well, sticky."

"I don't know," Hewitt said. It was working. "Maybe you
just better wait till Carla gets home—"

"Hell, man," said Cado. "She ain't coming home, she
done *absconded*."

"What's that?" snapped Hewitt, the .22 back at attention.
"She's gone?"

"Looks like it," I said. "No clothes, no personal stuff anywhere. You didn't know? You can check it out, if you want."

"Okay," he said, waving the gun like a garden hose and
walking toward the bedroom. "You guys stay right there, got
me?"

The poor little guy was really shaken. Cado made let's split
gestures at me, and I waved him down. Damned if I wanted to
die backshot escaping from an enraged octogenarian.

He came back from the bedroom a little smaller than he'd
gone in. The gun was stuffed in his belt.

"Your name's Garmick?" he asked. "Better let me see that
license."

"Garnish," I said, handing it to him.

"And you?" he said to Cado.

"Hey," said Cado before I could think of anything. "Look at the way I'm dressed. Undercover. Can't be carrying papers, dig. Name's Molina, from Harry's L.A. office."

"Hmm," said Hewitt, too distressed not to buy it. "Look. Are you boys on the level? I mean, about not trying to cause Carla any—trouble?"

"Bruce—Bruce, right?" asked Cado. "When you were in the bedroom, did we split? Or try to roust you? Come on—what do *you* think?" I sighed, and lit another cigarette.

"Well—well, okay. Can we talk at my place—next door? I can make some tea. Thalberg? Thalberg!" And with that the cat, a fuzzy orange-and-black-kielbasa, trotted back in and made a three-point landing in the crook of Hewitt's arm.

If Carla's bungalow was short on the personal touch, Bruce Hewitt's—identical on the outside—was like getting kicked upside the head by a mule. Every inch of wall space— really, I couldn't find any gaps—was covered with movie posters, magazine covers, newspaper headlines, all framed. *Life, Look, Collier's, Liberty, The Blue Dahlia, Young Man With a Horn, Carousel,* and on and on; news of VE Day, Ike's election, JKF in Dallas, that one with a triangle of black felt in the upper right corner, the way my Sicilian friends do it.

And cats: maybe a football squad's worth of cats, who grumbled amiably, making room, while their pal Thalberg decided how to rejoin them, finally settling next to a cut glass candy bowl on the coffee table.

"So," said Cado as we tried to find places on the sofa and Hewitt bustled into the kitchen. "I guess you like the movies, huh?"

The old man's laugh was pleasant—tinkly. "Ah, you noticed," he said. "Yeah, I like them. Fact is, maybe half those movies you see on the walls, I helped make 'em. You boys know what a gaffer is? Course you don't. You never stay for the credit roll, end of the film, do you? Well—oh, say, fellas," and he poked his little head out of his little kitchen, "it looks like I'm fresh out of tea. How about a little brandy? Myrna Loy, I'm *ashamed* of you! Mr. Garalic, just brush her off."

That last was addressed to a Siamese who had decided my lap was just about the nicest place on earth and was asking me with her amber crossed eyes if I'd respect her in the morning.

"Call me Harry," I said. "It's okay. I like cats." Lies, lies, lies.

Out came Hewitt with a tray—yep, a *Gone With The Wind* tray, Rhett and Scarlett and Atlanta in flames—with three purple-tinted ponies and a liter of Korbel. I wondered how long Brother Bruce had been fresh out of tea, like, maybe, since Apollo Eleven?

"Yeah, a gaffer," he said, scenting and sipping the Korbel like it was Courvoisier. "Forty years, and I must've worked with 'em all. The lights, you know."

"Oh," I said, "lighting director."

He snorted. "Lighting director my butt! Lighting director flounces on the set, waves his arms. 'I want shadows *here* and *here*, and let's have a nice soft backlight right *there*,' and goes to lunch in Westwood. Now, who do you think *puts* the shadows and the backlight there and there and there?"

"Uh—the gaffer?" I said. *Damn, I'm swift.*

"You *betcha*, Red Ryder," he said and poured himself another. "Forty years. Met Patti—that was my wife—on the job. She was continuity—you know, script girl?—on *Charlie Chan in Egypt.* You ever see *Charlie Chan in Egypt*?"

"Jesus," said Cado. "With Sidney Toler?"

"Warner Oland," the gaffer smiled. "Easy mistake."

"Yeah, but—that's *great*! You did that one?"

"Well, I was just an apprentice back then," he said, stroking a fluffy gray who was nosing his brandy. "But yeah, I had a hand in most of the setups. *No*, Cagney; *bad* for kitties." He saved Cagney's ass by draining his drink, and then endangered the poor kitty all over again.

"Uh, Mr. Hewitt," I said, shifting and trying not to disturb Myrna Loy, who was sound asleep with her claws half extended into my leg. "Could we take about Carla Bolero?"

If leather can blush, he blushed. And chuckled. "Ooops, sorry, Harry: you boys are busy. You know us old farts."

Actually, I like old farts: a lot better than most of the young shits and middle-aged turds I meet, and I was getting to like this one especially. But I did need to know what he knew about Carla before he brandied himself into a Saturday afternoon nostalgia nod (you do know about *those*, I hope).

"Carla," he said while Cagney alternately eyed the brandy and gave him love bites on his thumb. "Carla is a *lovely* kid, you know? I mean really *lovely*— *inside*, I mean. Look—" and he leaned forward, sloshing a little Korbel onto the nose of Cagney, who ran like hell for the kitchen—"I guess you fellas know how she makes her living."

"Well," I said—

"No, no, it's okay," he went on. "This town, people do what they do, doesn't mean they can't grow roses, you know what I'm saying? Where'd you say *you* were from, Harry?"

"Chicago," said Cado. Thalberg had joined Cado.

"Yeah. Well," said Hewitt. "We never talked about that, Carla and me. Never. I mean, I don't like that kind of stuff. Come to think of it, I don't even remember how I found out what Carla was doing. You just find things out, huh? Anyhow—" and he chuckled again, slyly, pouring himself a fourth—"I went to see one of her movies once, one of those places on Melrose Avenue. Geez Louise, it was *terrible.*"

"Mr. Hewitt. Bruce," I said, afraid he was losing it.

"No, really. *Terrible,*" he went on. "Some of that nonsense—look, I've lived in Hollywood my whole *life,* I *know* what people like to do with each other, and some of that stuff, I tell you, people just don't *do.* Silly. And the *lighting,* my God! The movie I saw, I promise you: one rack of baby spots, maximum, and I bet the jackass of a director'd never even *held* a light meter. Everybody's skin looked like wax."

"So you haven't met anybody she—ah—works with," I said. But he wasn't listening.

"Course, when I went to that movie, that was after Patti—my wife—was gone. Boy, Pat would've had a *fit.* So let's see: Patti's gone, uh, three years, so that means Carla's been here about five. Yeah: cause Patti was pretty sick those last couple of years, and Carla, she'd come over and bring meals, even read to Pat, you know? And—uh, and *after*—she kept coming over, you know, watch TV with me, help with the kitties. Hey, fellas, excuse me a minute." His eyes were tearing, and he lurched off toward the john. We heard water running.

Now I made let's split gestures to Cado, who shook his head.

"Hey, give it a little longer. We got time, and it's good for the old man to talk," whispered the Son of Satan.

"Sorry," Hewitt smiled, coming back. "A little more brandy?"

I was shaking my head as my designated driver said, "Sure, thanks," so I figured, what the hell.

"Yeah, the kitties," he went on. "There were only two before—when Patti was here. Ol' Thalberg, there, is eleven, and Greta—well, she's gone too, now. Excuse me, Harry, didn't you ask me something?"

"Huh? Oh, yeah," I said. "Did you get to meet any of her friends? People she worked with?"

"No, not really," he said. "Like I said, we were both kind of shy about her end of the business—I don't even think she knows *I* know—and she didn't have a lot of people over, anyway. Till lately—"

"What, lately?" I asked.

"Well, the last few days—week, maybe—there's been a lot of coming and going late at night. You know, cars, voices. I'm not nosey, Harry—I just sleep light. And last night— that's why I was so worried about you fellas—maybe one, two in the morning, there's noises. I get up, look out the bedroom window, and the lights are on in her house, some- body's moving around."

The next question I always hate to ask. "Mr. Hewitt," I said, "when did you see Carla last?"

He panicked, as I'd feared. "What do you mean, *last*?" His pony tipped onto the carpet. "You don't think anything's—I mean, Carla just *left*, right? I mean, she didn't say goodbye, but that's, well, sometimes people just *go*, you know?"

"Hey, dude, relax," said Cado, standing over him with a snake-tattoo hand on his shoulder. "All Harry means, you know, Carla's in some deep—ah, yogurt here, and we need to know how long she might've been gone. Right, Harry?"

I just nodded. I hoped Carla, wherever she was, had some idea of the pain she was causing this old man.

"Okay. Look," Hewitt said. "I guess I saw her last, what, five or six days ago. Sometimes I lose track of time, huh?" he smiled, looking at the Korbel out of the corner of his eye.

"Five or six days," I said. "You didn't think about knock- ing on her door, see if she was alright?"

"Oh, no," he said. "I don't want to be a nuisance to her. You know, sometimes old people can be a pain in the butt.

Say. If—when—you boys find her, you'll let me know, yeah? And, ah, tell her I say hello?"

It's a bad way to be, and we all get that way: he *really* didn't want to lose anybody else. Suddenly I knew—I mean, *knew*—that Greta the cat was buried somewhere in his back yard.

And it was time to go. I stood up—pissing off Myrna Loy in the extreme—and told him we'd let him know whatever we found out. My second brandy, untasted, was still on the table: I guessed it would find a home.

We were at the door when Hewitt said, "Oh gosh! Wait!" and bustled back to the desk in the corner, fiddling through a tossed salad of paper scraps.

"Yeah. Here!" he crowed, "Darn, I'm glad I remembered! Carla gave me this. Told me if I needed her, couldn't get in touch, I should call this guy, this"—squinting—"Reilly. You boys want this?"

We did. We sure as hell did. We thanked him again, told him we'd be in touch. I began to say something about how the .22 had scared me, and he laughed.

"Oh, *that*," he said, and handed it to me. "That there is the prop Richard Widmark used in *Killer's Kiss*. Careful, now—that baby's worth something." And we left.

Neither of us spoke till we got back to Cado's cycle. Then he said, "Okay, Chicago, what now?"

I lit a cigarette, gave it to him, lit another. "Fuck it," I said.

"Come again?"

"What," I said, "it's a complicated concept? Fuck it. You know? *Fuck* it."

"Oh," he said. "You mean mortality."

I looked at him. "On the button," I said. "Bro."

"Yeah," he said trying to keep his face straight. "*Fuck* it."

And we collapsed, laughing and hugging, for one of those twenty-second times that feels like two hours.

"So, really now," said Cado, wiping his eyes, "what now?"

"Oh, hell," I said, fishing for another cigarette and coming up empty. "We have to think. A phone booth. In a bar. With a cigarette machine. Fair enough?"

"Righteous!" he said, and kickstarted the pink pterodactyl. We idled down the residential street, so I could still talk to Cado.

"Hey!" I hollered in his ear. "Is *Charlie Chan in Egypt* really that great a movie?"

"Don't know," he hollered back. "Never saw the goddman thing."

$\triangledown$

CHAPTER THIRTEEN

So we wound up in a—what? Carrow's, Sizzler, Red Lobster?, the one that serves Heineken's anyway—at three-thirty in the afternoon, plotting our next step in the quest for, you should excuse the expression, Snow White.

"Or Rapunzel," said Cado, sitting two of those lovely beetle-green bottles across from me. "You think—could be—old Carla's getting the screw here, too? Like, you called her, so what if she just gets scared and decides to pack it in, chill out for a while?"

"Right," I said, putting my glass down a little harder than I'd intended to. "She panics, heads for the tall grass, doesn't give two shits about her daughter—remember her daughter, the one we're looking for?—and I just got my ass shot at last night because it's a big ass and the local N.R.A. was out testing some new assault weapons. Swift, Cado."

"Well," he said, "that old guy, Hewitt—"

"Uh *huh*," I said. "That old guy, Hewitt, says she's Florence Nightingale and she feeds his cats, for Chrissake, and every whore gets a Heart of Gold secret decoder ring when they graduate from whore finishing school. You go to the movies a lot, or what?"

Ever see a death's-head insignia outlaw biker *miffed*? He

poured some more beer, took one of my cigarettes, and grumbled. "Okay, it was a *thought*. So what now?"

"You tell me," I said, pouring the rest of my beer so that when the bottle was drained the foam stood maybe an eighth of an inch up from the rim of the glass and not a drop ran down the side. You think that's easy? "I'm tired. Plan one, we spend the rest of the afternoon here, find out just how much Heineken's they have in stock, and go home. Plan two, we try to get in touch with somebody at Sybaris Agency, see if they can tell us *any* damn thing, though on a Saturday afternoon I don't think our chances of finding somebody there are real dazzling. Plan three, we call this number Hewitt gave us"—I fished it out of my jacket and shoved it toward him—"and see if *this* guy can tell us something, or doesn't want to tell us something, or if he even answers his phone."

"Plan one sounds good," said Cado, fingering the scrap of paper.

"I was hoping you'd say that," I said. "Way I figure it—"

"Wait!" he said, looking at the paper. "Reilly. Damn! You know who this could be? This could be *Bobby* Reilly. Private number. Sonofabitch!"

I didn't know who Bobby Reilly was, so of course I asked him, silently watching plan one go down in flames. It's okay, I frequently have that experience talking to Bridget.

"Bobby Reilly!" Cado said. "Old One-Eye Reilly himself. You never heard of him?"

Well, I'm Czech, myself, but nobody lives in Chicago for very long without meeting a lot of Irishmen, and nobody meets a lot of Irishmen—at least, Chicago Irishmen—without hearing a lot of jokes and songs, sometimes it's hard to tell the difference, about One-Eye Reilly. One-Eye Reilly is the character, maybe the monster that, I guess, most Irish

Catholic boys between fourteen and seventy spend their lives
fearing, taking measures against, or aiding and abetting.
When they're not calling him "One-Eye Reilly," guys tend to
call it a cock. Women—and I have Janie the hooker's author-
ity on this—usually call it a weenie. And out of that semantic
dissonance—old Martin O'Toole loved using phrases like
"semantic dissonance"—old Martin O'Toole would have
probably said you could evolve the whole history of marital
discord here in the Western World.

"No," I said to Cado. "Never heard of him in my life."

"Jesus, Chicago," said Cado, shaking his head sadly.
"You heard of Holmes? Reems? Bobby Reilly's in *that* class:
that's how good he is. Motherfucker's *big*."

I let the hundred-and-one punchlines to that pass.

"Really big," Cado went on. "Fact, he was in one of those
movies that ol' Carla was in. Let's see: wasn't *The Sweeter
Elixir*, I don't think. No—yeah! *Spanish Delight*, that's right,
and *The Schoolmistress*, and—oh, wow, man, I'd almost
forgotten—*Gestapo Slaves*. A lot of movies: boy, you forget,
huh? Harry, we gotta call this guy. I mean, he fucks her. All
the time. On camera."

I'd nodded to the waitress for a couple more beers, and
she brought them, and, folks, they looked just terrific, and
now I knew I couldn't have mine. Phone call to make. That
made one wasted brandy at Hewitt's and one wasted beer
here. Go ahead: tell me there's a God.

You do things like this all the time: I bet you do. You dial
a number—tax accountant, ex-wife, dentist—because you
know you're supposed to, because it's the grownup, *mature*
(yeah, I hate that word, too) thing to do. And you wait, and
you wait, and you wait, all the time thinking "*Please* don't
let them answer, *please* don't let the answerphone kick in,
please let it ring just six times so I can hang the fuck up and

then when they call me and say "Where *were* you?" I can say, "Hey—goddam, I *tried*."

And, of course, I got Bobby Reilly's number on the third buzz.

"Hello. This is Rob," said, I guess, Rob.

"Mr. Reilly?" I said. "Sir, my name is Garnish. I'm a private investigator—"

"Okay," he interrupted me. "How'd you get this number? No. Never mind. You want to talk to my lawyer—"

"No, sir," I said. "Please hear me out. I got your number from a friend of Carla Bolero's, and all I want to do is—"

"Carla? Is she all right? Look, Mr.—"

"Garnish. Harry Garnish. Mr. Reilly, I don't know if she's all right. I'm trying to find her, talk to her; believe me," I lied again, "she's in no trouble. But she seems to have disappeared. And all I want to know is if I and an— associate—can come talk to you about her."

Silence. Then, "Okay. Look, I've got some things to do, but you can come by in, say, an hour and a half. Around five? You know how to get here?"

"No, sir," I said. "I've just got your phone number."

"Mattachine Garden Apartments, number 12C. That's on Crane Street, West Hollywood. Make it five-thirty. You can find it?"

I told him I was sure I could. And when I told Cado that he was going to meet one of his favorite film stars—can you say *actor* about that end of the business?—and gave him the address, he guffawed.

"So what's the gag?" I asked.

"No gag, little buddy," he said, still chortling. "You'll find out. So we got an hour to kill. Want to eat?"

I looked at the menu, told him to order me a hot pastrami sandwich, and carried my beer over to the phone booth. I called David's home number, collect, hoping Bridget would be back by now. She was.

"I'm afraid," I told her, "things are not exactly going what you'd call apace." She just grunted, not especially surprised, when I told her that Carla had skipped.

"The closest thing to a lead we've got," I went on, "is this guy—friend of Carla's—named Reilly. We talk to him in a while, and then I'm heading for the barn."

"Reilly?" said Bridget, suddenly interested. "Is that Bobby Reilly? The actor?"

People are always doing things like that to me when I've got a swallow of beer halfway down my throat. After a few seconds of strangled gurgling, I croaked, "Well, yes, Bridget, as a matter of fact it is. You—ah, know his work?"

"Oh, I've never seen it, but I've heard of him. He's very prominent. Dear—if he seems to have any information, or if he seems at all cooperative, do you think you could arrange, or suggest, for me to interview him also?"

Okay. Bridget wanted to meet a porn king. I mean, I knew this was California, and like all midwesterners I knew that California does weird things to you. But this was *Bridget*: and this was *fast*.

"Sure thing," I said. "And—uh—*your* day? How was your day?"

"Oh, very pleasant," she chirped (imagine a baritone sparrow—that's Bridget's chirp). "You wouldn't believe how busy a real estate office can be. David and Kim were on the phone, or talking to clients, constantly from the time we walked in the door. And, oh yes: David's main competitor appears to be something called Morningside Realty. He had a lot of phone calls from them, and he seemed annoyed about it. I didn't bother the boy about it, but perhaps you and I should speak to them tomorrow—just for background. And then, after lunch, Kim dropped me back here, and I've spent the afternoon—well, puttering around, you know. Have you had a chance to eat, dear?"

I told her I was just about to do that, promised her that, yes, I'd see about her meeting Bobby Reilly (weird—did she want an autograph?) and rang off.

Cado was demolishing a taco salad—that's fried tortillas, ground beef, guacamole, and about a half-acre of lettuce, if you're an outsider—and my pastrami, with a nice new beer, was waiting.

"Waitress says you made a good choice," he said as I sat. "Says the pastrami is nice and lean today."

Never mind that the words "pastrami" and "lean" are never, *never* used together in polite society east of the continental divide, or that my sandwich contained not just pastrami-lite and mustard but sliced tomato, mayonnaise, and—you really have to trust me on this—bean sprouts. Or that the pickle on the side was three sweet gherkins. I was hungry, I ate.

"Good?" asked Cado as I washed the last of it down with the last of the Heineken's.

"Amazing," I said. "I got a friend back in Chicago, Ben Gross, he wouldn't believe a pastrami sandwich could taste like this."

"Good," he said. "Let's ditty-bop. Chicago, you're gonna love West Hollywood."

And ditty-bop we did.

"Oh, yeah" said Cado right before he kickstarted in the parking lot, "*The Frog King*."

"Wha." I said.

"*The Frog King*," he said. "Another movie with ol' Carla and ol' One-Eye. Fairy-tale thing. She's this princess, see, never been laid or anything. And he's—well, at first he looks kind of like a big lizard, yeah? But then they start fucking and such, and he turns out, he's a fuckin' prince! Good movie. They do lots of weird shit."

"Right," I said. "Let's ditty-bop."

$\triangledown$

CHAPTER FOURTEEN

IF WEST HOLLYWOOD WAS supposed to astonish me on sight, it—or I—was missing something. It looked—well, residential, or as residential as anyplace in L.A. can look, knowing that those freeways are groaning away, big snakes in eternal peristalsis, just a long run away from wherever you happen to be.

Nevertheless, Cado kept grinning his coyote grin all the way to the doorbell of 12C Mattachine Gardens, a little maze of cinderblock duplexes that could have passed for a college dorm with a big, blue tile reflecting pool in what I guess was the central courtyard.

"Mr. Garnish?" The guy who opened the door was maybe six-one, six-two, and his hair and beard were orange, and I mean *Crayola* orange, which made sense because his eyes were a color that used to gas me as a kid because I never saw it anywhere outside a Crayola box: remember "magenta"? He was wearing a black silk turtleneck with a silver cross on a chain, and he had a crystal hanging from his ear that looked like one of those purple jellybeans that—again, in my youth—it seemed they only sold around Eastertime.

"Mr. Reilly?" I said, realizing, *of course: his jellybean matches his eyes!*

"Yes," he smiled, extending a hand. "Will you come in? And—ah—your friend?"

Cado introduced himself—as my "partner," what are you going to do?—and we marched into the living room. Piano music—pretty boring piano music—was coming from the speakers somewhere.

"Winston?" I asked.

"Yes, *Winter!*" Reilly said, cranking up his smile a couple of candlepower and gesturing for us to sit. "Can I offer you both some wine? Oh—this is my friend, Tedd: with two dees," he said with a special smile at Tedd, who returned it, not looking at us.

Tedd with two dees was perched on one end of one of the three sofas that bordered or defined the living room. He was holding a glass of white wine and he was wearing, over a pink T-shirt, a blue seersucker jacket with the sleeves pushed up past the elbows, the way they do it on "Miami Vice." His hair wasn't as orange as Reilly's, though it was shoulder-length, and his eyes, behind steel-rim glasses, weren't as shockingly blue: just almost.

Cado sat down and, grunting, reached for the bottle and one of the empty glasses on the table. I remained standing.

"Excuse me, Mr. Reilly," I said. "I assumed that our conversation would be private. This is sort of a—delicate—business, and the fewer people involved, well—"

"Oh, Tedd's fine," said Reilly. "And Carla's his friend, too."

"Yeah, fine," I said. "Still, I wonder if we couldn't—"

"Don't think we can," said Tedd, looking at me for the first time. "To be honest, Mr.—Garnish, is it?—I'm here in Rob's interest. I assume you know his profession, so you must realize that he's open to a lot of innuendo, negative publicity, like that. I'm here as witness, to make sure that nothing said gets, well, misreported later."

Maybe I was tireder than I thought, or maybe the third Heineken's hadn't been such a great idea. Anyhow, "Look," I said to Reilly. "I honestly don't give a leaping shit about your publicity, negative or whatever. I've flown three thousand miles here, been shot at and arrested, bounced on a fucking motorcycle down here from Santa Barbara, and I just want to ask you some questions. Now, can't you just ask your fruit buddy here to run around the corner for a few minutes—get his vibrator recharged or something?"

"Tedd?" said Rob, still smiling at me.

"Okay, Rob," said Tedd, put down his glass, rose, and walked past me toward the door. He was a short guy.

He was also a fast guy. My feet went out from under me, my chin decided to point toward the ceiling, I was *lifted*, and then I was on my back on the sofa, Tedd standing over me, behind my head, smiling down and pulling my arms into a pretty good imitation of a pretzel. Under my back.

"Now tell your friend," said Reilly, "that if he wants to join the fun, I do Tai-Kawn-Do three days a week, and if he *does* get through me to you, you won't be playing the piano for a while, anyhow."

I glanced at Cado. Cado was pouring himself another glass of wine and staring at the prints on the walls.

"Okay," I said. My arms really hurt: the sonofabitch was *strong*. "Tedd with two dees gets to stay."

And they both laughed: a really *friendly* laugh. And Tedd tugged a little at my arms.

"You don't get it," he said. "It's *attitude*, man. It's *language*. I'm a *fruit*? The word, my dear sir, is *gay*; or, if you wish, in Rob's case, *bi*." He tugged again, and damn! it hurt. "But *fruit*? *fag*? You know any *niggers*? *cunts*? *kikes*? *greasers*?" Tug, tug, tug, tug. "*We* don't. Come on: I think you

could use some wine, now." And he let me go, poured me a
glass, and sat back down.

My arms worked, a little jerkily, to get out my cigarettes
and light one. Reilly silently placed an ashtray on the coffee
table.

"So," I said. "You guys are both—uh—I mean—"

They both laughed again. "As a pair of three-dollar bills,"
said Reilly. "Most of the people you're likely to meet in this
apartment building are, too, as a matter of fact. You didn't
get the name?"

"The name?" I said.

"Mattachine," said Reilly. "The Mattachine Society, in
the nineteen-fifties, was the first American political organization of gays—we were "homosexuals" then, which is not
only overclinical sounding, but as semantically meaningful
as a traffic jam. If that makes you uncomfortable, I'm afraid
there's not much we can do about it."

"Well," I said, taking a sip—a gulp, who's kidding whom?—
of wine. "You could accept my apology. Seriously. I usually act
like an asshole only when I'm drunk or tired." And I meant it.
Funny: in my business, you hear a lot of decent people called
a lot of shitty things—things that hurt, things that deface. But
then, you get a little tired, a little mad, you let your guard down,
and what do you do? It's like keeping loaded guns around the
house, dig?

"Accepted. Seriously" Tedd laughed, pouring us both
some more wine.

"Chicago," Cado said, "sometimes you're almost real." I
think it was a compliment.

"So," said Reilly, as George Winston finished running
major chords and the invisible tape clicked into—goddam!—
the amazing Bud Powell playing "Un Poco Loco." "What's
going on with Carla?"

I gave him the same number I'd played with Hewitt: sensitive matter, Carla potentially in trouble, but me meaning her no harm at all, her not being in her bungalow, etc.

He stared at me. "First off," he said, "I don't think I believe you entirely, Mr. Garnish."

"Harry," I said. "With two r's."

"Okay," with a chuckle. "But I *don't* believe you. May-be it's just the curse of your profession, or maybe it's because you mentioned that you came down here from Santa Barbara. That's where Carla's ex-husband lives, isn't it?"

Harry, I thought and not for the first time, you dumb dork.

"Of course," he went on, "you can't agree or disagree with that without telling me more than you want to. So let me tell *you* why I'm going to tell you as much as I know and help you as much as I can. Mainly, because I love Carla—no, don't smirk, I *do*—and so does Tedd, and so do a lot of people in our—circle. You want the fag-joke cliché? Okay, I love her 'like a sister.' But I *do*: like *my* sister. Ahh, *screw* this. You wouldn't understand."

"Maybe not," I said, taking a chance and I *hate* to take chances. "But maybe I'm trying, and if I don't it's because *I'm* fucked up. Okay: I'm working for Carla's ex because the ex is about to get remarried and Jennifer— his and Carla's kid—has disappeared and the ex believes Carla kidnapped her and that's a *heavy* rap, and Carla's done beamed up to planet Tylenol as far as anybody can tell. If you help me find her, the best I can promise you is that I can try to keep her ass out of the Place *if* I find her before the Feds get the scent, which they haven't so far. You like that story better? A little more, Tedd?"

"Much better," said Reilly as Tedd poured. "Thank you. Because Carla could never—*never*—do the sort of thing you're tracking her for, and that means she must be in danger, herself. Are the police looking for her?"

"You're kidding," I said. "I'm calling the cops because a porn queen—sorry, man—skips with her rent already paid? You want to help, tell me when you talked to her last."

He thought. "Not for a week, at least," he finally said. "I've called her, I don't know, two or three times, left messages on her machine, but she hasn't called back."

"The machine was working, though?" I asked.

"Oh, sure," he said. "I just assumed—"

"Okay, fine," I said. "What did she—the machine—say?" I lit another cigarette, and then noticed that I had one already smouldering in the ashtray.

"Say? God, just the usual—you know, 'This is Carla, leave your message after the beep,' like that. Why? Is it important?"

"How the tell should I know?" I said, sitting back, disappointed. Something was scratching at me, but I didn't know what. "I told you. I'm an asshole."

"No," grinned Tedd, offering me some more wine, which I shook off. "Just a homophobe."

"Wha," I said back.

"Homophobia," he said. "A social disease, but in some cases—cheer up, Harry—curable. Now, do you want my take on this scenario?"

It's only guys in California and Washington, D.C., who say "scenario" instead of "scene," am I right?

"Why not?" I couldn't help grinning back at him. "I did give you permission to stay."

"And don't think I'm not grateful," he said. "Okay. Rob won't bring this up because he's shy, but he'll let me do it because he knows you should know it. You walk around West Hollywood—you know West Hollywood? I didn't think so— trashing Carla Bolero, you find yourself bound and gagged with your butt roasting on a Weber Grill. She is *loved*, man—"

"Hey," I said. "This is nice to know, but—"

"But bullshit, man!" said Tedd. "Shut up and listen. She's what you want to call a 'porn queen.' Damn straight she is. She fucks and sucks and gets herself into *weird* positions that *nobody* could enjoy, and she acts like she enjoys it. In public. For money. And what do you do for *your* money? Or the president of Standard fucking Oil? Or Chrysler? Or—"

"Tedd," said Rob Reilly.

"Tedd, my ass," said Tedd, and then chuckled. "Sounds like a punchline, doesn't it? Okay, sorry—sometimes I get hyper. The point is, Harry, the lady has a lot of friends, and she's got them because she *is* a lady."

"Right," said Reilly. "And that's why we hope you find her. Because if she needs help, we're here. You'll call if you find out anything?"

"Oh, sure," I said, "and it looks like I'll find out something useful about the time I qualify for Social Security. Look, dammit, so far all I know is that everybody in Santa Barbara thinks she's the wicked witch of the west and everybody in L.A. thinks she's Mother Theresa on a rocket sled, and she's not here and I'm tapioca out of places to look or things to ask. Do you guys know *anybody* I can talk to? I mean, ah, boyfriends? girlfriends. That is—" and, I swear to God, I blushed.

They laughed again. These guys laughed a lot. "Okay, Harry," said Reilly. "There are some—of both, don't be embarrassed—and I'll give you names if you want, but I don't know if they can help you. There's also—let's see— there's Father Koponen, he's the pastor at the Church of the Advocate, we go there quite a bit—"

I couldn't help myself. "Church?" I said.

"Oh, yes" Reilly smiled. "And sing hymns and take communion."

"Not me," said Tedd. "I'm a *kike* fag." And Cado roared a laugh that managed to say "Whoa!" and "Fuckin *Aay*" at the same time, and they gave one another the thumbs-up sign.

"Yeah," I said. "Father Koponen, swell. You got a phone number for him? Now, anybody else? Hey—what about her agent, somebody from this Sybaris Agency?"

All the smiling and laughing disappeared from the room, just the way a tape runs out (the tape had, in fact, just run out, with the last chords of Keith Jarrett playing whatever it is Keith Jarrett always plays).

"That would be my agent, too," said Reilly, pouring himself his first glass of wine. "His name is Kawin. Jerry Kawin. He's not an especially nice man, and I know he and Carla don't like each other. But then, you're not looking for testimonials, are you?" The smile, a little tentative, crept back. "Sure, let me write down his private number for you. You can tell him I gave it to you, not that it will make much difference. Expect to be treated—ah, discourteously."

"It's what I live for," I said, taking the slip of paper he offered me. "Thanks. And whatever I find out, I'll let you in on it."

I gave Reilly a card with David's number, we shook hands all round, and Reilly let us out while Tedd fiddled with the tape deck that had been all along concealed under the coffee table.

"Nice dudes," said Cado as we reached his cycle. "What now, we call the agent?"

"Fuckin *Aay*," I mimicked. "On a Saturday night, we see if this guy that books skinflicks every day is just spending the evening at home with a beer and reruns of "Star Trek" instead of out somewhere getting banged like a gerbil on speed, and if he *is* at home we just boogie over there and ask him the same stupid shit questions we've been asking all day and get the same stupid shit answers. Goddam, Cado, you're sure on top of *this* thing."

It was just dusk, so I could see he was hurt and puzzled. He gestured for one of my cigarettes, and I just stared back.

"Hey, what, Chicago?" he said. "You pissed at me?"

"Me? Pissed?" I said. "We go in there, goddam Tedd trusses me up like a turkey, damn near breaks my arms and gives me a lecture to watch my fuckin' language, for Chrissake, and you sit on your ass and grin and drink wine. Pissed? Me? Jesus!"

"Oh," he said, and smiled and shook his head. "Okay, you're pissed at yourself. Harry, man, you know you had that coming. You did call him a fruit, you know."

"Yeah," I said, "so—"

"So," he said, "this is West Hollywood. Okay, I should've told you. You walk around here in the daytime, you see lots of old married couples, and lots of guys with guys and women with women, and they're all friendly and comfortable. Gays and old folks, dig? They moved here because they could afford it here, and because nobody gives 'em shit here. You think they don't protect that? Hell, Chicago, you ever think about the word, *community*? You ain't gonna see more community than this. You say 'fruit' here, you best be buying an orange. C'mon: gimme a cigarette."

The hell with it, I gave him one. "Yeah," I said, "but you're—"

"What," he laughed, lighting up. "A biker? Big bad macho queer-basher? Hey—*you* go to the movies a lot? What if I told you I was gay?"

"Uh," I said.

"So what you want to do?"

"Uh," I said.

"How about we head back for Santa Barb? We can fuck around some more tomorrow, after a good sleep, okay? Talk to Lady Bridget about what next. Yeah: jump on, grab on me, and *vamanos*, baby."

"Cado," I said as he started the machine.

"Yo," he said.

"Are you?"

"What?"

"Are you—uh, gay?"

He turned and the failing sun made his grin technicolor. "Makes you fuckin' think, don't it?" he said, as we sputtered and then hummed and then roared up the coast, into the night.

$\triangledown$

CHAPTER FIFTEEN

I *TOLD* YOU CALIFORNIA was disorienting. We'd been to two parts of the city. Okay, not the greatest, not the best, not the friendliest city in the world, but let's face it folks, everybody in the world *knows its name.* And now, I thought, I knew it less well than when I'd left Chicago. Somewhere around—what? Universal City? Burbank?—anyhow, somewhere around where 101 becomes officially the Ventura Freeway, I risked looking back.

Spangles floating in a shallow dish. Strings of lights, red, yellow, green, strung out every which way, moved through by white lights, stopping and moving and stopping again, and all of it without *any* idea of a center, where the lights were moving to or where they were moving from, except the lights give you the idea that *they* know where they're going, and all of it ringed by the dark lumps of the hills, which are maybe, you think, just bored by the whole thing, and waiting.

And why, I thought, trying to keep awake and not lose my hold on Cado's belly, why would anybody in his right mind build a city *here,* where those mountains and that ocean would make any city look ridiculous, temporary? Oh, so *this* is the point where Highway 101 becomes the Ventura

Freeway? Right, tell that to the mountains, I'm sure they'll be impressed: cute streetplan.

"The sea is a form of ridicule": that's a line of poetry Ben Gross quotes to me once in a while, always looking at me after he quotes it with his mouth twisted in an expectant grin like I'm going to clasp my hands together and fall to my knees and shout, "Oh, God, yes, Ben, now I see!"

But, driving up out of that city and looking at its brave and foolish lights twinkling between the edge of a continent and the biggest ocean on the planet, for a minute I think I did see.

So it was a place where the gays and the porn stars went to church and acted nice even while they were bending the shit out of your arms, and where the cops made apologetic social calls to hassle you, and the bikers quoted Oscar Wilde. Okay, I figured as we passed the sign SANTA BARBARA NEXT 12 EXITS, it made sense. It wasn't just loopy, it was simply *opposite*: is there something like an ethical mirror-image, where everything stays somehow the same but is altered? Even directions, for crying out loud. In Chicago, you know you're heading north when the lake is always on your right; here, the Pacific was permanent *west*, not *east*. *Up* the map was now *down* the map, and everything worked out just the same, except for my own internal compass, which after forty-odd years in the *other* city was too damn set to reverse.

Cado executed one of those fancy skid-and-fishtail stops in front of David's house—right out of the movies, and nearly throwing me into some kind of big damn thorn bush—and throttled down to a low purr.

"That's it, Chicago," he said. "Catch you in the a.m."

"What?" I said. "You're not sleeping here tonight?"

"Negative. Think I'll boogie down by the fig tree, check out some of my pals, read the aura. Been away two days, you know?"

"Yeah, sure," I said, a little disappointed. "What is this 'fig tree' anyhow, some kind of shelter?"

He threw his head back and laughed and, as he laughed, twisted the handlebar-accelerator so that his bike laughed with him.

"Chicago," he finally got out in gasps, "you are—you are fuckin *something*! Yeah, it's a shelter. You ever see a tree that wasn't a shelter? It's a fig tree, man—the famous Moreton Bay Fig Tree, south end of town. *Big* fuckin' fig tree. Used to be one of the tourist attractions, like, you know, 'Golly, Martha, just think, they say ten thousand people could stand in the shade of this tree,' shit such as that. Except now, alas, the tourists just don't go there much anymore."

"Oh," I said. It had been a simple question, I thought, and I was tired.

"Nope. Verrry sad. Grreat pitee," he said, rolling his r's like Omar Sharif in *Lawrence of Arabia*. "You see, sahib, the poor peoples, the peoples who cahn't afford no homes, they think, oh goodness, we sleep under great fig, it gives shelter to ten thousand, they say. But the white folks, all rajah landlords and all mem sahibs on vacation from Kansas, think it not pretee. So: no more tours. Until," slipping back into his own voice, "the fuckers find a legal—nope, a workable—way to roust us out of there."

"That's not fair," said David, walking into the light of a streetlamp, with Bridget and Kim following. They were all in bathrobes, so I suppose Cado's laughing-motorcycle trick had awakened them. In a maroon bathrobe with the collar turned up and that Peter Pan haircut tousled from the pillow, Kim could have probably singlehandedly forced repeal of the Mann Act.

"Hey, David," crowed Cado. "Guys. We wake you up? Sorry."

"That's really unfair, what you were saying," continued David. "It's so easy to talk about the big bad landlords and the evil, greedy realtors, and the poor defenseless homeless, isn't it?"

"Hey, David," said Cado.

"David," said Kim at the same time.

"No," said David. He was really angry and, since I didn't like him, I was enjoying it. "I know you tried to help us and all, and I'm grateful. But you—you people should know that you have a—a distorted view of things. This city is *people*, people who work hard to make themselves a life. You think they're selfish just because they don't want a lot of—well, they only want to be at peace. You call that selfish? You think all anybody cares about is profit margins?"

Cado smiled and fished a cigarette—actually, the whole pack—out of my pocket. "Well, little brother," he said, "as a matter of fact, that's just what I believe. But, hell, we're not gonna convert each other tonight, are we? See you tomorrow."

"Wait!" shouted David as Cado rolled away. "If that's what you think about me, then—"

"Then why am I hanging around trying to help? Cause I'm doing a *koan* on you, baby. Ask Miss Bridget. I bet she'll know. Later!" and he was off.

We walked back to the house in silence, except I noticed that David was still fuming, Kim was looking worriedly at David, and Bridget—well, Bridget had that smile on her face she sometimes gets which is not exactly nunny-contemplative and not exactly streetsmart-wiseass, but a combination of the two. It's unnerving: like sitting across from a Madonna who's just drawn to an inside straight and made it.

Another confab around the kitchen table, with milk all round except for yours truly, who decided to memorialize that untasted brandy back at Hewitt's place, but nobody had much to confab about. Bridget had told them about my meeting with Hewitt, and when I told them what I'd learned from Bobby Reilly, which was next to nothing, we just sat and stared at the big empty place growing in the middle of the table.

"I don't know," said David finally. "I just don't know. Maybe—maybe Jennifer just has run off someplace. It happens, doesn't it?"

"And then what about C—Carla's disappearance?" asked Kim. "David, you can't mean you just want to—to *wait*?"

"Honey," he said, "what *have* we been doing? Harry and Bridget here haven't—sorry, Harry and Bridget—been able to come up with anything about Jen. So Carla's gone. I hope she never comes back. Does she have Jen? I don't know, but if she does, maybe now only the police have the resources to find her—to find them both. Why don't we just call Inspector Carroll—Lieutenant Carroll, whatever— tomorrow, tell him Carla's gone, and let him take it from there."

Everybody was quiet, especially me, who was restraining myself from observing that that was just what I'd told them they should be doing forty-eight hours ago before I, for Chrissake, got shot at, busted, sleigh-ridden to L.A. and back, and trussed up on a sofa.

"And besides," he went on after a while—ever notice that? the last guy to talk before a silence always feels *responsible* for the silence—"besides, I'm not sure I like this Cado being involved. Let's face it, if Harry hadn't talked with him when they were—detained—things would be a lot simpler. I can't place my confidence in him."

For no very good reason except, I suppose, I was tired, I was about to give David a graphic description of just where I thought he *ought* to place his confidence, and how he could get it all crammed in there, when Bridget spoke.

"It's late," she said. We've all had a trying day, and tomorrow may be just as trying. Why don't we sleep on David's suggestion, and talk about it when we're all fresh?"

"Well—" began David.

"Trust me, dear, it'll be best," said Bridget. "And believe me, tomorrow you won't be quite so bothered by what Mr. Molina said. You don't want that to cloud your judgment, do you?"

He flushed, but mumbled agreement. As we were breaking up to get ready for bed, Kim told Bridget that David and she usually went to nine o'clock Mass, and asked her if that would be all right.

"Oh, thank you, dear," said Bridget, "but there are some things I have to do tomorrow, so Harry and I will probably be gone before you leave for Mass."

Which was the perfect end to the day. Not so much because I knew that if Bridget was skipping Sunday Mass she was still hot about this—to use her word—"case," but mainly because I'm convinced that even *thinking* about waking up before ten a.m. on a Sunday is a major cause of cancer.

I stripped, turned out the light, and turned on the TV. Morton Downey, Jr. was calling some guy a wetpants liberal sissy who made him want to puke. Flip. A preacher was talking to the camera about how you should beware of preachers who use the TV to "feed their pockets and their lusts." Flip. The Late Show was just beginning: Sidney Poitier in *Lilies of the Field*. Great! I turned the volume down to just barely audible, slipped under the covers, and hit the prenatal position, sure that, whenever Bridget woke me up, I'd anyway be asleep within five minutes.

$\triangledown$

CHAPTER SIXTEEN

OKAY, I *KNOW* THAT the days of the week are arbitrary and have to do with economics and religion and national customs and such: Ben Gross loaned me a book about all that once. But now *you* tell *me* that Sunday, from the time you get out of bed till the time you crawl back in, is *not* the one day in the week when you feel like you're walking through invisible Jell-O.

I won't tell you what time Bridget woke me up, it still gives me a headache. David and Kim were having breakfast in their bathrobes—different bathrobes from the ones they'd worn last night, I noticed, inwardly shaking my head—and Bridget, fully dressed, was washing her dishes as I walked into the kitchen. I turned down Kim's offer of waffles and bacon, and said a Coke and three Excedrin would suit me fine.

"David has decided not to call the police, Harry," said Bridget, towelling a coffee cup.

"Well, not today, anyhow," said David. "I think Bridget's right: if Carla *isn't* involved in Jen's disappearance, calling the cops might just point them down a blind alley, don't you think?"

I don't think he really wanted my opinion, but what the hell, I was feeling generous.

"David," I said, "I don't think a goddam thing. If I *thought* anything, I wouldn't be in this f—in this business. Do I think you could be putting your fat in the fire for withholding information from the Man? Or that if you *do* tell the Man, the Man will know that I've been poking around in things after he politely asked me not to? Or that it's one helluva note when the civilians start deciding what the professionals should and shouldn't know? What, you tell your dentist how to do root canals? Okay by me, sport: I'm a tourist."

David's mouth was open to answer, and he was leaning forward waiting for me to finish—don't you *love* it when guys do that?—when Bridget sailed back from the sink with a cute little—okay, a cute big—smile/pout on her face.

"Oh, Harry," she said, "you're always such a grump in the morning. Don't mind him, David, he's just not awake yet. But now, we really should be off. Kim, dear, if Mr. Molina comes by before you and David go to Mass, would you give him this?" And she handed Kim an envelope. "You can read it, of course—it's unsealed. I just ask him to meet Harry and me at this famous fig tree around noon. And if he hasn't come by the time you leave, could you just tape it to the font door?"

Kim took the envelope. "Of course," she said. "But, Bridget, what are you and Harry doing this morning?"

Reassuring, beaming, don't-you-worry-Suzy-you'll-do-just-*fine*-at-the-piano-recital smile. With a loving pat on the head, yet. "Dear, if anything comes of it, you'll be the first to know. It's just drudgery that may or may not turn up anything. You'll be at the office all day after church, won't you? Good. And now, Harry?"

The rescued rented Datsun was in the driveway, Bridget gave me the keys, and we drove away.

"Okay," I said as I turned onto San Roque, the nearest

main drag off David's street. "Not that I know what the hell you think we're doing, or why you bolloxed David into not calling the cops—which, by the way, I think is exactly what we should be doing. But could you at least tell me where we're going?"

"Eleven-hundred block of State Street," she said, without a trace of her smarmy manner at the Pescatore breakfast table. "Morningside Realty. It's Sunday, so you can probably park on the street. Harry—" and she turned toward me— "did you ever read any fairy tales?"

San Roque, I knew, hit State, but I couldn't figure whether the eleven-hundreds would be a left or a right turn. It felt like it should be a right, so I decided on a left.

"Fairy tales?" I said at a stop sign two blocks from State. "Not that I remember—unless you want to count *Tarzan* and the Tower Commission Report. Why, Bridget?"

"Oh, no special reason," she said. "I was just wondering if you know the story about *The Frog Prince.*"

I was at State, took a left, and saw that the street numbers were going down from nineteen-hundred. Sonofabitch! Just keep thinking *reverse*, and *anybody* could cut California.

"The Frog Prince?" I said. "Oh, yeah, that's the one where the girl kisses the frog and he turns into—hey, that's odd! You know, Cado told me yesterday—"

"It should be just along here," she said, looking out the window. "Yes, there, on the right. Now, Harry, can you park on the street?"

In a rented car on a Sunday morning, I really didn't give much of a damn if I could or couldn't, so I did. "Done," I said. "Now, before we go in, do I get a hint as to why we're going in?"

"Oh, Harry, I'm sorry," she said. "I'm afraid I'm—a little preoccupied. I told you yesterday that Morningside seemed to be David's biggest competitor. So, when I was home alone, I made an appointment for us to talk with one of the agents this morning—a Miss Rice," looking at a scrap of paper she fished out of her purse, "District Sales Coordinator."

"Wow, a real high roller, huh?" I said, but my irony is always wasted on, or by, Bridget. "And what do you expect to find out here, for crying out loud? And come to think of it, why didn't you tell David and Kim that we were coming here? Bridget—you don't by any chance know something you're not telling me, do you?"

She smiled. "Oh, Harry, I know you're the one with the detective experience. But we *are* rather at a dead end, at least for the moment, so let's just see where idle curiosity takes us, all right, dear? Ah—it's just ten o'clock; let's go in."

It's what I've come to call her Angela Lansbury mode, and it pisses me *off*.

Morningside Realty, nestled between an Indian restaurant and a store that looked like it sold, for Godssake, nothing but candles, was the kind of place that, if I ever could buy a house, would embarrass the hell out of me because I'd know I could never afford a setup as elegant as the rental office itself. The reception area, only a little smaller than my apartment, was all in yellow and rose, with Toulouse-Lautrec posters and, instead of the usual instant coffee hotplate, two small electric samovars—*electric* samovars?—marked COFFEE and DECAF and an array of doughnuts that would satisfy the night shift of a decent-sized precinct house. Bridget told the receptionist—in realtor's uniform, natch, a blue blazer and one of those white blouses with the ruffled thing down the front that looks like a hyperthyroid lasagna noodle—who we were. She said yes, would we wait a moment please, and Bridget, snagging one of the really serious looking crullers, sat on one of the two sofas.

About two-thirds of the way through the cruller—say, two minutes—Meryl Streep walked in and said, "Miss O'Toole? And Mr. Garnish?"

Okay, it was Emily Rice; or so she said. But that haze of hair the color of summer and that skin that was always just about to blush but never quite did, topping a tall black suit that made it look all the brighter, and an air that said, "If this isn't how a duchess walks, it's how she ought to"—you could have fooled me. As a pal of mine said after we'd seen *Sophie's Choice*: "Goddamn, she sure as shit *is*."

She led us to her office at the back of the store, past a scattering of desks with, I guess, District Sales Coordinator wannabees talking on phones or showing couples books of listings. There was a big chart on the wall in this section, with names of salesmen and their sales records for the month grease-pencilled in, making the place look like a successful bookie's.

We sat across her neat desk, complete with a V.D.T. and a stick-on stuffed Garfield clinging to its side, as Bridget de-crullered her lips with a napkin and I noticed that I'd been holding an unlighted cigarette in my hand since my first Emily Rice sighting.

"Now, Miss O'Toole—" she began.

"Please, it's Bridget," said Bridget.

"And Harry," I hurried, feeling like an ass as I said it: swell, Garnish, welcome back to the freshman mixer.

"Fine," she said with a tiny smile. "And I'm Emily. So, Bridget. When you called yesterday, you said you had some"—she glanced at one of the three notepads before her—"yes, some 'urgent and confidential' business to discuss with me, that it had to do with our relations with Pescatore Realty, but that—ah, let's see—'no violation of confidence on either side' would be involved. Well!" and she folded her hands over the notepad and turned the smile on high beam. "I have to tell you, first, that you were lucky to catch me in the office yesterday—weekends are crazy in this business—and second, that your request sounded a little— well, is 'unorthodox' too strong?"

"Not at all, Emily," said Bridget, "though I think 'flaky' might be closer to what you mean. But you did agree to see us."

"Well," she said, glancing at her lapel watch, "it so happens I have—let's see—just under a half-hour free this morning, and, frankly, I'm intrigued." High beam again. "What in the world is this all about?"

"I was rather hoping you could tell me," said Bridget. "You see, Mr. Garnish—Harry—and I are private investigators. We work in Chicago, but we're out here trying to help David Pescatore find his daughter, who simply disappeared a few days ago."

Great investigative approach, I thought: real subtle. Old Martin O'Toole, back in his North Shore rest home, would have chewed through his I.V. tubes.

"Oh, no," said Emily. "David's daughter? Little— unh—"

"Jennifer," said Bridget.

"Jennifer," said Emily. "But this is awful. Have the police been called? Is there anything I can do for David?"

Call me weird. But, by me, sexy *and* maternal is a can't-lose parlay.

"That's kind of you," said Bridget. "But everything that can be done has been done. It's just that—"

"Then I don't understand," said Emily. "Why do you want to talk to me? I mean, you don't—you can't—think that—"

"Oh, of course not," said Bridget. "It's just that—to be honest, Emily, we've come to an impasse. I can't think of a

single stone left to turn, and the local police *are* a bit
disturbed by our involvement in this at all—"

Aces, I thought. If there was another way to blow our
credit as questioners, I couldn't think of it. Bridget's technique was about as confidence-inspiring as the Surgeon
General's Warning on a pack of cigarettes. Maybe less so.

"So," she went on, making the grave a little deeper, "we're
here in desperation. I know that your company and David's
have been involved in some sort of transaction lately, and
one that seems of some concern to you both, judging by the
number of phone messages from Morningside David got just
yesterday. I didn't want to bother him about the details—the
poor man has enough on his mind as it is— so I thought, if
you could tell us anything, anything at all—" she trailed off.

Emily smiled. "Well I don't see how this can possibly help
you, but it's no great secret, either. Morningside is trying to
buy some land that Pescatore owns: about fifteen acres, just
north of the city. We have strong interest, and some semi-
firm commitments, from a number of chains who would like
to see a new mall grow up there. And David's company—
David, actually—is dragging his feet, asking a ridiculously
high price, and trying—well, this *is* a secret, I suppose, but
one everybody knows anyway—to negotiate for a block of
condos on the land. It's as simple as that—and, I'll tell you,
a very big pain in the neck."

"But I don't understand," said Bridget. "Why can't you build
condos *and* a mall? Or come to some kind of compromise?"

Emily's eyes—did I tell you they were green?—took on that
cozy glaze people get when they're about to explain the
intricacies of their own private bag.

"You don't understand Santa Barbara," she said. "This
town is the damnedest combination of boom and bust you
could imagine. It's paradise on earth—haven't you read our

brochures?—but paradise comes with a large tag these days. The city is pricing itself out of range, even for the sort of people we *want* to attract. So they're building to the north: suburbs of the choicest suburb of L.A., if you will. What we're planning isn't just communities, it's the future. The whole shape of what is going to keep on being one of the dream locales in America."

"Nathanael West," said Bridget.

Emily laughed. "Okay," she said, "you got me. *Day of the Locust*, and maybe you're right. What's the line? 'They had come to California to die.' But if we're selling fantasies, at least we're up front about it. And for this fifteen-acre property—unzoned as yet, which is a developer's godsend—we happen to have the backing and interest of some people who want to see a mall there, and David has some people behind him who want to see condos. But his people's commitment isn't as firm. But, for now, he owns the property."

"So it's a range war," I said.

She looked at me sharply. "You know—it's Harry, right?—you're *right*. Except in this range war, the farmers and the ranchers both win. In the end."

If that was the way it was, I thought, then that made the renters and buyers and shoppers in the deal the cattle.

"And now," she said, looking again at her lapel watch—

"Oh, of course," said Bridget. "Thank you so much for your time, Emily. May we call you again if—well, if anything develops?"

"Absolutely," she said, rising to scoop us out of the office. "And I'll contact you if I think of anything that might be helpful. You will tell David how very concerned I am, won't you?"

And like that, and like that. The Datsun, of course, had been ticketed. Bridget looked at me and clucked.

"Relax," I said, filing it in my inside jacket pocket. "After drunk and disorderly and probable obstruction of justice, this can't add more than a week or so to my sentence. I'll write every day from Folsom."

It was as I was starting the car that I realized I didn't know where we were supposed to be going next. And when I asked Bridget for a flight plan, she just stared at the windscreen and told me to drive around for a while. I asked her if she would like to stop somewhere and have a cup of coffee, just sit and think. She said okay, listlessly. I was rolling south on State Street which , the farther south you went, became more and more the fantasy Santa Barbara Emily Rice had been talking about: cobblestone and tile sidewalks, shops of fake adobe with red tile roofs, early Ricardo Montalban. You could almost read the legend, like on one of those medieval maps of the world: "Here Dwelleth Tourists." But on Sunday morning they all looked forlorn, debutantes between proms, waiting for the next dance to start.

About eight blocks down, she suddenly said, "Pull over here!" I did.

"Swell," I said. "Now what?"

"I'm ready for that coffee now. And I'll buy you a beer, if you like."

This strange power I have over women.

$\triangledown$

CHAPTER SEVENTEEN

W<small>E WALKED INTO A</small> place called J. Michael's Pub that, for once, lived up to the "pub" promise of its name: comfortably dark, though the whole front was open to the street, with a bar and tables of real, scarred wood, and a jukebox (I always check out jukeboxes) that had, besides the top 40, some Dorsey, Shaw, Ellington and even—how'd they get that?—Gerry Mulligan's "My Funny Valentine." While Bridget took a table and ordered, I punched up Gerry, "Song of India," and "Satin Doll."

"You realize that we're getting nowhere, don't you?" I said as I sat down. "What's our next step—talking to Jennifer's scout leader?"

"Harry," said Bridget as her coffee and my tomato juice arrived. "How did—"

"Just a minute, Bridge," I said, and asked the waiter, "How much extra for a raw egg, Worchestershire Sauce, and Tobasco?"

He grinned. "No charge, Mac. Boston?"

"Chicago," I said. "Same place."

"Yeah. And the chaser?"

"Maybe later," I said, and, looking slightly disappointed, he went off.

"Harry," Bridget said patiently, "how did Mr. Reilly strike you?"

"He didn't," I said. "Tedd did."

"Come again?"

"Dumb joke. Forget it. Well, let's see. He's gay, for one thing." I stared at her.

She stared back. "And?" she said.

"Well," I said, "I mean, he lives in this all-gay apartment house, dig? And—"

"Harry," she sighed, and it was the Bridget O'Toole-attack-sigh. "I wonder if you realize how much psychic energy you've wasted over the years playing Shock the Nun. Here—maybe this will disabuse you." And she fished into her handbag and brought out a magazine, putting it on the table between us.

It was called CREAM SCREEN, and on the cover was a blonde with a *mean* expression, a whip in her hand, wearing a mask and a leather bikini. Oh, yeah: shot from below. And across her belly it said: XXXX! YOUR FAVORITE HUNG STUDS AND HORNY BI-BABES!! ALL NEW AND ALL HOT!!!

"Carla and Bobby Reilly are on page forty-seven," she said, and I automatically turned there.

My timing as usual was perfect. As I found the page, a voice at my shoulder said, "Goodness! And on a Sunday!" The waiter, of course, grinning like Wile E. Coyote with my Tabasco.

"Go back and read your *Watchtower*," I told him, "and when you finish the next page, bring me a Beck's." He chortled away.

"Damn, Bridget," I said. "You didn't buy this, did you?"

She smiled and—sonofabitch!—I realized she'd just won a round of Shock the Garnish.

"As a matter of fact, dear, I found it at the back of David's closet"—huh?—"and now, if your nerves are settled, perhaps you can tell me about your meeting with the young man whose picture you're staring at."

I usually don't do three things at once, but I managed to tell her about my trip to Reillyland, not excluding the thrill-packed Tedd-coaster ride, while cracking the egg into my tomato juice, and ogling—love that word, been doing it since high school—Bobby Reilly and Carla doing—well, lots—on page forty-seven and forty-eight and forty-nine and, single-shot double-page spread, fifty and fifty-one.

There was something about Carla's eyes. Okay, go ahead and laugh your ass off before you read on. But there *was* something about her eyes, and her smile, even when she and Bobby were in positions where I wasn't sure anything could, well, *happen.* I mean, everybody's seen the K-Mart ecstasy, fake-orgasm look: about as convincing as Sammy Davis singing "My Way," right? But Carla's expression, even when she was *doing* that, had something more. What? Intelligence, good humor, maybe even a little self- mockery. Ever make love with somebody who thought it wasn't just great and earthshaking and fun but also—which, face it, it *is*— funny? And, yes, Bobby's expression radiated the same kind of feeling. I don't know what the Supreme Court's definition is, but I'm not sure you could even call what I was looking at "pornography." I mean, they still both looked like *people.* And I realized that this was the first photo of Carla I'd seen.

I also realized that I'd been silent for a couple of minutes, that my Beck's was sitting, unpoured, at my left hand, and that Bridget was studiously *not* clearing her throat.

"Uh, right," I said, lighting a cigarette and closing the magazine, cover side down. "Sloppy lighting. They probably didn't have a professional gaffer on the shoot." I poured some beer.

"Perhaps not," she said. "What should we do now, Harry?"

Lucky for me, I had swallowed my beer. "You mean that?" I said.

"I mean that. After what you say about Bobby Reilly's information, I'm not sure we even know who—or what—Carla Bolero is. At least—even despite what she does for a living—I don't think we can take David's opinion of her with full credence. And I'm beginning to be concerned that her disappearance could mean that *she's* in danger. I just don't know," she sighed. "Could I have some more coffee?"

I signalled to my pal, who was lounging by the bar with that vacant waiter's stare—the same one lizards have while they wait for the next fly to come within tongue range.

"Listen," I said. "When we were driving down here, you asked me about 'The Frog King.'"

"'Prince,'" she said.

"Whatever," I said. "The Boss Frog. Why'd you ask about that?"

"Oh," she said as her coffee came. "It's just been in the back of my mind for a while—even before Jennifer disappeared. Goodness, Harry!" and she stared at me. "I keep forgetting, you've never even met Jennifer. She's a lovely child. Certainly, shy. Her father's been, I suppose, overprotective, overanxious for her; I think Carla—the divorce—devastated him. But she's so fond of Kim. She really blossoms around Kim, Harry."

"That's nice," I said. "The Frog King?"

"Well," she said, "You know the story. A princess loses a treasure in the lake, a frog promises to retrieve it for her if she will grant him a wish. She agrees, and the frog brings back the treasure. But the promise he exacts is that she will welcome him in her father's castle."

"I thought he wanted her to kiss him," I said. This was

going nowhere, but Boston Blackie had brought another Beck's with Bridget's coffee, so what the hell.

"Oh, no," she said. "In later, sanitized versions perhaps. But in the earliest versions, it's important that the frog insists on being invited, *by the princess*, into her father's house."

"That's important, huh?" I said.

"Harry," she said, giving me, swear to God, exactly the stare my old man gave me the time I installed a new battery in the Nash Rambler and got the positive and negative wires reversed. "Harry. A maiden loses a valuable object which can only be restored to her by an ugly, amphibian life form. And then, to consolidate her gain, she must bid that creature welcome within the doors of her father's house. Gracious: what do you think the story is *about*?"

"Unh," I articulated.

"You really *are* a prude, aren't you? It's about sexual initiation, of course. And, for a Western fairytale, it's remarkably feminist. The maiden, remember, is *guilty* of nothing. It's just that, at a certain age, things begin to happen to her—things she doesn't understand, and of which she is quite naturally frightened. At first, when the Frog Prince is announced at the door of her father's castle, she refuses to have him admitted. But then, when she explains to her father what he is doing there, her father tells her she must keep her promise and welcome the Prince in. *In*, Harry."

"Yeah, yeah," I said. "I get it. And then she kisses him and he turns into Tom Selleck, right?"

Her laughter—really—sparkled. "All right," she said. "If you wish, then she kisses him and he tells everyone that he's been under an enchantment from a wicked witch until he can be kissed by a maiden in his frog form. But it's the

welcome, not the kiss, that releases the enchantment; allows
the man to become fully himself just as the woman allows
herself to be herself."

"Just like Sleeping Beauty," I said, finishing my beer.

"No!" she said. "Honestly, Harry, you surprise me. Sleeping Beauty—poor Barbie doll—can only sleep until she's
awakened by Prince Charming. What a life *that* is! But our
princess—the Frog Princess—has to *face* what's happening
to her, and choose to become part of it. I suppose that's why
the story has been on my mind. Jennifer—and Kim—are
both on the verge of such an important— passage—in their
lives, and I've been hoping so hard they will both be able to
face it, and let it make them stronger."

"Sorry, Bridget," I said, lighting my fourth cigarette. "Now
you're sounding like ten p.m. on Sunday TV. Jennifer's still
gone, and we don't know where the hell to look for her, or
what particular frog's got her in his clutches. Do frogs have
clutches?"

"I think they got mandibles or something," said the
waiter, hovering over our table. "You folks want something
else?"

Bridget insisted on paying the bill, explained to the waiter
something about the difference between insects and am-
phibians, and, while we waited for the change, told me:

"No, Harry, I think I'm over my dejection. Thank you so
much for asking me about the Frog Prince. We're not
through! At least, I can see a way to keep threading our way
through this— this *silliness*." That's a very bad word in
Bridget's vocabulary: you don't want to hear its equivalent
in Cado's or mine.

I didn't know what I'd done so helpful, though I did
suspect that, as usual, I'd be sorry I'd done it. I asked her
where we were going next.

"Why, to the fig tree," she said. "I have to meet Mr. Molina and you have to handle a few items yourself this afternoon. I'll tell you about them on the way."

Bridget always forgets to tip. She's not cheap—*au contraire*, as she likes to say—but all that nun training just can't be, don't you know, wiped out. I mean, they don't even usually *pay*, you dig? So, as she lumbered out of J. Michael's, I slapped a five into Boston's palm.

"Hey, Mac, thanks," he said. "It's Christmas or something?"

"Celebration," I said. "I just solved a kidnapping and I don't know what the hell is going on. They give you a name?"

"Schlenz," he said. "Mark."

"Harry," I said. "You're enough of a pain in the ass, you should be waiting at the Palmer House."

"I love you, too," he said.

"Yeah. Next time I come here, have the Beck's on the table before I sit down."

"Fuck I will."

"I figured. Be good." And I walked into the sunshine where Bridget was waiting.

$\triangledown$

CHAPTER EIGHTEEN

THE FIG TREE IS maybe a ten-minute drive from Morning-side Realty and the candle shop and J. Michael's carefully tattered elegance; one hell of a ten minutes. Ted Turner can save his money colorizing *The Grapes of Wrath*: just reshoot the damn thing under the fig tree.

"What did Ms. Rice say?" asked Bridget as we walked into the small park under the fig tree's shadow. "Ah, yes: 'we're selling fantasies.'"

Bums and winos and vagrants and whatever you call them in *your* neighborhood all have this special look: you've seen it, the loser's version of the thousand-yard stare. If you've ever been outside enough that you have to cadge the bread for a bag of Fritos or a beer, you know how hard it is to look in the eyes of the guy you're bumming from. Because you've got to believe that sooner or later you'll be back in the groove, cool and flush and fighting, and you could maybe stand *this* guy a friendly brew, dig? But not the *real* losers. Their eyes meet yours, and what their eyes say is okay, let's drop the bullshit about I'm "down" on my luck; I'm *out* of my luck and I'm *here* and what do *you* want to do about it? It spooks hell out of the citizens because they think it's a kind of assault. Actually, it's a kind of—what?—innocence?

The thing is, though, that in Chicago or the Apple or
D.C., the losers occur singly or at most in small packs.
Winter keeps them as far apart as the warm-air gratings on
the sidewalks, anyway. But in the earthly paradise you can
sleep out the whole year round, and congregate.

We walked among clusters of families—kids chasing kids
with that skinned-cat kids' laughter—and men and women
just sort of wandering (freedom's just another word for
nothing left to *do*) and a few guys who looked like under-
studies for Jesus nodding out over brown paper sacks. Wood-
stock without the fun: it was only the kids who didn't have
the thousand-yard stare.

Cado was at the opposite end of the park from the tree's
giant trunk, leaning against the peppermint monster and
having Pepsi and Taco Bell burritos with a guy and a girl.
The guy had a blonde flattop and a full biker uniform,
complete with tattoos. The girl had a dark brown ponytail
that would have made a Shetland vain and a—okay, call it
a *presence*—that would have convinced Mr. Levi and Mr.
Strauss that their lives had not been misspent.

"Hey, Chicago," Cado boomed, raising his can. "Lady
Bridget! Meet Mitch and Lisa. They're up from San Diego
on their way to—can you feature this?—*Utah*! I been telling
them you're cool."

Shy nods all around, although Mitch looked at my jacket
and tie like he thought I could be a practical joke of Cado's
at his expense.

"Utah!" said Bridget. "Salt Lake City?"

"Yeah," said Mitch, as if he did not think it was one of
the great ideas of western man. "Lisa's into archaeology."

"*Anthropology*," she said, whipping her ponytail. "God,
Mitch. I'm doing a thesis," she explained to Bridget. "On
city planning and belief systems. Like, you know, religions?"

"I see," said Bridget, her eyes brightening. "And have you read *The Book of Mormon*, dear?"

By now, I can sense a Bridget-episode a mile away. I saved the day.

"Hey, Bridget," I said. "Sorry, but if I'm going to do all the stuff we talked about in the car, I'd better get cracking."

"Right," said Cado, draining his can and banking it into a trash bin about fifteen feet away. "Lady Bridge, tell me what you want to do, and we can boogie too."

"Well, Arcadio," she said, a little crestfallen, "I was hoping you could take me a few places on your machine."

"Righteous," he grinned. "Just name the places. Hey— you ever ride one of these? It's a little, you know—bumpy."

"When I was stationed in New Mexico," she said—maybe huffily—"I took my little Vespa into town twice a week from our school to collect the mail."

"Well all *right*, mama," he laughed. "Let us eke *go*. Mitch? Sweet Lisa? You going to be by here tonight? Good. We catch you up on the flip-flop. Harry? Old Davey's pad around sundown, yeah?"

I didn't wait to watch Lady Bridge climb on Cado's bike, so don't expect me to describe it for you. I just grunted the mutual so-longs and strolled back to my car through Loser Nation, thinking about a kinder, gentler America while some of the thousand points of light dozed over their Thunderbirds, dreaming, I guessed, of—what else?— California.

And then, in the middle of the park, I had a smart attack. Or an almost-smart attack. Ever have one of those? You're walking along in the ordinary haze and all of a sudden zap! or bang! or click! everything falls into sharper focus and you *see* what's been bothering you, you *see* how simple it was all along.

Sort of. Maybe talking with Bridget had jogged my memory, or maybe looking at her magazine had. Whatever, I remembered that something Bobby Reilly had said had bothered me when he said it. What came back to me wasn't, dammit, *what* he said, just the same feeling, the way you can sometimes remember a toothache or a hangover. Something about Carla, something about something Carla had *said*—

I'd stopped and lit a cigarette, trying to get my fingers around it, it was so damned close, when one of the Jesuses came up to me and began explaining how the planets evolved from the sun and the sun evolved from the galaxy and the galaxy evolved from the eye of God, and so on. He was pretty thrilled about it all, so I told him thanks and slipped him a couple of singles since I believe research ought to be funded. But whatever it was I'd been about to remember had gotten lost in the space warp. Running various changes under my breath on my favorite word, I walked back to the car to begin filling Bridget's shopping list.

First on the list was finding Pescatore Realty. Bridget had given me careful directions—it was at the northern end of town, on a main drag called Calle Real—so naturally I found it with only two stops, at a Mobil and a Unocal, to get help. That's one way California is *not* different. Stop at any gas station in any strange town for directions, and you get, "Yeah, go right out here, take a left on Flimfram, two lights, right on Wuzzlits, and you can't miss it," and you *do* miss it, am I right? I think gas jockeys keep secret score: little drawings of screwed-up out-of-towners on the wall underneath the nude calendar.

So: David's command bunker in the great Condo-Mall War wasn't as ornate as Morningside HQ. More functional: very chromey and angular, very tense to tell you it was *new*, like, no dust bunnies in the corners *here*, man. And Muzak.

While I was waiting for the receptionist to fetch Mr. Pes-
catore, I was trying to figure out what the hell I was hearing.
It was the 101 Strings or somebody like that playing Stevie
Wonder, "For Once in My Life."

"Mr. Garnish," said Kim, interrupting the Free Stevie
Wonder letter I was composing in my head. "I'm sorry, but
David's out of the office for a while. What can I do?"

On her, the real estate lady suit—even the noodle cravat—
looked good. I'm just a sucker for *cute*: did I ever tell you
that I discovered puberty in the old Grant Park Theatre
watching Audrey Hepburn in *Sabrina*?

"Call me Harry, please," I said. "Well, it's a little vague,
but Bridget wants me to do a few things, including what she
calls 'appreciate the situation.' So if you could manage it, I'd
like to start off with a private office where I could make a
long distance call, and then, if you're going to be around,
maybe you could help me start appreciating. Okay?"

"Oh, sure," she said. "You can use David's office. Come
with me."

Kim usually looked worried when she talked to me—*cute*
worried, of course—but just now I thought there was an
extra vertical crease between her eyebrows.

"David's out on business, huh?" I asked as I settled in his
chair and lit a cigarette.

"David doesn't—I'll get you an ashtray," she sighed,
bopping into the next office and back.

"Thanks," I said. "Out on business, right?"

She knew I'd guessed, so she had to tell me.

"David went to have a talk with Lieutenant Carroll," she
said. "He had to! Lieutenant Carroll called here first thing
this morning, and he couldn't just lie to him! We *tried* to
get in touch—"

"It's okay," I said, though it really wasn't. "I've got to

make this phone call, and then we'll talk about this. I'll be
with you in, maybe, a half hour or so: no interruptions,
right? Now go sell some fantasies."

"Beg pardon?"

"Nothing: turn of phrase," I said as she closed the door.
And then, speaking of fantasy salesmen, I got out the paper
Bobby Reilly had given me and dialled the private number of
Jerry Kawin, President of Sybaris Agency, Inc.

CHAPTER NINETEEN

I HAVEN'T HUNG OUT with that many big-time show business people, unless you want to count watching guys hug and kiss on the "Tonight" show, or drinking and shooting pool with Tommy Eifler, who went to high school with me and weighs more than Bridget for Chrissake. Tommy runs—or ran, before his cardiac—a topless bottomless place on Rush Street in Old Town called, I promise you, The Dangle. While Kawin's private line buzzed, I decided that he'd probably respond more like Tommy than like Frankie or Dino or Liza. I wasn't wrong.

"Hello? This is Mr. Kawin's residence," said a woman's voice, "Can I help you?"

"I hope so, ma'am," I said, trying to get back that aw-shucks, hopeful altar-boy tone. "I need to talk to Mr. Kawin, and his friend Mr. Reilly—that's Mr. Bobby Reilly— said it would be okay for me to call him at this number. My name's Garnish, Harry Garnish. Maybe Mr. Reilly told him I'd be calling?"

"Well," she said, "I'm not sure Mr. Kawin is here just now. Could you hold a minute, please?" I said sure, and started counting.

Whenever they tell you they'll be back in a minute, start

counting; if you get to fifteen or so (one kill a dog; two kill a dog; like that) before they come back, somebody's taking you seriously enough, you didn't waste your quarter.

I was up to *twenty* kill a dog when a voice like a carpenter's plane on hardwood said, "Garnish? Kawin. Talk to me."

"Hello, sir," I said. "And thanks so much for making time for me—"

"Yeah, yeah. I'm a fuckin' prince, I know it. Listen: Bobby calls me last night, says you're looking for Carla. Okay, *I'm* looking for Carla. I'm looking for Carla, what, a week, week and a half. Bobby says you got a hair up your ass, something about she kidnapped a kid, which I tell you, my friend, is strictly bullshit because I *know* the bitch. I did six, seven pictures with her and she's too fuckin nice-nelly—you feature Mary Tyler Moore doing spread shots?—for that bullshit, not to mention too goddamn cagey or too dumb to pull it off, same difference.

"So." It was, I think, the first time he'd taken a breath. "So," he went on, "Bobby tells me he thinks anyway *you're* not bullshit, which he may be a faggot but he's got a good head—hey! *good head*, you got that? Mwaah!"

"Mr. Kawin," I said while he strangled on his laugh—

"Yeah, yeah,' he said. "I'm okay. So here's the plan. I got to find Carla, I got some gigs for her, very tasty gigs, but I need cops on this like I need another asshole. I would not, however, be what you call *averse* to her getting a little publicity, especially if it's on the, hey, sticky side, catch my drift?"

"Mr. Kawin," I said, lighting another cigarette. "What I need—"

"Hey, right, I'm *coming* to that. Jesus, you got to catch a train or something? Of *course* you need, who doesn't *need*? What I figure, you find her, you're already on this thing, you bring her back in, some photos, if they're the right photos, wouldn't hurt, and I can sell her next flick with some very *nice* advance spreads— hey, *spreads*, mwaah—she gets richer, I get ten percent of richer, seashells and balloons all around, and you get, what, five hundred fish from me on top of whatever you're getting from her ex-dork. Whaddaya say? Talk to me."

I wasn't sure I could. Bridget had spent all those years telling me I was "foul-mouthed"; and before I'd talked to Kawin, I'd thought the concept was a myth. Live and learn. I cleared by throat, and began, "Mr. Kawin, I think you may have misunderstood why I'm calling. I—"

"Okay, okay," he said, "I won't dick you around, one *thousand* fish, and I can't go higher than that and save my own nut, God's truth."

"Look," I said. "I appreciate the offer. But you don't get why I called. The fact is, I don't have the slightest idea where, or even how, to look for her. I was hoping that *you* could, maybe—"

"Say what? You're asking *me* for help? Reilly says you're a fuckin' *detective*, yet; says you're on her trail, and now you want me to do your fuckin' job for you? Jesus, bubbie, I'm a busy man, you know? What do you think—"

"Goddamnit, Kawin, forget it!" I shouted, thinking: just make believe you're talking to Tommy Eifler. "You can't pull your head out of your ass far enough to see what I'm telling you, then tuck it back in. How the fuck you think detectives work, with a ouija board? Go see a movie, for Chrissake: I mean one where people get out of bed once in a while. We ask people questions, dummy, and then we put the answers together and then we either find or don't find what we're looking for. Aah, the hell with it. You're a busy man, you don't have time for this shit. Tell you what. I happen to know the cops have just gotten interested in your pal Carla, so you just save up your time for answering *their* questions. Cause *they* got *lots* of time. So long, Jerry baby."

"Hey, wait! hey, Harry," He chuckled the way you do—or I do— when your bet's just been seen and raised. "Look. I get a little stressed out sometimes, you know? Sure, I understand your problem, I just don't see why the fuckin' cops should get in all this, I mean, couldn't you do something? Okay, okay, that was dumb. So what can I tell you?"

"Okay," I said. "For openers, you say you haven't seen Carla in a week and a half, right?"

"Seen? Hell, I haven't *seen* her in maybe two months or so. We do all our business by phone or mail. I been trying to get in touch with her, maybe a week, is all."

"But I thought—"

"Don't tell me. You thought us guys and gals in the business all lived together and when we weren't making movies we all had orgies at the Crisco factory, am I right? What you think, Harry, I'm short and bald, I'm wearing an aloha shirt open to the navel and a coke spoon around my neck, yeah?"

"Well—"

"Yeah, *well*. Look, man, this is a *business*. We got some wild asses, we got others, off the set you'd think it was Beaver Cleaver, whatever. Just like the insurance business, except we ain't selling insurance—"

"Don't tell me," I said. "You're selling fantasies."

"Hey, that's *good*," he said.

"Right," I said wearily, "but the thing is, I need to know who Carla hangs around with, who she might confide in— besides Bobby Reilly, who thinks she's aces. Now, according to her ex-husband—"

"*That* putz! Harry, my man, whatever whatsits, David, told you, figure sixty percent of it's what makes the grass grow green. You tell me I got *my* head up my ass. I bet he told you how Carla got sucked into the business, he wanted her to have a real career, he was shocked, and blah, blah, blah. Now, come on, baby, you think he didn't know what the fuckin' score was?"

I was silent.

"Listen," he went on, "you want my opinion, one of the reasons she stuck in the business was to rub the son-ofabitch's nose in what he'd set up for her. Like that name, Carla Bolero. She let him know—and this is one true fact— she let him know, far as she was concerned, Karin Bryant was *no more*. Damn!" and he chuckled, "she may be a bitch, but she don't take shit, you know?"

I figured that, for Jerry Kawin, this was about the equivalent of a Kiwanis Auxiliary Woman of the Month award. "Yeah," I said, "I can buy that. But about her friends— "

"Can't help you there," he said. "We didn't, aah, hang out a lot together. Strictly business. Same with the directors she worked with, most of the people in the business. Funny chick. Guess you're out of luck, huh?"

"I don't know. But thanks, Mr. Kawin. Sorry I hollered at you."

He laughed. "Hey, you got my fuckin attention, didn't you? And it's *Jerry*. So look, what about our little deal?"

"Wha?"

"*You* know. Like, if you get lucky and find her, you give me some notice, let me set up a little publicity? They're waiting for her next contract."

"Well," I began—

"Okay, okay, I can see you're a businessman, too. What about a little taste up front, not the whole—wha'd we say, five hundred?—but a retainer, hey?"

"Well," I began again—"No. Wait. Yeah, why not?" I got

out my wallet and thumbed through for a slip of paper. Found it. "Okay, Jerry." I said and read him the address on the paper. "A guy named Hewitt, Bruce Hewitt lies there. If you send him, say, fifty bucks worth of cat food and a quart— make that two quarts—of Korbel brandy, I'll clue you in as soon as I find out where Carla is—*if* I can do it without hurting Carla. How's that? Talk to me."

"Well . . . yeah, I guess. Is this a joke?"

"Nope," I said. "Have the card say, 'From an Admirer,' and I'll do what I can for you."

"You want a receipt?"

"Jerry, *are* you short and bald with a coke spoon?"

"No!" He sounded hurt.

"Then I don't need a receipt. Ciao, baby: shine on." That's showbiz talk.

Kim wasn't exactly lurking outside the door to David's office, but I got the impression she'd been on what they call a tight orbit during my chat with Jerry Kawin. She glanced, not annoyed but maybe a little apprehensive, at the cloud of smoke I'd left over the desk.

"So," I said, lighting up. "David not back yet?"

"N-no," she said, "as a matter of fact, he had some other business to take care of after—uh—"

"Right. And idle hands are the Devil's workshop or something, aren't they?"

"You know," she said under her breath, looking around at the bustling realtors. "I don't know why you dislike David so much. Maybe you dislike me, too: you certainly act like it. But I have to tell you that he's a *wonderful* man, and I don't think your attitude is any help at all in this awful business."

Her lower lip was trembling, and I felt—it's not unusual— like a cow pie in a hotel lobby. Would *you* want to make

Shari Lewis cry? Or, for God's sake, Lamb Chop?

"Look," I said, "I'm sorry. You're right, I act like an asshole. I must have been an abused child, isn't that what all the assholes say these days?" She smiled a little. "Anyway, believe me, I don't dislike *anybody*. Well, maybe old ladies who take thirty items through the express checkout lane." She swallowed a chuckle. "So I'll watch it. Fair?"

"Fair. Harry." And she held out her hand. "Now, you said Bridget wanted you to just sort of look around the office? What can I tell you about our business?"

"To tell you the truth, Kim, you could start telling me if there's anyplace near I can snag lunch. And if you could please join me."

"Well," she said, "I don't usually eat lunch—"

"Hey," I said. "We just made friends, I need to talk to you, I'm hungry, it's on expense account and you're the client. What the hell?"

She had a *really* nice laugh. "What the hell," she said. "Let me just tell Marcie to take my calls. Do you like Mexican food?"

In Seattle they probably ask you if you like rain.

CHAPTER TWENTY

"E$_L$ POLLO LOCO" MEANS "the crazy chicken," and Californians think it's such a wild gag that they gave it to, I'd guess, every twelfth restaurant in the state. This particular crazy chicken was at the other end of the tiny shopping center from Pescatore Realty. Kim ordered a glass of herbal ice tea and the "New Age" salad, which actually made me look at the menu and this is what it said:

> *New Age Spinach Salad.* Fresh Spinach leaves combined with Sliced Mushrooms and Almonds all tossed in our Low Calorie Vinaigrette Dressing. BE HEART SMART!

I sighed, felt *old*, and ordered two beef tamales with refried beans and a Dos Equis.

"So what do you think, Kim?" I asked as our drinks came.

"Please?" she said. "What do I think about what?"

"Anything. Everything. This is one hell of a way for you and David to get ready for your wedding, and I know Bridget's been telling you to buck up, have faith, and like that. But *I* can tell you, and I think you ought to know, that things are going nowhere."

"But," she said, "the police—"

"The police," I said, "are interested when anybody disappears, and they're extra special interested when folks like you and David hire people like Bridget and me to do a job they're sure they can do better, and they're usually right about that, by the way. I don't think old David's having the world's comfiest chat with Lieutenant Carroll right now. That's okay. The most Carroll can do is tell me and Bridget to bugger off, and what I'm telling you is that we've *been* buggered off. Look: did you *really* expect us to accomplish something, or what?"

She stared at her New Age salad, sorting the almonds from the mushrooms with her fork. "Harry," she said finally, "do you know who is the most important person in the world to me?"

"Well, uh," I said, "David, right? David and Jennifer?"

"I hope this doesn't shock you," she said, "but it's Bridget."

It was my turn to separate the beef from the tamale with my fork.

"It's the truth," she said. "When I went into the convent, I was a *mess*." She smiled a little at the memory. "I'd been on the street, I'd done drugs, I'd done— well, lots of things. Bridget never told you that, did she? I knew she wouldn't. So I came there wanting—oh, hell, I don't know, wanting just to leave everything behind, just to be *clean* for the longest time: clean and *quiet*. Did you ever want something like that?"

"Well—sure," I mumbled.

"Then you know how much it means. But Bridget—she'll always be Sister Juanita to me, you know—" her smile, I swear to God, could have sold beef jerky to Hindus— "Bridget helped me find out that I was looking for those things in the wrong place and in the wrong way—at least, for me. It's

not just that she's so sweet and caring— *you* know that,
Harry. It's that she's so *strong*. Strong for *you*, for what *you*
need. Oh, I *do* love David. And Jennifer—well, she's like a
chance to take care of myself when I was her age, you know?
But Bridget . . . I'll tell you, Harry, if I ever thought I'd let
Bridget down, I don't know what I'd think of myself." Her
big eyes were moist.

My tamales, by the way, smelled great, and I was really
hungry. But how the hell do you give kindly-uncle advice
with your mouth full of cornmeal and steak chunks? I leaned
across the table and took her hand.

"Kim," I said. "Believe me, Bridget would be—uh, touched
to hear how you feel about her. But, I'll tell you, kid, she'd want
you to be a little more—what?—a little more solid with
yourself, dig? I mean, you don't have to *please* her, prove
anything. Isn't that what she really told you?"

She smiled, teary, and nodded, putting her other hand on
mine.

"Right," I said. "And that means, right now, you've got
to admit a couple of things. You've got to face the fact that,
good person or not, Bridget isn't going to be able to do a hell
of a lot more for you here. No, wait—come on, don't sniffle
up on me. All we know is that Jennifer's gone, and Carla's
gone; but we really don't even know that those two are
connected. And there's been no ransom note, none of that
stuff, and that means the trail couldn't be colder. Now you
just might start thinking about this: that Jennifer *is* a
runaway—now come on, stop that, that doesn't mean she
hates you or anything. You just might have to go ahead with
the wedding, go ahead with your life not seeing Jennifer
for—well, maybe for a long time."

Honest: I'm so damned *good* at stuff like that, I ought to
be, maybe, Leo Buscaglia's dialogue coach. She bent her head

and sobbed, her forehead on our joined hands.

My timing was right up to speed, too. "Kim?" said David, standing over us and looking at me with one *mother* of a curious face.

We all said, at the same time, "What have you been saying to her?" "Oh—David! Is everything all right?" and "Hey, David! Sit down, man!" And then we all tried to answer one another's questions at the same time. By that time David was seated, with Kim's hands in his. He got to solo.

"Well, Harry?" he said. "What have you been saying to Kim? Marcie said you two were here."

"Not much," I said, finally getting to my tamales and beer, now both about the same temperature. "Just about what I figure John Carroll has been telling you—and by the way, David, cheers for standing so firm on that one. We're dead-ended six ways from Christmas. Looking for Carla is probably a waste of nervous energy. Bridget and I didn't have much of a hand to begin with, and that's all played out. You probably—sorry, man, but it's on the table—have a runaway, pure and simple. Comments?"

Cado and Bridget, as far as I was concerned, could be tooling all the hell around Santa Barbara checking out laundry lists and discussing fairy tales and X-movies. This was the real tapioca, no place to go, and at least, I thought, old Hewitt would walk out of the deal with some snacks for Cagney and Thalberg and some nice nods for himself.

David was trying to look stern. I thought—I hoped, anyway—he was remembering getting sucker-punched in L.A.X.

"You know," he began, staring at a point on the table midway between us. "I wasn't too crazy about this way of proceeding since Jennifer—from the beginning. As you said, Harry, there are plenty of good detectives in California. But Kim loves Bridget, and Bridget knows Jennifer, so—when

you were called out here, I confess I was even less enthusi-
astic. And to be honest, Harry, what have you done? You've
gotten arrested, you've dragged in this punk biker who calls
me names—"

"Say what?" I said.

"Your good pal, Cado! You heard him last night, he called
me a *Cohen*. You know, all real estate people are Jews! He—"

But I was cracking up. "Jesus, David!" I laughed. "You've
got a tiny bit of an anti-Semite problem there, but I think
you got some hearing loss with it. Cado didn't call you a
Cohen. He said he was doing a *koan* on you."

"Doing a what?"

"*Koan*. *Ko-an*. It's a riddle, a puzzle. Like, a Buddhist
monk asks the head monk, uh, 'Oh great master, what's the
secret of life?' And the master, instead of answering the guy's
question, stands on his head or smiles and farts or twists
the guy's nose. That's a *koan*. It's supposed to teach you
something without telling you anything."

He stared at me. "You're making this up," he said.

"David," I said. "*You* work with Bridget as long as I have
and try not to pick up stuff like that. Trust me. I think what
Cado meant, you were gassing about the community of solid
citizens and suchlike, and here's this biker dude trying to
help you, just to help you. Like, you know, 'Blessed are the
losers, for they might save your ass.'"

He looked like he'd rather have been called a *Cohen*.

"Wonderful," he said. "Tell your friend how grateful I am
for his moral lesson. Meanwhile—"

"Meanwhile," I said, "you're frustrated, angry, nothing is
turning out, and you wish we'd just get the hell out of your
life. You're right, and I'm seriously sorry, man. I hope like
crazy Jennifer turns up. But hoping like crazy is what I've
got left."

"David?" It was Marcie, the girl from the office. "Sorry to bother you, but we just got a call for Mr. Garnish. The gentleman said it was urgent, Mr. Garnish should call him right back, and he said it was about—about Jennifer."

She had the message slip in her hand. "Gimme," I said.

It was Bobby Reilly's number.

CHAPTER TWENTY-ONE

"Bobby? HARRY HERE. WHAT'S happening?"

"Hey, thanks for getting back to me so fast. I didn't know *who* I should call, really, but—"

"That's okay, let's hear it."

David and Kim and I were in David's office, and David had one of those gizmos on his phone that allowed you to broadcast the call and talk back from anyplace in the room.

"Well, it's crazy," he said. "You know, you coming to see me just yesterday and all, but—well, I got a telegram this morning. From Carla. I think."

"You *think*?" I said.

"Yeah. It's a little funny," he began—

"For God's sake, what does the telegram *say*?" That was David.

"Harry, is that you?" asked Bobby.

"Jennifer's father," I said. "Bobby, read the telegram."

"Oh. Okay. Here it is: 'Dear Bobby. Thought Jen and I could get away, but won't work. Am going away. Jen safe Room 209 Coronado Hotel, Santa Barbara. Tell everyone I'm sorry. Love, Carla.' And that's all."

David and Kim were halfway out the door. "Hey, dammit!" I shouted at them. "Bobby, hang on second. Look, you're going right to the hotel, right?"

"What do you think?" said David.

"Swell," I said. "But do yourself—do *Jennifer* a favor. On your way out, call Carroll's office. Make sure he or whoever's there knows what's going down, and that they'll be at the hotel. If this is for real, believe me, you'll want the cops in from the start."

"Why can't *you* do it?" asked Kim.

"Because I'm not done here and because it's better if you alert the fuzz. Now *go*."

"Okay, Bobby," I said as they closed the door. "I assume you heard what I was saying just now."

"Oh, yes indeed; something about the authorities, wasn't it?"

I smiled. "Sorry, but they've kind of dealt themselves in since we talked. I just wanted you to know that—"

"That they'll be coming to talk to me and that they'll want to see the telegram and know all about my relationship with Carla. And that because of my—profession, this could lead to some unflattering speculation in the press. It's all right, Harry. The Moral Majority has already assigned me a cell number in hell. Know what we call their TV broadcasts? The Falwellian Tube. I just wish I could be sure Carla's all right."

"That was the other thing," I said. "What did you mean, it's from Carla you *think*?"

"Oh," he said, "maybe I'm just a little unhinged by this whole thing. Let's just make sure the poor kid is at the Coronado."

"No," I said, "let's not. Something struck you as 'funny,' you said. I'd really like to hear what's funny, Bobby."

"Well, that's just it. 'Dear Bobby,' she begins. But my friends—no offense, Harry, I mean my *close* friends— call me 'Rob.' 'Bobby' is, you know, for the movies. Silly, I suppose: Carla has to be at wit's end by now—"

He kept talking but I didn't listen. There's a special tingly chill you get when you *realize* you're in the middle of someplace you don't want to be: a flasher in your rear- view, an overdraft you didn't expect, a lover who wants *out*. The tingle begins at the back of your skull and washes, in its own sweet time, down to your fingers.

It was about names. Public frogs were princes to their friends, it all depended on what you called them. The Orrington bartender was "Torch" to the regulars. Arcadio was "Cado" to his brothers. Jennifer was "Jen" in her family. And Carla called Bobby "Rob," just like—yeah!— Tedd had called Bobby "Rob."

But that wasn't it. Why the tingle? Something about names and something about talking with Bobby and Tedd about Carla, and *about Carla who always said 'this is Carla' on the tape when Bobby got her answer machine.*

So what? Goddammit, *Carla* was her fuckin *name.*

The name she took, said Jerry Kawin, to hurt David. The name she took as a way of saying 'Karin Bryant is no more.'

But not the name she'd used with me. Not the name she or somebody used when I called her number that first time. "This is Karin Bryant," the voice on the tape had said. The voice on the tape that wasn't in her answer machine when Cado and I searched her apartment. That was what had been nagging me about my conversation with Bobby, and that was what had frozen me, what I had almost gotten hold of under the fig tree before Jesus came up to explain the birth of the universe to me.

The voice on the tape had not been the voice of Carla Bolero.

Now if I only knew what the hell *that* meant.

"Harry, are you still there?" Bobby sounded puzzled.

"Yeah—yeah, man. Sorry. Look, are you going to be at that number for a while?"

"Well," he said, "I can be. What is it?"

"I don't know," I said, "but it's something. I'd appreciate it if you could stay close to the phone, Bobby. I'll get back to you as soon as I can."

We rang off. I put out a cigarette I didn't remember having lit, and left the office. There, waiting for me outside the door, was Marcie, looking worried.

"Mr. Garnish?" she said. "David—Mr. Pescatore—said I should wait till you were finished with your call."

"Problem?" I asked. "Do you know if David called the cops before he left here?"

"Well, that's just it, you see. He did, and the police said they'd been looking for you—trying to get in touch with you, that is—all morning, Lieutenant—uh—"

"Carroll," I said.

"Yes, that's right. Lieutenant Carroll said to tell you— well, to ask you—to wait right here. They're sending someone to pick you up and take you to Cottage Hospital."

"Say what?"

"Well," she said with that nervous, embarrassed look people always get when they're about to drop bad news on you—as if they're responsible—"well, you see, there's been an accident. With your friend. Miss—uh—"

"O'Toole?" I asked, feeling suddenly queasy.

"That's right, Miss O'Toole. I'm awfully sorry, Mr. Garnish. Can I bring you some coffee while you wait?"

I told her no, thanks. She didn't know how serious the accident was. She didn't know when the cops would be here to pick me up. I was sure I didn't want a cup of coffee, thanks again. I had one cigarette smoking in an ashtray and I had just lit another one. Sure, thanks, a glass of water would be nice. And while she went off to the water cooler, the front door opened and in walked—of course—Officer Helgerson, his face as blank as ever.

"Are you ready, Garnish?" he asked.

And I told him I was, in a nice warm shower of relief. Cops are always cops, you see, at some deep level. And I could have been a suspected axe-murderer and horse-thief, but if Bridget had been seriously hurt he would have—I'd bet on it—called me "Mister."

$\triangledown$

CHAPTER TWENTY-TWO

IT WAS ALMOST A pleasure to ride in the back of a cop car without cuffs on, but unless you've ever ridden in the back *with* cuffs, maybe you don't understand what I mean.

Helgerson had said, "Are you ready, Garnish?" His partner in the front seat, a very *large* Ken doll in blues, wasn't nearly as talkative, so the ride to Cottage Hospital was mainly what you might call meditative. I think—no, I hope—old Helgie kept waiting for me to ask him what was going on, so that he could grunt back that I'd find out when we got there, so I kept on not asking him and he kept on getting pissed off because I wasn't asking him. You know how it is: most of the time the world is playground recess, fifth grade.

Or maybe I was playing jackass poker because I was still nervous about Bridget and figured I might as well wait and get all the bad news at once instead of driblets: you know, "Dear Fred, the cat is on the roof and we can't get her down," like that. Who knows?

Anyway, I was *really* relieved when we parked by the Emergency Room entrance—that eliminated either Intensive Care or the Big One—and even more so when I saw, sitting outside one of those curtained-in cubicles they have,

160

a scraped-up but grinning Cado with his friends Mitch and Lisa.

"Hey, Chicago! They found you," began Cado.

"Shut up," said Helgerson, ushering me through the curtain.

Bridget was sitting up in bed with a potato-pancake size bandage over her left eye and her left arm in one of those gauze and metal, weird-angle things that make you look like you're doing a bush-league Boris Karloff. Smiling, yet: though her lips looked a little bruised and puffy.

John Carroll was sitting beside her. His lips were thin, and he wasn't smiling.

"I hope you feel good about all this, Mr. Garnish," said Carroll.

"Beg pardon?" I said. There was only one chair in the cubicle, and he was sitting on it. I think he wanted it that way.

"Lieutenant," began Bridget—

"*Excuse* me, Miss O'Toole," he snapped, and Bridget fell silent. I've seen Bridget interrupted that way maybe three, four times since I've been working with her. She doesn't take it well. I could see her eyes—okay, eye—focus on Carroll, waiting for him to say something that would allow her to pounce, the logician from Hell.

"'Beg pardon' is about right," he said, turning back to me. "As far as I can see, you and Miss O'Toole here simply lied to me. I warned you against getting involved in the search for Jennifer Pescatore. I told you that we were perfectly suited to do everything that could be done. Now Mr. Pescatore came to his senses—finally—and told me this morning that you had been digging around in L.A. and that you had come up with exactly nothing."

"I know all that," I said. "And I'm sorry if you feel like we lied to you, but I don't see what the hell damage we did."

"Oh, I'm sure you wouldn't, Mr. Garnish"—again with that slight emphasis on the *you*—"and I suppose there's no way I can officially penalize you; especially in view of Miss O'Toole's accident—"

"Yeah," I said. I get pissed when people call me *you* like that. "I was going to ask about that, you know? It's kind of been on my mind."

"I'll get to that," he said, and Bridget's eye got a little narrower. "The point I'm making is that you *could* have jeopardized an investigation with your haphazard questioning. You're only very lucky that you didn't. And, as you can see, your meddling—I'm sorry to use so strong a word, but that's what it is—your meddling was just fortunate enough to have been unnecessary instead of counterproductive. While you were being brought here, Jennifer was picked up at the Coronado Hotel by her parents— well, Mr. Pescatore and Miss Molloy—and two of our officers. She's fine, and she'll be back home soon, after a little preliminary questioning. So, if Mr. Pescatore had some to us in the first place with his suspicions about his ex- wife—"

"If David had come to you in the first place," said Bridget with *Gotcha!* written across her puffy face, "you would have proceeded—if you did proceed—by questioning the same people Harry questioned. Except you could not have; you would have had to ask the Los Angeles police to cooperate with you in the investigation. So the people with whom Harry spoke would have been, instead, confronted with grim-faced uniforms or plain clothes, with all the daunting panoply of officialdom. They could not have told you more than they told Harry and Arcadio; and they certainly might have told you less. And when Mr. Reilly received his telegram from Carla Bolero, would he have called you as readily as he called Harry? Or would he have called David—and wouldn't David then have most likely just retrieved his child, leaving *you* to learn about it later, looking even less efficient than you do already? Remember that Harry insisted David call you when the telegram arrived: that's how you knew he was at David's office. Come now, Lieutenant, wouldn't all that have been what you like to call 'counterproductive?' And by the way, could you arrange for Harry to have a chair?"

I don't know if Bridget made any sense. But I did once see Alfie Nicolosi pick up five hundred bucks by sinking three balls in three separate pockets on a four-cushion—that's *four*—shot in the Bambi Bar in Skokie. And the expression on Carroll's face was a lot like the expression on the face of the guy Alfie had suckered into making the bet on the shot.

"Richard?" he said to Helgerson, who I'd forgotten was in the room. Richard grunted, went out, came back with a folding chair for me, and at a nod from Carroll went back out again.

"The fact remains, Miss O'Toole," he said, "just as a matter of your own safety, if you hadn't been—well, still working on the case, you wouldn't have been injured this morning."

"Yeah, about that," I began—

"Hush, Harry!" she snapped at me.

"Balderdash!' she snapped at Carroll. "You sound like the kind of parent who tells a child, 'See, Johnny, if you'd been doing your homework, you wouldn't have fallen out of that tree and broken your arm.' I certainly hope you're not that kind of parent."

"It's nothing, Harry," she said to me. "As Arcadio and I were pulling out of the park, we were sideswiped by a van—a purple van, as I remember. We were thrown onto the grass, thank the Lord, and Mitch and Lisa were right there. Lisa stayed with me while Mitch called 911. The van didn't stop, and poor Arcadio's motorcycle is damaged, but it had nothing"—glaring at Carroll—"to do with the business at hand."

"And as *for* the business at hand, Lieutenant Carroll," she said, turning her attention back to him and *knowing* she was on a roll. "It's very interesting that you choose to be here, scolding and attempting to intimidate me, rather than picking up and interrogating Jennifer. And since intimidation won't work, why don't you just ask? Carla Bolero is now an official suspect in a kidnapping. Harry and I—without interfering in your work, mind you—have been proceeding on that assumption somewhat longer than you. You would like to know what we have discovered, if anything, about Miss Bolero. And of course we *will* tell you, because not to would be an obstruction of justice. You could have simply asked at the beginning. You may ask now."

He smiled at her, and it was the first time I'd seen him smile so that you could see his teeth.

"Miss O'Toole," he said, "were you ever a policewoman?"

Bridget smiled back. "I taught seventh grade, sir," she said.

Just then a doctor—well, a guy in a lab coat, with a stethoscope, and an idiotic "How are we today?" smile—came in and told Carroll and me we'd have to leave for a few minutes while he checked on "our young lady here." I didn't look at Bridget, but the eyebrow and half-grimace Carroll gave me as we rose to leave told me he was getting a pretty good fix on what our young lady was like.

Cado and Mitch and Lisa were still sitting outside the curtain, mumbling and grousing to one another. Helgerson was standing across from them, at something like parade rest. Lisa jumped to her feet as soon as we came out.

"We going to stay here all day?" she snarled at Carroll. She had a cute snarl. "At least you could send out for beer and pizza, something."

Carroll looked genuinely embarrassed. "Oh, I'm sorry, Miss—"

"Lisa," said Lisa.

"Yes," he said. "You've given your statements, have you?"

"A damn hour and a half ago," she snorted. Cute snort.

"Well, then, please excuse me. I've been preoccupied. You and your friend are free to go. Mr. Molina, I'd appreciate your staying."

"Wouldn't have it any other way, chief," grinned Cado.

"And Lisa," said Carroll as she and Mitch were walking away. "Here." He handed her a ten. "For beer and pizza, with apologies. Compliments of S.B.P.D."

"Well—" she aw-shucksed, then snagged the ten and flashed him a—you got it—cute smile.

"Good shew, Inspectah," said Cado, doing a terrible Peter Lawford. "If I stay longer, do the rates go up?"

"Mr. Molina, please just sit there and wait. I'll have some things to talk over with you later. Mr. Garnish, would you like to step outside and have a cigarette?"

"You're really good, you know?" I told him when we were outside and I'd lit up. "I've never seen the same guy do bad cop-good cop."

He smiled—he may have even meant it—and, to my surprise, took a Parliament out of his breast pocket, lit it and poised it like a conductor's baton.

"That's a very smart lady you work for," he said, and then glanced at me. "But you probably prefer with, don't you? Anyway, Harry. May I call you Harry? Anyway, I don't want to try to divide you and your—aah, partner. But as long as we have this opportunity . . . If there's anything you, your-

self, might want to tell me. After all, you did the real
questioning, as I understand. So—well," and he trailed off,
staring at the end of his Parliament.

"As a matter of fact, Lieutenant, there is something—
kind of a funny something—that I just picked up on before
you sent your pals to pick *me* up."

"Yes?" he said. He was one of those guys who register
excitement by trying like hell not to register excitement. He
stared at his cigarette like there was a prize for guessing the
strands of tobacco in it.

"But I might as well tell you and Bridget—my partner—at
the same time. The doctor ought to be done with her soon,
and that way I won't have to explain it twice."

He just shrugged and kept on smoking, not looking at me.
After a while he said, "Ready?" and we both ground out our
smokes. I caught him out of the corner of my eye "son of a
bitch" to the pavement, and we went back in.

It's the Garnish Method: do unto others as you know,
sooner or later, they're going to do unto you.

$\triangledown$

CHAPTER TWENTY-THREE

THE DOCTOR WAS JUST leaving as we got back to Bridget's stall. He looked at me strangely when I asked him, "And how *is* our young lady doing?" said she was all right, all things considered, bad sprain, nothing broken, could leave as soon as Lieutenant Carroll was through, and blah, blah, blah, and bustled down the hall.

"Molina, you might as well come in with us," said Carroll. I noticed that Cado was limping.

Bridget's arm was now in a sling and the potato pancake was off her eye, revealing a righteous mouse the color of Pepto-Bismol.

"Mama Bridge," said Cado. "That eye matches my hike!"

"Hello, Arcadio," she said. "Are you feeling all right?"

"If we can dispense with the greetings," said Carroll, "Garnish says he has something to share with us. Garnish?"

So I told them about my big discovery, about how Carla never called herself, as Kawin had told me, Karin and how Bobby Reilly had said she always said "This is Carla" on her answering machine, how the telegram had been addressed to him as "Bobby" not "Rob, which is what he said she always called *him*, and how *that* was the thing that started me thinking about the whole name business in the first place . . . and the more I talked the more I felt like an ass.

You ever do that? Get an idea, I mean, that feels solid as pig-iron, the kind of idea where you say to yourself, "Goddamn it, Garnish, you be *good*"; and then you start to explain it—they say "share it" in California—and watch it turn into Kleenex? Of course it helps a lot if the people you're sharing it with stare at you like you're a dead picture tube, which is the way Carroll especially was staring at me.

"Uh-huh," said Carroll when I had limped to a finish. "And that's it?"

"Well—yeah," I said. I was remembering how Bandit had looked after he'd proudly brought a dead bird to my door and I'd give him my reaction.

"And you're *certain* that when you called the Bolero number, the voice on the answering machine said 'Karin,' not 'Carla'?"

"Well—yeah," I said. Bandit hadn't come back for week after that.

"And you realize that Jennifer, who should be—"checking his watch—"who should be home by now with her father, corroborates that it was her mother who took her away, and her mother who deposited her, yesterday afternoon, at the Coronado?"

"Well—"

"And you're sure it *wasn't* the mother, and all because you're *sure* a recorded message you heard two days ago, before you were arrested for drunk and disorderly, used what you say is the wrong one of the lady's two names."

"Three days ago," I put in helpfully. When you holler at Bandit, what he does is he lays on his back and waves his paws in the air.

"Why do you keep Garnish on the payroll, Miss O'Toole?" Carroll asked, getting to his feet. "Is it for entertainment value?"

Bridget only said, "Will there by anything else, Lieutenant? I'd like to get to David's and see Jennifer."

He sighed. "That will be all for now. We *will* talk again. Molina, you can go, too—just don't try to leave Santa Barbara."

"Without my bike?" said Cado. "Hell, chief, you know us crazy obsessed leather metal freaks. But, don't you know, Miss Bridge and I need a ride to David's. And come to think of it, old Harry here probably got to be driven back to where you snagged him, too. You got a couple of spare squad cars, or you got taxi vouchers, or what?"

Carroll just stared for maybe fifteen seconds. "I'll tell Helgerson to arrange transportation for you all," he said finally. "And now, if you'll excuse me, I have work to do."

When he'd gone we stared at one another in a kind of communal shrug. Bridget began hefting herself out of bed and Cado rushed over to help her. I had just about worked out my apology to the two of them for sounding like the king of the dork people and had cleared my throat to begin when Carroll came back through the curtain.

"It seems," he said, handing me a slip of paper, "we're in the answering service as well as the limousine business. This lady was trying to reach you at Pescatore Realty, Garnish, and apparently insisted that they call the message through to the hospital. Once more, good day."

I looked at the slip as he went out. It was Emily Rice's name, a number, and the note "Please call before 6:00." It was 5:15.

"Bullshit," I said after I'd read it aloud, and crumpled it to throw away. I know: I've said she was a stone fox. And besides her, checking out Mitch's Lisa, Kim, and Carla Bolero's contributions to CREAM SCREEN *had* kept the Garnish glands on at least yellow alert all day long. But it had been a *long* day. And I was still feeling pretty damn dumb about my attempt to play Little League Sherlock with Carroll. And—I'll tell you the truth—stone foxes almost never call me up for reasons I wish the stone foxes *would* call me up. Make that "reason." So "bullshit," I said.

And "No, Harry, don't!" said Bridget, leaning on Cado's arm. "If you're not too tired, dear, I really think you ought to call her back."

"Bridget," I said, "it's over. I *am* too tired. I just want to go home, say hello to little Jennifer, have a sandwich and a six-pack or two, and fly back to Chicago after a ten-hour nap. What the hell can Emily Rice tell us now?"

And what she did was The Pout. The Pout is to Bridget what "Born to Run" is to Springsteen or the floating lay-up is to Magic Johnson: a trademark, a patented masterpiece, something you can't, no matter how hard you try, defend against. I've never quite figured out the receipe, but it's part Jewish mother—"I asked you once, I wouldn't break my own heart asking you again"—part seventh-grade blackmail— "your parents would be *so* disappointed if they knew how you were behaving"—and part secret ingredient— something like, "Oh, if Father were still running the agency, *he'd* know how to convince you to do the right thing." The only difference this time was, I'd never seen her do it before with one eye swollen half-shut and the rest of her face trying to decide how purple to get in the next few days: must've hurt.

So "Yeah," I said. "Is there a pay phone anywhere around here?"

There was just down the hall. I told an increasingly pissed-off looking Helgerson that we'd all be ready to go real soon, and punched up the number on the slip.

"Mr. Garnish—I'm so glad you called," said Emily after her receptionist put my call through.

"Yeah," I said. "It's been kind of a busy day."

"I've heard!" she said. "They told me when I tried to reach you at David's house. Is Jennifer all right? Is Miss O'Toole all right?"

They'd told her, I thought, a hell of a lot more than it was their business to tell her. But maybe Californians just naturally liked to share. Anyway, I assured her that all the troops were in marching formation, and then—okay, maybe with a *little* bit of dry-mouth—asked her why she'd been trying to get in touch with me.

"Oh," she said, with—I swear to God—a giggle. "Well, maybe now that everything has been resolved, it wouldn't mean much. But, to tell you the truth, I thought I was a little short with you and Miss O'Toole this morning. You understand, our business is so *crazy* on weekends, and— well, I thought maybe you and I could get together and fill in any blanks I left this morning. Of course, now that Jennifer has been returned—"

"Well—" I said.

"Well—" she said. "I guess there's probably no point—"

And let it hang there. Christ! I thought. This was about as subtle and sophisticated as conversation at a freshman mixer. I felt like I should be scuffling my feet and asking her what her major was.

"Yeah. Well, but—yeah," I said, setting a personal best record for Dopey Come-Ons. "You know, if it's okay with you, we could probably still set a couple of things straight. If you have, you know, the time."

"Oh, sure," she said. "Look: we could meet, maybe have dinner—I've been working all day, I'm starved—in, say, forty-five minutes? An hour? Okay? Do you know J. Michael's Pub? On State Street? They have *wonderful* margaritas."

Go ahead and ask: was it the Garnish gonads, in spite of

everything, or was it the mention of J. Michael's that made me set up the date? Or was it just that, when you get tired enough, you just let the next thing happen because you figure, screw it, I'm not in control of this bullshit anyhow? Beats the hell out of me.

Anyhow, horniness had to be at least part of it, because as soon as I parted the curtain and walked back into Bridget's cubicle, Cado put on a rat's ass smirk and said, "Hey—looks to me like Chicago's in love!"

I gave him what I hoped was my best glare and told Bridget— talking *only* to Bridget—what was going, as they say, down.

"Oh, good, Harry," she said, The Pout replaced by The Approving Nod—which was just a little less effectively executed with a broken face. "Now, when you and Miss Rice are together, I wonder if you could introduce a certain topic into the conversation."

"You mean Videodrome?" asked Cado.

"Well, Cado!" said Bridget, trying to smile at him like he'd just demonstrated the law of infinite Primes at the blackboard. Except that in her present condition the approving smile looked more like an attack grimace.

And "Wait a minute!" said I, feeling—big goddamn change—left out. "What the f—what the hell is Videodrome, and why am I supposed to bring it up with Emily—with Emily Rice, I mean?"

"Oh, dear, it's nothing, really," said Bridget—and I don't have to tell you how you feel when people lay that kind of line off on *you*. "It's a local rental store—you know, tapes and things like that—and it's actually where Arcadio and I were going to visit before—well, before the accident."

"And you want me to ask Emily about this?" I said.

"Well, Chicago, see," said Cado, not noticing that Bridget

was giving him a one-eye glare, "Lady Bridge found out that Videodrome is, like, owned by the same, what you call, conglomerate that owns—guess what?—Morningside Realty."

"No shit," I said, and now I was talking only to Cado. "And just when did Lady Bridge find all this out?"

He finally caught what was going on, and got shy. "Well, man," he said. "You dig, I'm just along for the ride—"

"I found it out yesterday," said Bridget, "while you and Arcadio were in Los Angeles."

"Yeah," I said. "But how did you find out that there *was* a place called Videodrome? And how come I haven't heard any of this before? And how come—especially now, Jennifer's *back* for crying out loud—you want me to bring all this crap up?"

Then came the hook. "I don't, dear," she said, "if you don't want to. You're right, the case is closed, and there are only a few minor bits of information that Miss Rice might be able to supply. The whole business about Videodrome is probably irrelevant, anyway—I just thought it might clear up some things. Nothing of substance. Just go and have a good time, Harry."

I love it. "Just go and have a good time, Harry." I didn't want to go in the *first* place, and now I was going and I was supposed to go and not worry about Videodrome, which I wasn't even too sure what it *was*, and on top of everything else I *was* getting a little of that good old feeling—you know the one I'm talking about—that "Gawd-*damn*! Maybe tonight's the night I get lucky" feeling—and if I was going to make the meeting at J. Michael's in time, I had to get driven back to my car fast so I could drive from there to J. Michael's fast.

So—with no more questions—it wouldn't have made any difference anyway—we all split up, got our rides back to where we were going and agreed to meet back at David's after "everything"—"everything" being my date with Emily.

That's what I said, my "date" with Emily, as in those early, zit-studded, never-been-laid days when every time you went out with a girl your mother and father and cousins would give you half-serious, half-giggling advice that made you wonder if sex was worth it. That's what Bridget had pouted me into feeling—with the added advice about "Videodrome." I promised myself that I would by God not bring up Videodrome.

$\triangledown$

CHAPTER TWENTY-FOUR

Emily was sitting near the back of J. Michael's wearing maroon slacks and a maroon silk blouse with a collar as big as Batman's cape and her hair pulled back in a ponytail. She still looked like Meryl Streep—or like Meryl Streep's impression of Richard Chamberlain's impression of Hamlet, which was more than okay by me.

"These really are great." She smiled at me, lifting her margarita. "You've got to have one."

"Thanks," I said, "but I'd rather have a beer. Hey—do you mind if I go play the jukebox?" Fact is, it *did* look great: but I've never been able to put the concepts "margarita" and "one" together. And I wanted to keep my head clear enough to remember not to bring up Videodrome (see—what did I tell you?).

While I was choosing the menu at the box somebody tapped me on the shoulder.

"You're working your way up in the world," said Mark Schlenz, out of his bartender's uniform and dressed in a jogging suit, nodding in the direction of Emily's table. "What, your approach gets better as the day wears on?"

"What, you live here?" I said, trying not to grin.

"You could say that. I'm part owner of the place. You

175

solving another kidnapping, or—" glancing again at Emily—
"you planning one?"

"Great," I said. "A filthy mind *and* a fuckin' capitalist. A
fuckin' capitalist who accepts five-dollar tips from innocent,
working-class tourists. You mind if I finish feeding quarters
to your record machine?"

"Be my guest," he said. "In fact, damnit, *be* my guest. It's
Larry, right?"

"Harry."

"Right. The hell, you're a funny guy and you bring interesting ladies in here. Your drinks are on the house, okay?
The dining part, that's my partner's business, you pay for
that and if I were you I'd steer clear of the clam chowder,
S.B. ain't Boston, if you get my drift. It's still Beck's?" he
asked, turning and signalling to the bartender.

"Beck's and another margarita for the lady," I said. Emily
had finished her drink and was looking at me with that
quizzical—I love that word—half-smile and half-frown people
get when they're wondering why the hell you're not spending
time with *them*, and you don't know the answer either.

"Hey—one more thing," I said as Mark turned to go back
to his booth. "I know this is going to sound stupid, but does
the name 'Videodrome' mean anything to you?"

Yeah, right. My promise to myself. But remember, I'd
promised myself not to ask *Emily* about Videodrome. And I
was asking Mark about Videodrome, right?

He stared for a minute. "Yeah," he said "*Videodrome.*
Movie. David Cronenberg directed. James Woods, what's her
name from Blondie, Debbie Harry. Gross movie. Guts, gore,
all kinds of weird shit. Why?"

"No," I said—getting a little worried that Emily might be
getting a little worried, her smile now hardening from quizzical to "*what* the hell?"—"no, I mean the *store.*"

"Aahhh, the *store*," he said, breaking into one of those hey, we're all guys here together and I *know* what you're talking about smirks that can make you, if you're in the mood I was in, wish you had a phaser you could set on "stun," like in "Star Trek." "Well, buddy, if you ask, you gotta know, am I right?" he asked. I was quiet. "Yeah. It's on Anacapa Street. That's—oh, hell, your lady friend can find it. Very heavy tapes: I mean, tapes you couldn't find, your basic Sam Goody's, like that. Planning a pretty serious evening, huh? Just ask the lady: I bet she knows." And, with a go-brother punch on the shoulder, he was gone. I walked back to the table, where Emily was sitting with a fresh margarita and a cold Beck's and a glass across from her. The jukebox was playing my first selection: "In the Mood" by the Glenn Miller Orchestra.

"Sorry about that," I said as I sat down. "I was here this morning, after Bridget and I talked to you, and I struck up a conversation with that guy. He's—"

"He's the bartender and he owns fifty per cent of this place," she smiled. "J. Michael's is kind of a Santa Barbara tradition. But Mark doesn't usually make friends that fast. You must have some special talent. What were you two talking about, anyway?"

And suddenly I was as *shy* as a kid on a date. "Oh, nothing much," I said. "Just what tunes to pick on the jukebox, shit like that, you know?"

You want to know how sucked-up and turned-around I was? I mean, just because she looked so damned fantastic in that outfit, *knowing* how fantastic she looked? I kicked myself for saying "shit" in front of her. *That's* how sucked-up and turned-around I was.

"Oh," she said, and sipped her margarita. "Well, I like Glenn Miller. What else did you pick?"

And like that. We talked about music—she was surprised I liked the Kinks (I think she was surprised I knew the Kinks). We talked about current events—she was glad to know Bridget was all right, couldn't understand hit and run drivers, Santa Barbara was really getting congested, etc. We ate: Mark hadn't been kidding about the clam chowder. We talked about Chicago—she was a native Californian and thought a real winter must be—har!—romantic. We talked about a lot, except anything to do with anything. When I took out a cigarette after the chowder bowls had been taken away, she asked me if she could have one. When I struck a match for her, she cupped my hand in both of hers. Once again, I proved that Pavlov had been right on.

"Mmmm," she said, exhaling. "I've quit, officially. But sometimes these things are so damned good. I guess I'm just a naughty girl." Her eyes twinkled at me while I did another full Pavlov.

"You know, Emily, this is really nice," I said, pouring Beck's number three (*Nice*? I thought: Jesus, maybe I should have been doing margaritas after all.) "But—well, you did say that you wanted to talk about—you know, what we were talking about with Bridget this morning." A-plus for inter-rogator skills, am I right?

"Oh," she said, and put out her cigarette. "I'm sorry. I must have been boring the pants off you."

Repressing the urge to tell her to hold the second part of that thought, I told her no, no, I was just afraid *she* might have other things to do, I didn't want to waste *her* time, and—

And it was her turn to tell me that she was really pretty much through for the day, and that she'd like to talk some more—about David and other things—if I had the time. But there *was* one more stop she had to make, wouldn't take a minute, and could she possibly get a lift from me, since her car was in the shop, she'd had one of the girls drop her off at the pub?

The game is endlessly surprising and absolutely predictable. With nearly infinite variations it follows a course as surely preordained as that of a dropped stone. And the only way to resist its seduction is not to begin play.

That's what Ben Gross, eyes shining, told me after one of the many times he waxed my ass at chess.

So I half knew and, what the hell, half hoped that I was having a number run on me. At my age, I'm supposed to know better than to go along? Wrongo. At my age, you're a damnfool if you still think there *is* such a thing as "knowing better." Once you begin play.

I ignored Mark's grin and thumbs-up signal—about as subtle as a gag on "Sesame Street"—as we walked to my car.

The stop we had to make was up in the hills, a "fourplex condo," Emily said, where she had to check if the electricity was on in one of the units. And—maybe because they think it's more atmospheric for the tourists, like being in a forties film, Santa Barbara doesn't put a whole hell of a lot of streetlights up in the hills.

We found the place, anyway. I've never been too clear on the idea of what a "condo" is: something between an apartment, which I have, and a house, which I don't need, except that if it's a condo, the I.R.S. doesn't rape you once a year for the great American sin of not *owning* something. So "condo" is sort of like safe sex or voting for president: making believe you're doing the real thing without actually believing you're doing the real thing.

And speaking of the Real Thing, this place looked like it was designed for nothing else. No shit. The "fourplex" turned out to be a big damned concrete box perched on the edge of a hill so that you could see the stars, the ocean, and the lights of the town from *somewhere* in each of the condos (I would have called them "townhouses") in the setup. In the particular condo we went into, the stars, etc. were most visible from the back patio, which is where Emily led me by the hand as soon as she'd turned on the entryway light.

"It's a demonstrator," she said as we sank into those wicker chairs that look like big damned dried apricots. "We think we're going to be moving a lot of these. What do you think?"

"I thought you liked to build shopping centers," I said, not really very interested in a real-estate seminar—she'd kicked her shoes off when she sat down. "I thought David was the one who liked to build condos."

She laughed. "See? That's what I wanted to get clear with you. I was afraid, from our conversation this morning, that you might have the impression that we were in some kind of—what did you call it?—a 'range war.' Believe me, Harry, in a market as fat as Santa Barbara, competition doesn't really exist. Whatever happens, David's company and Morningside are going to do just fine, and we both know it. Ooh, it feels good to get out of those shoes. Are you comfortable?" And she planted her feet on the table between us.

I told her that I felt just peachy, and noticed that my tongue had thickened, and knew that it wasn't three Beck's that had done that.

"Say," she said brightly—just struck by a brilliant thought, dig?—"we usually keep the fridge in our demonstrators stocked with goodies for prospective buyers. Would you like me to see if there's some wine, beer? I mean, I know you're driving, but—"

"Tell you what," I said. "I don't like drinking and driving. But, right now, I don't know *when* I'm going to be driving, or am I getting this all wrong?"

She smiled and shook her head. Her breasts, I thought, were rising and falling a little rapidly. Mine sure as hell were. Endgame, I thought: foreplay in the fourplex.

"Check," I said. "So you tell me how long you think it's going to be before I drive anywhere, and then I'll decide about the drink."

"Well," she said, sliding down in the chair and wriggling her toes—is it just me or does everybody think that's a turn-on?—"I think we may be here for a while, Harry, don't you?"

"And in that case," I said, "who the hell wants to waste time on a drink?"

In a single motion, or what seemed to *me* a single motion, she: laughed, unbuttoned her blouse, settled on her knees beside my chair, started undoing the buttons on my shirt, and gave me her tongue.

She kissed with her eyes open. She *smiled* as she kissed, if you follow me: remember what I said to you about the photos of Carla Bolero?

We giggled and fumbled our way into the bedroom. She stripped and lay back on the bed. Why do women always look so damned graceful doing that? I struggled out of my clothes, feeling as usual about as suave as a pelican with a hernia, and snuggled down. And, having executed two Pavlovs, decided—or maybe that's not quite the word—to do a Harry Garnish.

"You like this?" she smiled, guiding my hand down her thigh.

"Mwgufth," I replied. *You* try to say "marvelous" and nibble at the same time. More nibbling, more guided stroking.

"Hey, Harry," she whispers then. "Anything you especially like—you know, anything unusual?" I don't think it was a quiz.

So I raise my head, smile back at her—God *damn!*—and say, before I know I'm saying it, "You mean, like some of the stuff you see from Videodrome?"

That was it: the full Garnish, with the two oak-leaf clusters. You don't want to know the number of Beautiful Moments I've screwed up—yeah, that *is* the word— opening my mouth at the wrong time and for the wrong reason, ever since puberty and I first shook hands. The total tonnage could probably swamp the U.S. Seventh Fleet. *Coitus interruptus*? Hell, I could probably make the Olympic Team.

So she sat straight up, the smile all gone, and nearly dislocated my jaw (don't ask).

"Is that supposed to be a crack?" she said.

"Hey," I said, putting my hand on her tummy. "Relax. Things were getting—"

"Things were getting really nice," she finished for me. "Things were just fine, and then you make a crack about Videodrome. I thought you *wanted* to make love." If you've never seen the look that goes with that line, I can't describe it for you.

"It wasn't a crack," I said, noticing that I was starting to whine. "Jesus, Emily—I was just, I don't know, trying to keep the mood going. What?"

The mood—and you know these things the way you know room temperature—had by now packed its bags and taken off for a vacation on Catalina.

"So what about Videodrome? What do you know about Videodrome, anyway?"

Swell. I figured, I'd blown my own chance to be Conan. Second best was being Dr. Watson, but second-best was what I had.

"Nothing," I said, sitting up and not even trying to lay a hand on her. "I mean, they rent videotapes, and I heard somewhere that Morningside had a share of their ownership. Look, Emily, don't you think we can just—"

"No. I think this wasn't such a good idea," she said, and she was on her feet, pulling on her clothes. She could have been changing after a workout on the Nautilus. "If you can get up, we should smooth out the bed."

I did, and we did, and then I realized that she was dressed and I was still naked. She didn't speak while I got dressed.

But I never learn. "About Videodrome," I began as I pulled on my jacket—

"Jesus, you're really a trip, aren't you?" she laughed. "Harry, it could've been fun. But if you want an interview, you call me at my office—or have your fat boss call me. And I'll tell you—either one of you—no. Now, are you ready to go?"

Never readier, I thought. "Well—what the hell, you need a ride. I'll just drive you home, okay?"

We were at the front door by now. She smiled. "Well, thanks a lot, Galahad. But my own condo is just next door. 'Bye, now."

CHAPTER TWENTY-FIVE

I DROVE BACK TO David's, taking only four or five wrong turns on the way, and got there, I don't know, eleven, eleven-thirty at night. Tired. Feeling about as significant as a used lunch-baggie. Trying to remember who was the last person I'd talked to back in Chicago, where I knew what the score was. Oh, yeah: Janie. Janie with her out-of-town John in the Orrington Bar. Now Janie, right now, would have been a lot of fun to be with. Just have a couple of beers, talk, like that, you know? Homefolks.

The lights were on and the music was playing and the Eewoks would have been dancing on the lawn at David's, except I suppose the Eewoks had an exclusive contract with Vegas. Anyhow, the prodigal daughter had been returned— she wasn't even that damned prodigal—and David and Kim, I saw as I came in, had opened the champagne and killed the fatted Brie.

"Harry!" said David, smiling and extending a hand. I hadn't bothered knocking or ringing the bell. "Well, thank God, it's all over. Can I get you a drink? Oh!—Harry Garnish, would you like to meet my daughter, Jennifer?"

And there she was, the little grail-child (*is* there such a thing as a grail-child?), sitting on the sofa with David and

184

Kim and Bridget and—you're not going to believe this, but I swear to God—the Carpenters' "We've Only Just Begun" on the stereo.

She had a half-finished Coke in front of her, and a plate with a wedge of cheese and some grapes and a slice of apple, and *boy* did she look like her mother.

Not like her mother at fourteen: like her *mother*, or at least like the picture of her mother Bridget had shown me. When she looked at me, there was all the intelligence— and something else, something past intelligence, a kind of sad *knowing* she was intelligent and not giving a damn about it—that I'd seen in those dark eyes in CREAM SCREEN, and there was the same tense, dancer's tone in her body, with her knees crossed and one hand holding the other's wrist at the joining of the knees. She was wearing a black sweater—and she already had breasts—and a plaid skirt down to the ankles. She could have been a freshman at St. Mary- on-Tweed's School for Young Ladies, except she was, don't you know, and she sure couldn't help it, a stone *fox*.

Okay. Go figure that I'd just been kicked out of bed by a dynamite lady closer, let's say, to my own age, so my first impression of Jennifer wasn't exactly under what we would call ideal test conditions. And, if you want, go figure that I'm just the kind of dirty old man that digs the bud as much as the flower. (Notice how we get poetic when we start to talk about the *really* embarrassing stuff?) So happens that's not the truth ("Yeah, sure," you snort)—though I *do* always get this special, strange rush when the Beach Boys come across my radio singing "I wish they all could be California girls." Putting all that aside, the fact *is* that Jennifer Pescatore/Bolero was, if you'd spent the last three days looking for her as a poor lost and maybe endangered waif, stunning— and a little scary.

"Hi there, Jennifer," I said, rising to the occasion.

"'Lo," she smiled. It was cute: the kind of smile you always gave to friends of your parents when they came over on Christmas Day, and you hadn't the slightest idea *who* they were, but you knew they were people, maybe The Boss, to be greeted with respect and happiness they were *there*. So you made believe, on top of making believe that you loved everything you'd gotten for Christmas (you never did, you know), that they had made your day by barging in and demanding, in the voices of Roman soldiers, peanuts and seven-and-sevens.

That's the kind of smile it was.

And it worked. She stopped being a cashmere Lorelei and, for a moment at least, turned into a fourteen-year-old kid who had been through one hell of a bad time. Maybe it was just that at the end of saying, "'Lo," the edges of her smile began to tremble and melt, and her eyes started to tear up, and Kim—another stone fox who could not, whatever she tried, deny her stone foxness—Kim put her arm around Jennifer's shoulders, and stared at me like I'd interrupted— no, that's not the right word—like I'd *violated*—some private pact.

"Thank you for trying to find me, Mister Garnish," said Jennifer, after the general weirdness and discomfort of my entrance on the scene had been digested (sort of the way you digest one more slice of cucumber when you've already got a case of the hiccups). "I'll always remember how kind you were—you and Bridget—how hard you tried. Oh, Daddy!" she cried, jumping up and hugging David, who had just come back from the kitchen with a Lowenbrau Dark for me.

I took the Lowie from his hand while he patted Jennifer's hair, and sort of stood there, feeling dumb. That was it. Three thousand miles and three, four days of getting shot at, busted, almost laid and generally confused up the hoo-hah, and now the lost was found, "the nightmare was over," as the dorks on TV like to say, and there we were in just another California living room, with chips and dip and beer, just living in the U.S.A. as Chuck Berry says. I mean, you ever wonder what happens *after* Dorothy says, "Oh, Auntie Em, there's no place like home" and the music comes up and we fade to black? Next morning she's still got to milk the same goddamned cows and Toto goes to the pound, is what happens.

David took Jennifer back to the couch, where she sat between him and Kim, being stroked and hugged by both of them and beaming from one to the other in a way, I guessed and was a little mad about it, I'd never be beamed at by a kid. He started telling me how maybe he'd said some harsh things, but he was so concerned about Jen, and so forth. And I mumbled how it was no harm done, everybody was tense, the important thing was that Jen was back, and so forth. And then we were all out of things to say again.

"So," I said finally, always the life of the party. "Where's Cado?"

"Cado stopped by, Harry," said Bridget—her bruises had by now ripened enough that she was starting to look like a welterweight after a bad night—"but said he had to take care of some things. He'll come by tomorrow."

"Oh." *Four* kill a dog, *five* kill a dog . . . .

"Well," I said, "it's been too much day for me, folks. I'm hitting the rack—oops, that's Jennifer's room."

"Oh, no, Harry," said Kim. "We've made up a cot in our room for Jen. We want her to stay right with us for a while."

"And Harry," said Bridget. "I know you're tired, dear, but could you possibly take me out for a nightcap? I'm still worked up about everything that's happened, and the night

air might help relax me. And I think Jennifer should have
some time just with her family, too."

Kim and David protested that there was plenty of juice in
the house, and of course Bridget wasn't intruding. Bridget
insisted that it would be good for her and everybody else.
Nobody said anything like, hey, have a heart, Garnish is
dead on his feet—not even me, because I was trying to
remember when Bridget—Bridget, for Chrissake—had *ever*
wanted to go out for a nightcap.

"So," I said as we climbed back into the Datsun, "what's
this all about, and *please* don't tell me you want to go to J.
Michael's again."

"No. There's a place that stays open twenty-four hours,
called Ricardo's," she said. "I have directions. Now, Harry,
what was your meeting like?"

So I told her as we drove. Well, okay—in my version, we
only got into heavy petting—remember when they used to
call it "heavy petting"?—and when I mentioned Videodrome— deliberately, since I'm your basic ice-cold manipu-
lative interrogator—it was Emily who seized up and yours
truly who called a suave end to the whole thing. In principle,
an accurate report.

"Hmmm," said Bridget when I'd finished. "Is this Calle
Reál? Yes—turn left here. Harry, do you know what Midrash
is?"

"Say what?"

"Midrash."

"You mean that dip stuff you get with pita bread in Greek
restaurants?"

"No," she said. "That's hummus. Midrash is retrospec-
tive rabinnical storytelling: interpreting a story by elaborat-
ing on the story to make it more understandable. I just
wondered if you'd heard the word."

"No," I said, feeling a little squirmy. "I thought you meant that dip stuff from the Greek restaurants."

"Here it is—Ricardo's," she said.

Ricardo's had a neon palm tree outside. Inside it had an unhappy-looking bartender who reminded me of the Mock Turtle in Wonderland—and the people you'd expect. There was an older guy at the bar who looked like he was trying to decide whether he could manage to walk out the door, or whether another shot would help. (If you've ever been in *that* bag, of course, you know what he was going to decide sooner or later.) There was a lady at a table with one cigarette in her hand and another smoldering in the ashtray who looked like she might be wrestling with the same problem. There were two kids in his and hers official punk outfits and matching blonde hair sprayed in points that would have made a stegosaurus weep, trying to sit in each other's laps and eat each other's ears at the same time.

"Bridget, how the *hell* did you hear about this place?" I was starting to ask as my eyes adjusted to the swirling lights from the reflector globe in the ceiling.

And then my eyes adjusted, and I shut up and followed Bridget to the booth at the back where Cado and Bobby Reilly were sitting, drinking coffee and waiting for us.

CHAPTER TWENTY-SIX

"CADO. BOBBY," I SAID, sitting down and lighting a cigarette. "What's, like, up?"

"It's Rob," said Bobby, winking at me.

"Yeah. Well, I can dig that," I said, smiling at the filter of my cigarette and feeling—it had been a while— pretty damn *good* about myself. "So. We going to take over City Hall, rekidnap Jennifer—what?"

"We are going, Harry," said Bridget, "to do something perhaps silly and certainly unpleasant, and we're going to do it because we think something is terribly wrong. And I— well, to be perfectly frank, I don't at all like what I think we may discover. But Arcadio and Mr. Reilly should know what *you* found out tonight."

And she proceeded to tell them about my meeting with Emily. *This* time around we had had dinner at J. Michael's, gone back to the demo condo, checked the electricity, sat and had a nice civilized drink, and when I had mentioned Videodrome she had as Bridget put it "expressed anxiety, concern, and discomfort," and that had been the end of that evening.

Midrash, my ass, I thought.

"Yeah," said Bobby, when she had finished. "Well, I know

that Videodrome is a big distributor for—well, for our kinds
of movies." That with a glance at Bridget, who looked about
as embarrassed as she would have been sitting in on a
discussion about automatic transmissions.

"I mean," he went on, "they sort of specialize in our kind
of stuff—you know, you want to see a film like that, if you
live in this part of the state, Videodrome is where you go."

"Wait a minute," I said. "I thought you could get that
stuff at any rental place."

"Oh, sure," said Bobby. "It's probably fifty, sixty percent
of the total rental business. But—"

"But Videodrome, you see," said Bridget, "specializes in
a more—well, *special* version of the product. And as I
understand it, the store features an appropriate—decor—for
its clientele."

"Yeah," said Cado, grinning like a coyote into his coffee
cup. "Like in the movie."

"What," I asked, "whips and chains and rhino-horn
jellybeans, or do they just pimp?"

"A little of both, in fact," said John Carroll, who had just
walked up to our booth. "Miss O'Toole. And I assume you
are Mr. Reilly?"

"Thank you for coming, Lieutenant," said Bridget. "Please
sit down."

Helgerson wasn't with him. "Where's your pet walrus?"
I asked. "Or is this a social call."

"A damned late one," he snapped, looking at his watch.
"Sorry, ma'am," to Bridget. "But Molina here caught me just
as I was checking out to go home. My wife had made *coq au
vin* and had uncorked a Cabernet we put down five years
ago. She had sent the children to her mother's place in
Montecito. She was not amused when I left right after
dinner. So I hope this is as earth-shakingly urgent as Molina

said *you* said it was. I sincerely do," he said, lighting a Parliament.

"Lieutenant. John," said Bridget, smiling. "I'm sorry—really I am—to have ruined your evening. But—come on, now—you wouldn't have ruined an evening that special unless *you* thought it was worth coming out here, now would you?"

"No," he said, simply. I was beginning to like him again. The only defense against an O'Toole, father or daughter, is absolute lack of bullshit, and he was learning fast.

"So," Bridget went on, "you were saying about Videodrome."

"Well," he said, "Garnish has it about right. They specialize in X-rated tapes, and in a lot of X-rated things that are beyond the pale, which they get away with renting because of some 'private card club' scam they have going, which so far the courts can't seem to break. You don't see their ads in the paper, and they don't have a big display box in the yellow pages. They advertise through magazines that only a special kind of customer buys, and they sell those same magazines in their stores. The whole thing's got a kind of secret-society thrill about it that, let's face it, a lot of their customers really like. They thrive, and they're very hard to bust—and make it stick."

"McBugger's," I said.

"Okay, if you want," said Carroll. "And, since the customers—men and women—know why they come into the store in the first place, a lot of, let's say, friendships are begun there. It's a perfect setup, in a way: like a singles bar with no cover charge and with a near-guarantee that *everybody* browsing there is browsing for action—for *some* kind of action."

"And you know that they and Morningside Realty are

corporately connected?" asked Bridget, and then blushed. "Oh, dear," she said. "I didn't mean to make a pun."

But Carroll wasn't giggling. "How did you know that?" he asked.

"Well," she said, in her all right, I'll explain the difference between an oblique and an obtuse angle just *one* more time voice, "when we were in Morningside's offices—goodness, just this morning—I noticed that some of their stationery listed them as a subsidiary of something called *Synergy, Inc.* And the—is it called a logo?— the logo is three lines converging into an arrowhead. Like this," she said, doodling on her napkin and showing to the group:

"That is also the logo," she went on, "with the same little trademark stamp beside it—you know, the 'R' in the tiny circle—on the special membership cards for the Videodrome—what do they call it?—oh, yes, the Videodrome 'Fantasy Fellowship.'"

It was my turn. "And where the hell, Bridget," I asked, "did you see a Videodrome membership card?"

"At David's," she said. "In one of the kitchen drawers, if you want to know, along with credit-card receipts, bits of junk mail, and a Videodrome receipt for rental of a tape. *The Frog King.*"

"Well," said Carroll finally. "Congratulations, Miss O'Toole; *we* found out the connection by accessing Videodrome's corporate returns and having one of our accountant-types spend a week at his terminal running down their claims on tax loses and deferred-return investments. It was a lot of tedious work."

"Well, of *course* it was, Brother Carroll," chortled Cado. "You all be workin for the *city*."

"And none of that," went on Carroll, just glaring at Cado, "really explains why I'm here. Companies own other companies, and some companies are all owned by one big company. It's a new world, Miss O'Toole. A vegetarian restaurant and a meat-packing firm can both be managed by, and trade money through, a conglomerate owned by a Buddhist who made his fortune in sushi. All that matters is the profit margin. Now, I've told you what, apparently, you already know. Will you please tell me why I *am* here?"

Bridget smiled. "Certainly, Lieutenant. And first, you should know what transpired this évening when Harry met with a certain person from Morningside Realty—in fact, you gave him the message that set the meeting up."

And—you got it—we heard again the story of my date with Emily. I won't even try to tell you how it came out *this* time, except to say that it sounded like the whole damned meeting between us could have been carried on across the goddamned Straits of Gibraltar, by semaphore.

"And that's it?" said Carroll when she was finished. Funny, I was thinking the same thing myself.

"Oh, come, John," said Bridget, shaking her head. "You know you're uneasy about this whole thing—*that's* why you're here, even if you don't want to admit that Harry's news about the answer machine messages and the "Carla-Karin" thing *did* impress you. It certainly impressed Mr. Reilly here enough for him to drive—at some risk to his own reputation, by the way—all the way up here from Los Angeles. Speaking of reputations, what is happening with the press?"

He sighed. "You probably just missed them at Mr. Pescatore's house. We tried to keep Jennifer's recovery as low-profile as we could, but you know the press. I got a phone call—and gave a 'no comment' answer—in the middle of dinner, but it's like trying to shoo off locusts."

"Right," said Bridget. "So by tomorrow the *News-Press* and maybe even the *L.A. Times* will be screaming about Jennifer's kidnapping and return by the mysterious, unfindable porno-queen star—isn't that the way those people talk?—and you're not really sure you want the Santa Barbara Police Department supporting a story like that, are you, John?"

He looked around the table, but Bridget was the only one not staring into a coffee cup (Cado grinning, Bobby Reilly frowning, me watching from under my eyebrows). He lit another cigarette, sipped some coffee, and stared Bridget back.

"You have an idea, I suppose?" he said.

"Sort of an idea," she said—and she wasn't smiling complacently, having outsmarted the cop, the way I expected her to. She was frowning. No, damnit, she looked like she was almost going to cry. A crying Bridget was not an experience I wanted to have.

"I'd like you," she said, and took a sip of Bobby Reilly's coffee without even asking him, "I'd like you to hold yourself and Officer Helgerson free tomorrow for a phone call from me or one of my associates, and free tomorrow evening—or the next evening, too, that would be Tuesday— for a little gathering. I know this sounds mysterious, Lieutenant—John—but I *would* appreciate your granting me the favor." She was still staring at Bobby's cup.

"All right, Miss—all right, Bridget," said Carroll. "Somebody will be at the phone and in touch with me all day. I'd better go home now." He laughed. "There should be some wine left. Maybe you should, too, don't you think?"

He left, and the four of us sat for a couple of minutes, not

saying a thing, until the lady came by and asked us if we
wanted more coffee. We all said no and started that squirm-
ing you do when you're about ready to split.

And then Bobby Reilly said, "Miss O'Toole: Carla's dead,
isn't she?"

And Bridget said, "Please call me Bridget. Do you have a
place to stay for tonight?"

"Yeah. A friend," said Bobby.

"Good," she said. "We'll be in touch tomorrow. Harry?
I'd like to go home, now. Cado, thank you so much for
everything."

I drove her back to David's, and I didn't say a thing on
the way. For Christ's sake, I was *tired*.

$\triangledown$

CHAPTER TWENTY-SEVEN

WAKING UP MONDAY WAS as pleasant as finding your I.R.S. forms for the year in your mailbox, but then waking up Monday is always like that. I'd slept till, thank God, ten, realized that the house was completely quiet, pulled on some clothes, stumbled toward the hall john, and thence into the kitchen. And there were Cado and Bobby, drinking coffee.

"Hey, Rob." Cado smiled as I sat down and lit a cigarette. "You ever see that movie, *Dawn of the Dead*? Look at ol' Harry here."

I told him to do something to himself that he thought would be impossible to pull off. "So where is everybody?" I asked, "not to mention what are you two doing here?"

"Waiting for you," said Bobby. "Kim, David and Jennifer are all down at the *News-Press* office. I guess the reporters were all over here last night, while we were meeting. David fought them off promising an interview this morning, along with the police. I guess the TV people are going to be there too, and some L.A. press. Bridget went along to—well, you know. To *help*," and he smiled a little smile.

"Yeah," said Cado, "and everybody sort of agrees that there ain't a hell of a lot of need to advertise that they called in private dicks from Chicago."

197

"Especially since the private dicks from Chicago didn't do a whole hell of a lot," I said.

"Well, yeah, that, too." Cado shrugged. "And also, Lieutenant Carroll—he was by here, what, seven-thirty this morning—didn't see much reason to get Rob here involved unless the press folks start rooting around. You know, why link Jennifer up with—uh—"

"With a bunch of porno-film scuzzbags," I said, looking at Bobby, who grinned at me and gave me a thumbs-up. "Right. And that was *Carroll's* idea, not David's?"

"Hey, man, I just got here after he left," Cado said, stroking his moustache. (Actually, a moustache like that you petted.) "But I do see your point. Anyhow, that's how David said it all went down."

"And after everybody left," said Bobby, "Cado called me, told me that Bridget wanted me to come over here and wait for her to call—she said it would be around noon, one—and that she might have a favor to ask then."

Well, I thought, Monday morning had come through again. Like Larry, Curly and Moe, we were being quarantined from public view and all we had to do was sit around the house for a few hours and wait for marching orders from Attila the Nun. And Cado and Bobby looked like they were willing and happy to do just that. Well, they hadn't known Bridget as long as I had.

"Tell you what, gang," I said, reaching the telephone book down from the kitchen shelf. "I don't really dig laying low, and in spite of all the foofaraw last night about multiple ownerships and rental slips and shit, I really don't see that we've got a hell of a lot more to do. I mean, dig: the kid was missing, the kid's back. I didn't have a goddam thing to do with it, and, you know, what the fuck?"

"But Carla—" began Bobby.

"Carla, my ass!" I said. (And why, I wondered, was I getting all of a sudden so mad?) "Look, man, she was—she's your friend, but I'm sorry, I never—I haven't met her. Oh, yeah—I forgot to tell you, you two take a great picture together. You guys use oil, bacon grease, what?"

"Harry!" barked Cado, and now he *did* look like a mean-mother biker. "You are way the *fuck* out of line, ace." Bobby just stared at me. I opened the phone book, and my hands were shaking—not because I was afraid of Cado.

"Check," I said, flipping to the yellow pages, not wanting to look at either of them. "Shitty thing to say. Really shitty. Sorry, Bobby."

"Rob," he said. That's what he said.

"So what I'm going to do," I said, staring really hard at the yellow pages, "is, I'm going to find a travel agent some-where close—yeah, this'll do it—and get me some tickets back to Chicago for maybe Wednesday, and then find some-place to pig out to a big lunch and boocoo beers and amble back here when Bridget's got her act together. You guys come along, okay? I'll spring for lunch. Bob—Rob?"

He smiled. "Thanks, Harry. Maybe tomorrow? I'm sort of tired today, not real hungry. But maybe Arcadio—?"

"Naah," said Cado. "That's okay, Chicago. We'll stay here. You just try to get back by two or so, huh? Hey—you want a good rib place? Woody's, right down the street from the fig tree."

I looked at him, and then at Bobby. *Arcadio? We'll stay here?* Cado reached around to the stove, poured another cup of coffee for Bobby, and put the pot back on the stove. They both were looking at me.

Okay. Well, *you* remember playground ethics. You tell the guys that don't want to play your game that you're going to leave, and you'd better by God *leave*.

"Okay," I said. "Well, you guys enjoy. Hope something good's on cable." Nobody smiled.

Complexity really sucks, don't you think?

So I strutted out to the Datsun, started cruising toward where I figured the travel agency should be from the address in the directory, and learned something about myself: that sometimes I could remember stuff I'd read in the yellow pages even when I thought I was looking for some other stuff. Because, almost before I knew it, I was parked in a public lot on lower State Street right across from the Santa Barbara outlet for Videodrome.

$\triangledown$

CHAPTER TWENTY-EIGHT

IT DIDN'T LOOK MUCH like a video store from the outside, but maybe that was the point. Between a bicycle shop and a classy-looking cocktail lounge, it had one of those big, dark glass storefront windows you see in jewelry shops where they figure, you're rich enough to walk in, you don't *have* to see the kind of ice they carry. No big Rush Street-style sign, either—you know, disembodied hooters and a GIRLS! GIRLS! GIRLS! flashing on and off. Just a polite little lettering in gold—VIDEODROME—and the three-pronged arrow logo.

It didn't look much like a video store inside, either: no big cardboard cutouts of Roger Rabbit or Batman, no posters of new releases on the walls. It looked, in fact, like the lobby of the kind of whorehouse I've always wanted to be able to afford.

Plush carpet, the hum of an air conditioner keeping it just a noticeable few degrees cooler than outside, and over that, just within audible range, the sort of gently rhythmic music you usually hear accompanying the humping scenes in the movies: you know, the sort of thing that can be played by a drum machine and a trained chimp at a synthesizer, or by Weather Report if they'd all just popped 'ludes.

And two clerks strolling around among the racks of tapes.

Some clerks. The blonde could have, for my money, doubled for Annie Lennox on her best day, and the oriental girl could have talked me, if I was Donald Trump, into *giving* all my holdings to Sony. I could tell they were clerks because they were both wearing name-tags, with the arrow logo, on their—and this is the truth, I *know* it was eleven a.m. on a Monday— backless red dresses with black leather sashes and slits *way* the hell up the sides.

"Hello, sir. May I help you?" The oriental girl smiled, gliding up to me. "Setsuko," her name-tag said.

It's times like that I usually remember I hadn't put on a fresh shirt that morning. I smiled at her. "Thanks, I'm just sort of browsing. Setsuko," saying it *"sets-* ko."

"Very good." She twinkled—know how some people can twinkle? "You speak Japanese?"

"Eeyay," I said. "I just remember *Shogun,"* and she laughed as politely as if she'd never heard that dipstick line before.

"Well," she said, "Mr.—"

"Harry Garnish."

"Harry. I like that. Sort of—forthright, you know?" Why fight it? "Are you a member of our special club?"

"'Fraid not. I'm from back East, actually, and a pal of mine just told me that I'd probably be interested in looking around your place. What club is that, anyway?"

"Oh, nothing much, really. You get access to our special collection, and we have some preview rooms in the back of the place, in case you'd like to, you know, check out the quality of the tapes, things like that."

"What, like listening booths? That's new—could I see one?"

"Oh, well," she pouted, "I'm not really supposed to let you back there without a membership card. Would you like an application? I mean, if you're going to be in town for a while—at fifty-five dollars entry, it's a really good deal."

"Sure," I said. "But can I just browse a while first?"

She said that would be fine, and shimmied back to look at papers behind the checkout counter. So I browsed.

There wasn't the usual arrangement of racks and racks of tape boxes hollering their contents at you. There was one large rack, labelled CURRENT AND POPULAR, right by the checkout, with all the recent PG to R movies just out of theatrical release, saying bravely, "I'm just a regular little old videotape store, see," and about as convincing as the cross around Tammy Faye Bakker's throat.

The rest of the place was divided into three, I suppose you'd call them alcoves off the central area. You walked into them under an arch, and inside there was a lower, false ceiling and dimmer lighting—one alcove had a kind of black-light effect—making it all feel kind of smarmy and private: except, of course, if, as in the first one I visited, there was a guy in a running suit and an even bigger beer gut than mine examining the cover photos as carefully, and looking around as furtively, as if he'd discovered the secret of low-tempera-ture fusion. Maybe, in a way, he had.

The other two were empty. And all of them were filled. Filled with what I kept thinking of as ghosts—no bullshit, and you know by now I'm not a poet. Ghosts of people screwing—dig, *really* screwing—all stacked up there on the shelves waiting to do it again—without the fun, if it *is* fun in front of a camera—for people who couldn't, or wouldn't, or didn't want to without a little encouragement—well, what the hell did *I* know? People do what people do, and that's all. Bobby Reilly was in the business, and he was a seriously nice guy. And who's jerking whose chain, of *course* I knew I was at least a little bit in love—"at least a little bit

in *love*"?—with Carla Bolero. And Jerry Kawin was probably
right, everybody was just selling fantasies, no harm done
unless you wanted to think so.

The third alcove, the black-light one, was, as I'd figured,
the one stocked with bondage and humiliation movies. Lots
of cassette-cover photos of very fine ladies in black lace and
black leather and *mean* goddamned smiles, and mostly
low-angle shots, in case you missed the point. And handcuffs—no shit, some of them *fur* handcuffs—and blindfolds
and some other pretty complicated-looking widgets, all of
them with those oversize plastic price-tag clamps they put
on music cassettes to keep you from ripping off the product.

Like I said, I'm not a poet. And I sure the hell am not a
preacher: the more time you spend on sex, the better for you
and the less time you have to do harm, is what my guess is.
But it all made me sad, maybe those damned fur handcuffs
with the plastic price-tags most of all. Sad for beer-gut in
Alcove One, sad for Setsuko and her blonde partner having
to act like every *zhlub* that came through the door was a rich
stallion, and for every poor *zhlub* that *did* fork over the
fifty-five fish to use the private viewing room (Christ! think
of the dry-cleaning bills), and for those TV preachers that
couldn't break the Big Sixth, as we used to call it in Holy
Cross Grade School, but *could* pay whores (like my pal,
Janie?) to do solo numbers while *they* whacked, and, dammit, said—not guilty, not angry, just sad—for myself, every-
time I'd buy a copy of a crotch-shot magazine and silently
make believe with the guy behind the counter that I wanted
to read the article about drug smuggling in Lapland.

Well, people do what people do. When I'd found myself
going into Videodrome, I'd had this really neat private-eye-
type scheme to browse a while, make friends with the people
behind the counter, and then pop the question, "Hey, do

you guys know my friend Emily Rice?" Then—what? They would all go ashen- faced, deny or affirm Emily's connection with the store or order me the hell out, and I'd have—what? Well, hey, at least confirmation that Emily's real estate business was as decadent as the porno business, and that they were in league with one another. But I already knew that, I hear you saying. Yeah, dig, but now I'd *know* it, and I could feel like I'd done some serious work, and in my business, that's not exactly your daily bread.

But for what? To bother Setsuko or her partner, who probably already felt like big sillies in those Madame La Fang dresses on a Monday morning? To reassure myself that I was hip, alert, above all this decadence?

I like that word. Ben Gross uses it a lot, and I once asked him what the hell he meant by it. "Ah, Harry," he said. "To speak precisely, it's a term of aesthetics, but I won't bore you with its fascinating history. Basically, dear boy, let's just say that it is an expression of rage and despair at never being able to experience—*nein*, to have—the Real Thing."

So I left the whips and chains alcove, and Setsuko came up smiling, application form in hand, and asked me if I'd seen anything I liked. And, what the hell, I asked her if she was going anything for lunch, and she fielded *that* like a pro, what a great idea but she had to meet a girlfriend for some power shopping. I took the application and told her I'd be seeing her again—she'd be looking forward to it, of course—and I was back in the sunlight heading toward my car.

I wasn't that far from J. Michael's. Maybe a beer and a sandwich would help the way I felt. But then, the way I felt, there wasn't much point in trying to stop feeling that way. I drove back to David's.

CHAPTER TWENTY-NINE

AND, WHEN I THINK about it, that's sort of when it was all over. I mean: it *wasn't* all over, you know that and I know that. But everything that happened afterwards, at least the way I think about it, has a kind of unreal, dreamy quality about it: the way I guess you feel when your jet is plunging 20,000 feet down into the Atlantic, and you keep thinking, hey, this is just like being in a damn *movie*, you dig? Or the way I felt when I was hiding among garbage cans and being shot at out behind Golden State Liquors. You tell yourself, this is a friggin' game, hey, and I'll just go with it till they bring the lights up. I don't know. I said goodbye to Setsuko— I wonder where the hell she is now?—and she in her silly damn dress and her sad job is like—what?—my *image* of the whole business.

So I got back to David's, and there were David and Kim and Jennifer and Bridget, all sitting around and complaining about how exhausting and intrusive the people from the press were.

"And where's Cado?" I asked Bridget. "And where's—"

"On errands," she said, sipping from a mug of hot chocolate. "And I thought you were going to be here for the same instructions, Harry."

Very strange, Bridget scolding like that, I thought. And she didn't look well, either. Her mouse by now looked like one of Bobby Reilly's jellybean earrings scotchtaped over her eye, but her hands were trembling a little as she put her mug back on the coffee table, and Bridget's hands are chubby enough, when you see them trembling, you *know* they're by God trembling.

"Yeah. Well," I said. Over the years that's become pretty much a complete code between us. What it says is, I maybe screwed up but at least I didn't do any serious damage, and she should let me alone about it because I'm already so jammed up with no clue to an exit door that I'll take her next suggestion without even being my usual pain-in-the-ass self about it.

Which is how it went down now.

"We're going out to dinner tonight, Harry," Bridget said. "All of us—and Lieutenant Carroll has agreed to come along, too. It's to celebrate Jennifer's safe return, of course, but it's also to satisfy the people from the newspapers, who would like to be able to photograph us all happily reunited. In fact, they came as close as they could to insisting that we do something like this tonight. Apparently Jennifer's return was just a little too late for a full-page spread in today's edition, and inconvenient for the kind of coverage the television people would like to give this event, also. So, if you can join us all, we are, in—" looking at her watch—"in three hours to be at the Coq d'Argent—is that right, David?—yes, the Coq D'Argent, eating and rejoicing and providing what I think people in the trade call photo opportunities. You can join us?"

Very weird, I thought. If you knew Bridget like I did, it was the closest to bitter you could imagine her being. I looked at David, who was just beaming at Kim and Jennifer, and at

Kim, who was looking anxiously at Jennifer, and at Jennifer, who was staring very carefully at a point on the coffee table maybe five, six inches from Bridget's cocoa mug.

"Sounds like a gas," I said. "That means I can, like, take a nap?"

It did, so I did. I've never asked Bridget what *they* did with the rest of the afternoon—I don't really give half a spasm, truth to tell. I snagged a beer from the fridge, swallowed the sucker like a sleeping pill, laid back on Jennifer's bed and started visualizing wild pigs—*little* wild pigs—nibbling their way through a cornfield. Don't ask why, it just always works for me. And after a while it was wild pigs and oriental ladies, and a little while later it was a knock on the door and Bridget asking me if I was ready.

So. Everybody looked just *spiffy* when I opened my door, in lots of tweeds and woolens and stuff that at least looked like silk, which made me happy I'd put on a new shirt and my favorite spider-belly-gray knit tie. For a bunch of people about to go and be photographed and filmed as a recently-happily-reunited family, they all looked about as happy as the couple in that painting, *American Gothic*. All except Bridget, and she looked about as unhappy as somebody looking at, and really digging, what was so sad *about American Gothic*.

You know the painting? The woman is staring at the man and the man is staring at *you*. And the woman is looking at the bastard the way I hope to God nobody ever looks at me, like, "*this* is what it was all for, this damn barn and that damn pitchfork?" And the poor bastard, who's so dumb he doesn't even know it's a painting not a photo, he could smile or drop the pitchfork or something, stares at you, but you *know* he knows his wife is watching him, and you know—hell, they show it in their hatred—that one time at least they came together and bayed at the moon, and that's *why* they hate. He stares at you, dig, and says something like, "It's all right, everything is under control, and the woman beside me is just as dedicated to making it all work as I am, and if we ever had sex, it was just to make babies, and we didn't enjoy it and *please* stop staring at me like that."

So I looked at Bridget and she looked at me and we nodded, and while I wondered what the hell was going on we drove to the Coq d'Argent.

That's funny, you know? I've never told Bridget that when I saw David, Kim, and Jennifer that evening I had this funny vision of the Grant Wood painting superimposed over everything. I wonder what she thinks. Sometimes I'm not sure if she and I really understand each other, or if maybe we just have separate needles on parallel grooves.

Whatever. The Coq d'Argent is one hell of a restaurant, and you're hearing this from a man who has spent most of his life eating out in Chicago, and if that doesn't tell you how good the Coq d'Argent is, then I might as well not have opened my mouth in the first place.

They did have dark beer—three brands, all of them good— and as we sat and let the photographer prowl around our table like a terrier at a picnic, snapping away, I sampled two of them, as did John Carroll, who had been waiting for us, and who seemed—I couldn't figure it out—more relaxed, more cheerful even, than anybody else at the table. He even winked at me and gave me a private thumbs-up when the waiter fought his way past the photographer and I ordered both the escargots and the paté de maison as hors d'oeuvres.

"I like delicate things," I told him. "In large quantities."

"And on expense account?" he asked.

"What are you, a cop?" I said, and we both laughed.

And that was about it for your basic dinner-table wit. The

back-in-Kansas effect again, remember? Carroll proposed a
toast to happy homecomings and everybody raised a glass.
And then he told the photographer to bug off, we'd be
available for interviews after the meal. And then we sat and
looked at one another and mainly at Jennifer, who looked
mainly at her menu.

I'd just finished the paté—the escargots, poor little bas-
tards, never even knew what hit them—the waiter was back
in order-taking orbit, and I was trying to decide whether to
play it safe with gigot, which *nobody* can screw up, or see if
when they said "bouillabaisse" they *meant* "bouillabaisse."
And Jennifer dropped her soup spoon into her soup bowl and
froze solid. Didn't say a word, just froze: but sometimes, if
you've noticed, people can freeze silent so that you can't help
but *hear* them.

Bobby Reilly was standing at the table.

"Mr. Reilly," said Bridget. "How good of you to join us.
"Sir"—to the waiter—"could you set one more place? Thank
you. David, Kim, this is Mr. Reilly, who was so important
to Jennifer's safe return. And Bobby, this is Jennifer."

David nodded hello as Bobby took a seat, but looked about
as healthy as when I'd fixed his chest for him at L.A.X. Kim
was staring at Bridget, and I hadn't believed those giant eyes
of her's *could* get any bigger, but they were now. It was an
almost—what?—*clinical* stare, like she'd never really seen
Bridget before. She started to say something, I thought, a
couple of times, but literally, physically swallowed her voice.
Hard.

"Hello, Jennifer," said Bobby, extending his hand across
the table.

"Hi," said Jennifer, keeping her little hands in fists on her
lap.

Bobby didn't smile ironically or shrug, just brought his

hand back. I thought about making a joke about the Ghost of Christmas Future, and then I thought about it again. The waiter asked us for our orders—suddenly gigot or bouillabaisse didn't seem to matter a hell of a lot—and David ordered, and Kim ordered, and Jennifer said:

"Nothing."

"Oh, come on, honey," coaxed David. "Wouldn't you just like a nice shrimp cocktail? Or—?"

"No!" she said, loud enough that the people at the other tables dropped their voices and turned their heads. "No! I'm not hungry, I'm sick! I want to go home!"

People turned back to their meals: another brat on a tantrum.

Kim was half out of her chair with her arms around Jennifer's shoulders. "I'll take you home, darling," she said. And, to Bridget, in a near-whisper that could have sliced fresh bread: "How could you—how could *you*— she's a *child*!"

And Bridget: "She's an abused child, Kim, and the abuse stops now. She knows Mr. Reilly, doesn't she? Knows that he knows her mother—"

And Jennifer, screaming now: "Cocksucker! Frog King! Motherfucker! Show us your big cock, why don't you!"

And Kim again: "Jennifer," but faintly, and sinking back down on her chair, beaten.

"Frog King!" cried Jennifer again at Bobby, while the rest of us—all of us in the restaurant—tried to break out of slow-motion, tried to think of what to do—or maybe where to go.

"Big cock!" she shouted. "Stick it in my mother, frog! I don't have a mother, Kim is my mother, going to be my mother! You fuck, fuck, fuck, fuck, but not my *real* mother, froggie, froggie—"

Carroll broke back into real time before anybody else. I'm
not sure how he did it, but he managed to flash his badge,
back off waiters and diners who were by now near def-con
four, stroke Jennifer's hair—she was collapsing into sobs—
and bring a glass of water to her lips. Sonofabitch moved like
a dancer.

David hadn't moved. Bobby hadn't moved. Kim raised her
face from her hands, looked at Bridget, and said, "If you
knew—if you *knew*—then why did you have to do this?"

Bridget, her hands trembling again, poured herself a second glass of wine from the carafe on the table. "Kim," she
said. "Kim, *dear*. I hope you believe I still mean that. I *didn't*
know. I'm not sure I know *now*. All I know is that it's time
for us to stop hiding things. And as for *this*"—gesturing with
her glass at the table, and at Jennifer, who now had her head
buried in Carroll's chest, and sloshing a little wine into the
bargain—"as for *this*, I didn't want a melodrama and neither
did Lieutenant Carroll. But what were we to do, Kim? Should
we have had you all in for intensive questioning, grilling, so
that Jennifer could be even *more* torn, wounded? So that *you*
could be more wounded? What were we supposed to do?"

I'd never heard up-against-the-wall panic in Bridget's
voice before.

Carroll had whispered something to a waiter while all this
was going on, and the waiter had headed out the front door.
He came back now with—you'll never guess—Officer Helgerson and another uniform.

"Jennie," said Carroll, tilting her chin up. "Can I call you
Jennie? Good. Look, honey, we have to go somewhere and
talk. Think you can do that? Kim and your Dad will be with
you, I promise nothing bad is going to happen. Can you do
that? Sure—there's a good girl."

"Headquarters, Lieutenant?" asked Helgerson.

"My house," said Carroll. "Nobody's under arrest, just radio on the way for a steno to meet us there. David? Kim? I think we ought to be going. We can all take my car. Miss O'Toole, sorry, but I'm afraid—"

"Certainly, Lieutenant," Bridget said. "I prefer that."

"Yeah," he said.

"Bridget," said Kim, standing up. "Bridget, I want you to know, I never meant to make fool of you. I never—"

"But you didn't, dear," said Bridget. "Now just go along with John Carroll. I have the house key, and we'll talk it all out when you get home."

And there we sat, Bridget, Bobby, and I, not saying a thing until the waiter, who'd for sure earned his pay this night, crept— that's the only word for it—back and asked us if there would be anything else.

What the hell. I ordered the bouillabaisse. And it was *good*.

$\triangledown$

CHAPTER THIRTY

CARLA BOLERO WAS DEAD, of course. She'd been dead when I'd stepped off the plane at L.A.X. She'd been dead when Ben Gross and I were celebrating the anniversary of the National League. And she'd been dead all the time I was learning about her and wishing I could get to know her.

That was the first thing Carroll told us when he came by the next morning, around ten. Jennifer, he said, was being hospitalized and Kim and David were in what he called—I'd never heard of it—"voluntary, minimum detention."

Bobby Reilly, who'd stayed the night, exploded when Carroll told us about Carla.

"Goddamnit!" he said, bringing his coffee cup down hard enough to break the saucer. "Carla's dead and they're in—what did you call it?—hell, they're being *kept after school*? What's going on here?"

"Mr. Reilly," said Carroll. He looked tired. "Believe me, there are going to be charges. And, if it satisfies you, some lives are probably going to be permanently—changed. Although, personally, I—" and he shook himself and lit a cigarette. "Sorry. Nothing. I've had hardly any sleep and I think I'm getting tired of my job. Anyway, we seem to have charges pending of assault, conspiracy, fraud, maybe black-

214

mail—everything but murder, if you like."

"Thank God!" said Bridget, getting very odd stares from Bobby and me, and a small smile from Carroll. "What happened, Lieutenant?"

"Part of it you guessed, Miss O'Toole. And—unofficially— thank you. As far as we can put things together— David and Kim are still pretty shaken, and of course they've called a lawyer, although they're driving him crazy because they *want* to talk—you know, Miss O'Toole, they're—it's funny—they're not bad people."

"I know that," said Bridget, blinking hard even with her moused eye. "Please go on."

"Right. As we can tell it, there was no kidnapping. Morningside Realty, you know, was fighting with David's company over some property to the north of town. And it seems that somebody at Morningside—David thinks it was Emily Rice, and we're trying to check on that—somebody, anyway, decided that a nice way to make David cave in on the deal would be to threaten to let his daughter and his bride-to-be know about Carla Bolero. Apparently, they threatened to have Videodrome mail some of the tapes."

"Jesus," said Bobby, and *really* shocked me by reaching across the table, taking one of my cigarettes, and lighting it.

"Well," Carroll went on, "what David did—at least what he says he did—was to tell Kim about the problem—she already knew about Carla, you know—and here the story gets, I don't know, a little hard to take seriously."

"No, it doesn't," said Bridget. "Here is where Kim—it *was* Kim, wasn't it?—rented a tape of Carla's, it would have been *The Frog King* of course, and forced Jennifer to watch it. Is that right?"

Carroll stared at her for a full minute. "That's it," he said finally. "How did—"

"Because I know Kim," she said, "and I know how desperately she wanted to *be* Jennifer's mother, to protect her innocence."

"Her *what*?" said Bobby, unbelieving. I said something else at the same time.

"Innocence," Bridget repeated. "To Kim, it would have been a way of, once and for all, banishing Carla from her life and from Jennifer's—*nobody* close to them could possibly be that awful—and bringing them safely together. Kim—this is *absolutely* confidential, Lieutenant—has repressed and exorcised her share of details like that from her own life."

"And it had just the opposite effect," said Carroll. "As— Bridget, I'm sorry—as any sane person might have expected. Where were you a week ago, Monday night?"

"Hey, goddamnit!" I said. "What is *this* shit? You better—"

"No, Harry," said Bridget, with what was almost a smile. "I know what he means. You're right, John. I was at the movies. I wanted to see a special screening of *Napoleon*— Gance's *Napoleon*?—it's four hours long and Kim and David didn't care to see it, so I insisted on taking a cab—"

"Right," he said. "Lucky for nobody. That was the day, apparently, when Jennifer decided to skip school and head for L.A.—she claims she hitched all the way—to see her mother."

And he stopped. Just stopped, watching his cigarette burn between his fingers. I got up, grabbed a Lowenbrau from the fridge, twisted the top off, and said, "And?"

"And Carla Bolero died that day," said Carroll.

"Jennifer killed her," I said, starting to gag on the beer.

"No," he said. "At least—look, damnit, she's *fourteen* and she's got tranquilizers dripping into her arm right now. *She* says that she confronted her mother, they shouted, they struggled, her mother fell against—something—the girl didn't know what to do, so she called for help."

"She called for help?" asked Bobby.

"She called Kim. And Kim told David she had to go out on an emergency real-estate matter. She drove to L.A. and—this is another hard part—" He swallowed. "She stripped and disposed of the body."

"With Jennifer watching?" asked Bridget quietly.

"Helping," he said, quieter. "Or so they both say. You see, we have no way of knowing—"

"We have no way of knowing," said Bridget, "how this all might have been averted, what Kim might have done—if I'd been there when she got the call."

"No," said Carroll. "Don't let that bother you. I mean, don't—look, this is hard to say right, but Kim is glad you weren't there. For the same reason she couldn't have just picked Jennifer up and then told you and David what had happened."

"And that reason is?" asked Bridget, her face looking like she was looking at something awful.

"Well," said Carroll, staring at his hands. "She says she would have been ashamed. In front of you, you know."

"Oh," said Bridget.

"Hey!" boomed Cado at the back door. "Okay if I come in? Brother Carroll, your office told me I could find you here, and have I got some *dynamite* shit for—" and then he saw our faces, clamped down instantly, and sat.

"We can't know," Carroll went on, ignoring him, "how much of this is fabricated. Except we did find the body, where Kim told us it would be. Under a hillock, covered with newspapers, behind one of the Dodger Stadium parking lots." He laughed a little laugh and not a pretty laugh. "They would have had to drive by the Police Academy to get there."

"*Chinga*," whispered Cado, sitting at my elbow.

I asked it before I knew I was asking it. "Dogs?"

He looked at me—yeah, angrily—and said, "Something. Something small."

"And the so-called kidnapping?" asked Bridget.

Carroll looked at her shyly. Really, *shyly*. "Bridget," he said, "Kim was terrified. Especially—well, especially of what you would think of her."

"Oh, dear," said Bridget.

"Yeah," he said. "So, in a blind shit panic—sorry, Bridget—in panic, she just left Jennifer in Carla's house that night, called David to let him know, I guess, a *little* of what was going on—at least enough that he knew Jennifer was all right. And drove home."

"Where David had already told me, when I got home, that he was worried because Jennifer was gone and Kim was out on a late closing." said Bridget. "So the whole kidnapping plot, blaming Carla, was—what? An elaborate device for covering their tracks by having two inept private investigators obfuscate matters?"

He smiled. "Nothing so Machiavellian. They were frightened, and like most frightened people they were just trying to move as little as possible while they waited for things to get better. A miracle, you know? And Kim—well, she thinks of you as, I don't know, a mother or a goddess, Bridget. She would have 'died'—that was her word—if you'd found out what she caused by showing that damned tape to Jennifer. She even went so far as to take out Carla's answer-tape— Jennifer had maybe, she didn't remember, left a message on it—and make a new one. But she used the wrong name on it— you were right after all, Garnish. As for the kidnapping business—" His smile turned to a frown. He knew what he was going to say, and so did I. So I said it, because I didn't really want to hear it.

"As for the kidnapping business," I said, "they wouldn't have thought of it—they wouldn't have *had* to think of it—except Bridget, here, insisted on trying to help and suggested that I, big damn ace private eye, fly out to help too, right? What the hell could poor David—Jesus, I never thought I'd say *that*—what the hell else could he do but go along, and make up a trail for us to follow?"

"He could have told the truth," said Bobby, quietly.

"No, man," said Cado. "Not when you're—what'd you say, Brother Carroll?—not when you're *shit* scared."

The phone rang, and Bridget got it. "Lieutenant?" she said, holding it out to Carroll. He talked for a minute and hung up.

"Kim and David are no longer in voluntary custody," he told us.

"What the blank?" said Cado, Bobby, and I, all filling in the blank in various colorful ways.

"I mean," he said, "it's no longer voluntary."

"Yeah," I said. "So who was it shot at me? And who sent the damn telegram to Bobby here?"

Carroll sighed. "Who shot at you is the assault charge. The other question, that you haven't asked, is who called you back claiming to be Carla and set up the appointment for you to be shot at."

Damn if he wasn't right—I hadn't thought about that.

"The phone call," he went on, "came from David's house. It was Kim, on David's business line, calling his home line. She even seemed a little proud of having pulled that off."

Right, I thought. And I had thought she was just pissed off because I didn't want to work on the case.

"The question of who really shot at you," he continued, "is a more serious one, and I shouldn't be discussing it with you. But I will. Bridget, which one of them was out of the house the night Garnish went to Golden State Liquors?"

Bridget stared at the kitchen table for a long time. Then she stared at Carroll, and said, "I can't remember."

"Sorry," said Carroll, "it won't do. You can remember that the logo of an insurance agency and a video rental store are the same, and you can't remember what happened the night your partner was shot at? I don't think you realize— "

"*No!*" she shouted, and everyone jumped. "I don't think *you* realize, John. I assume both of them are claiming to be the one who fired at Harry, just to scare us off. I assume both are claiming to have hatched the plot for Jennifer's miraculous return, and to have sent the telegram to Bobby. And you'll get no help from me in apportioning the guilt."

"Look, now—" he began.

"Don't you see," she said. "*There was no crime.* There was a pathetic, absurd tragedy. But there was the *fabrication* of a crime, there was deceit from people who are not deceitful, there was terrible psychic rape of a child by people who love that child, just because they were, as you say—" and I *knew* she was trying to say "shit scared," and she just couldn't—"frightened beyond endurance. And why? Because *I was there*, and then *Harry was there*, and in trying to help them we were co-authors of all this waste."

"Your friend Rosenberg," I said.

"What?" she asked, nearly laughing and as shit scared as I've ever seen *her.*

"That scientist you told me about," I said. "The one who said when you look at a thing you change it."

"Heisenberg," she sighed. I think the exasperation was good for her. "'The observer changes the conditions of the experiment merely by *being* an observer.' Harry, Harry. I hope you don't really understand how right you are. Well, Lieutenant?"

He cleared his throat and lit another Parliament. "Molina," he said finally. "You said you had something to tell me?"

"Well, yeah," said Cado, looking around nervously. "The thing is, Lady Bridge here thought that—well, Mitch and Lisa got a pretty good take on that van that scragged us, and they been asking around town, certain people, you know. And it looks like a van like that belongs to this dude who does deliveries and maintenance and shit for—guess what?—Videodrome. Unh—I can't tell at this point. Is that good news or what?"

And everybody laughed. I mean, the kind of laugh you share when you not only lost the state championship by five unanswered baskets, but the team bus blows a tire on the way back home and the spare is flat and it's raining and you're twelve miles from the next turnoff. In a weird way, it isn't the worst feeling in the world.

"It's news, anyway, Arcadio," said Carroll—the first damn time he'd first-named him. "It means that we're going to have quite a lot to talk to Miss Rice about. You must have scared her, too, Bridget, when you went to see her yesterday—no, Sunday—morning. She hadn't heard about Jennifer's disappearance till you told her? So, she must have assumed it had something to do with Morningside's squeeze play on David. We'll find out if she had a driver tail Bridget and try to put the fear on them."

"Bullshit," I said. "She's a smart lady. She could deny the whole thing."

He looked at me. "We'll find out," he said.

I believed him.

And we just sat there. For maybe a minute, maybe two minutes. Until we all turned our heads at once, as I remember it, toward a funny sound which was Bobby Reilly breathing very deep and very slow and trying not to weep.

"Sorry," he said, looking back at us. "It's just—it's Carla. You should have known her, Harry." And he stood up and walked into the back yard.

"Lieutenant," said Bridget after a while. "May I speak with Kim?"

"Well," said Carroll, "she really doesn't—I mean, in a way she's—she said she didn't want to see you," he finally got it out. "She says she's too ashamed."

"I know she is," said Bridget. "Would you please tell her, for me, that *I'm* ashamed, and that I really need to ask her pardon—and David's?"

"Sure," said Carroll. "I can do that. I'll call you this afternoon."

He left, and Bridget excused herself and went to her room to read. Cado and I sat and had some beer till Bobby Reilly came back in, and I said that the thing to do with the rest of a day like this was to find somewhere to get quietly and unbustably drunk.

Cado knew a place.

$\triangledown$

CHAPTER THIRTY-ONE

LIKE I TOLD YOU: no car chases in Maseratis, no shoot-outs (just one and a half shoot-*ats*, and I was the friggin' *at*), no mysterious ladies except Carla who was dead from the beginning and Emily Rice who could break your heart—or some part of your anatomy—but was about as mysterious as a Marlboro ad.

Emily, it turned out—I got this news after I got back to Chicago—*had* been spooked enough by our visit to, first, commission a driver to shave Bridget and Cado and, then, scared shit at having done *that*, to try and seduce me into an even stupider state of mind than my usual. But she never came up on charges: some kind of deal, who the hell knows? and Morningside Realty did wind up in full control of the famous territory, since Pescatore Realty basically got drowned in a scandal and legal fees and bad press you wouldn't wish on your best friend unless your best friend was the Ayatollah Khomeini and he's dead, anyhow.

Bridget did get to talk with Kim and David, not Tuesday, but the day after, and the day after, and so on. After three days of this—she'd been sort of avoiding me—she told me that she was going to stay on in California for a while, take care of David's house and affairs, and boy did that sound familiar, but that maybe I should get my ass back to the agency and what only foreigners would dare call the Second City.

Fine by me. I never saw Kim or David again. Bridget asked me to come along on that first meeting, but I was hung over and besides I didn't really need to see two people wringing hands and telling each other that love and trust could still win through and shit, now did I?

So I spent a few days haunting bars and restaurants with Cado and with Bobby Reilly, who'd decided to hang around Santa Barbara for a while. There were some good times. Nothing all that special, I suppose, but long afternoons of drinking beer, shooting pool at a quarter a rack and a dollar a ball—they both preferred shooting rotation, which meant they were human beings—and cracking up over really silly jokes about five o'clock and wondering where the nearest pizza place was.

And then on Saturday, one week after Cado and I got sprung from the tank, I flew home. Bridget couldn't see me off: she had to consult, she said, with David's lawyer about the disposition of their case. But Cado and Bobby insisted on seeing me off at L.A.X. Cado was in full biker regalia, which meant we had some space around us at the gate.

"Chicago," he said, giving me a very *hard* high five, "for a motherfucker, you're a good motherfucker. I don't write, you know? I just care."

"Check," I said. "You kiss Mitch and Lisa, they get back from wherever."

They were calling my row number. Bobby didn't say anything, just gave me a big hug, which I returned, and as I did his lips brushed my cheek.

Jennifer? As of the last I heard she's in a foster home in Santa Barbara, visiting her dad and his new wife every other weekend, and in therapy. As are dad and stepmom, released after a lot of lawyer's fees on recognizance and with periodic checkups from a court-appointed psychologist.

I never found out what they did about Carla Bolero's body.

So, when I got back to Chicago, and then to Evanston, I headed straight for the Orrington Bar. It was pissing sleet on top of snow, and the streets were the color of rice pudding you left in the fridge, uncovered, overnight, and it felt great. Torch was behind the bar.

"That was quick," he said. "California don't agree with you? The land of fruits and nuts?" He laughed.

What the hell, I thought, and I laughed along. "You got it," I said. "You sure as hell got it. Double brandy. Seen Janie?"

Janie, in fact, came by about an hour later. I bought her a Wild Turkey, told her all about my trip to Disneyland, asked her if she was on the job, got a no, suggested dinner, and like that.

Well, not quite like that. Nothing happened. I couldn't, you dig? And when I broke into a flop-sweat—don't tell me you don't know what *that* feels like—she kissed me on the forehead, got out of bed and put on my robe, brought me a beer, and said something very strange.

"Harry," she said. "You're not a trick, so I don't have to make you feel good. But you know what? Whatever it was that happened, it changed you. And—now don't get uptight, honey—I like the change." She kissed me again. "I never liked you more."

So go figure. Life started grinding along again. A few days later I bought a V.C.R. And—you got it—started renting tapes. Carla Bolero tapes, and watching them late into the night with Bandit and my two good friends, Ernest and Julio Gallo.

And, in time for the snowstorms of early April, Bridget came back. I eased off the brandy and the Carla Bolero tapes, and the sun came out and things got more and more normal. Janie and I get together pretty often now when she's not working, and a few days ago I got this sonofabitch of a letter—he's written me three, that I haven't answered—from Bobby Reilly.

Rob has AIDS.

If you have enjoyed this book and would like to receive details of other Walker mystery titles, please write to:

Mystery Editor
Walker and Company
720 Fifth Avenue
New York, NY 10019